# CRUSH

## The Love Story of Logan and Diana

## MARY OLDHAM

ISBN: 979-8-9859324-4-7 Paperback

Any references to historical events, real people, or real places are used fictitiously. Names, characters, and places are products of the author's imagination.

Story Editor: Sue Grimshaw, Edits by Sue
Grammatical Editor: Arleigh Rodgers
Cover Art: Lynn Andreozzi
Interior Book Design: Teri Barnett/Indie Book Designer
Author Photo: Tanith Yates

Printed in United States of America
By-Creek-Ity Publishing
Portland, Oregon

www.maryoldham.com

*To my sweet Vizslas, Ginger, Penny, and Maggie.*
*Your time on this earth was too short. Thank you to Mom and Dad, who*
*started me off young by bringing Ginger into our home when I was five. I*
*love you, my sweet fur babies. A part of my heart will always be yours.*

# PROLOGUE

*"Crush:"*
*Be gentle, press lightly to minimize the amount of tearing of the skin.*
*A brief but intense infatuation for someone, especially someone unattainable. -- Wikipedia*

They walked along the west edge of campus in the amethystine twilight of early summer.

The end of one more precious day together and one day closer to their forced parting.

"I'll be back by June 1st," Diana said, trying not to make it sound exactly what it was, almost a year away. Her voice held an edge of desperation, and she spoke too fast, but Logan was her everything. "But I'll make it back home before then. I should be back for Christmas. I just need to watch my expenses to make sure I can afford the plane ticket home. And you can come to visit. Philadelphia will be so fun! We can take the train to New York. I've always wanted to see New York City, the Statue of Liberty, and Wall Street, walk along Rockefeller Center. We could even go ice skating...Think of the fun we could have!"

She had been so excited about the thought of the business fellowship at Wharton. She would be going to an Ivy League school, for Wharton was part of the University of Pennsylvania. This was something she would not have dared to even think of a year ago. Her goals had been focused on paying rent, buying a new outfit every few months, and hoping to buy a car that wasn't held together with duct tape and prayers.

It had taken her possibly longer than it should have to notice that once her boyfriend, Logan, told her how proud he was of her at the beginning of their walk, he hadn't said much of anything else. She wasn't used to dominating the conversation. She wasn't comfortable with leading a conversation, especially the one they were having right now, a relationship conversation that was so one-sided.

Logan just smiled a tight-lipped smile that looked more tense than happy.

Stopping, she asked, "Are you okay?"

"I'm fine," he said, but he was looking past her, noticing the purple sky, and it disturbed her to her very core.

And if he was "fine," they weren't fine. Before she could protest that she knew he wasn't "fine"—for the mere fact that he hadn't taken her hand in his and had yet to make eye contact —he added, "I just don't know."

When someone said something like that, they did know, Diana thought. They just didn't want to say it. This was Diana's worst fears realized.

"What don't you know?" she asked as cold dread started creeping along her skin.

In the three months they'd been together, they'd never had a conversation that felt so strained and uncomfortable. Was he worried about missing her? She'd miss him like she'd miss an appendage, but they'd call each other. Heck, maybe they'd even write, and there were things like Facetime on computers that were becoming very popular. But had she said that? Or had he? She couldn't remember. The last few weeks were a blur of happiness and passion.

Their relationship was strong enough to handle this. He loved her. He'd often told her so, and she'd told him that she loved him. And she'd meant it with every cell in her body.

"What if you don't come back?" he asked, his voice unusually small, but it cut through the silence like a roar.

She didn't even let his words sink in because that potential reality wasn't her reality. Not come back? He was talking crazy. She loved him. How many times had she been in love? ONCE. He was the man she'd dreamed of her entire life.

"I'll be back exactly ten months after I leave. I'm not moving there. Not with you here. Not with what we have. Logan, damn it. I love you. You love me, right? What is going on here?"

These were the words that brought the greatest reaction from him. He scowled. It was an ugly expression she'd never seen on his handsome face and never wanted to see again. Did he not believe her? If he didn't want her to go, she wouldn't go. It was just that simple.

"Logan? I don't understand. If you don't want me to go, I won't go."

"For Christ's sake, you are taking the damn fellowship. It is a fantastic opportunity, which you deserve. No way are you missing it."

"Then what is wrong? Why are you so upset?"

He shook his head and finally met her eyes. "You're leaving. There isn't some sappy love story with one of us waiting for the other person to return. Our lives will change, but we will move on."

She'd never stop loving him. Was he saying he'd stop loving her?

"I don't understand. Two hours ago, we were talking about our future, and now it sounds like you're saying you aren't going to wait for me." As she heard her own words, the chill crept along her skin and led to full-on shaking. She was standing in the warm evening air, shaking like a leaf from the worst fear she'd known realized.

"Haven't we had a good time?" he asked, looking sad and resigned.

"We've had a great time, the *best* time," she replied, emphasizing the words. "It isn't over yet. It is just beginning."

"I've never felt this way before. I'll never forget you, Diana."

"Why would you want to?" she asked, her fear turning to anger. What was he talking about? They were perfect together. He was her best friend. You didn't walk away from what they had. Having never come close with any other relationship in her life, she knew how precious their connection was.

"I have something to ask you, something important," he said.

Her heart skipped a beat and struggled to right itself. Was he going to ask to marry her? This was the oddest proposal she could imagine but wasn't that what could make it great? She could see a future with him, growing old, having children, and all the wonderful moments. She knew he couldn't let her go.

She had known that she loved him, the way you know hunger or pain, joy, or elation. It hadn't been a conscious thought but an absolute knowing.

"What is your question?" she asked, softening her tone. He knew how to push all her buttons. That fact had been crystal clear to both of them for the hours spent making love on the soft mattress in his one-room apartment.

"Do you see yourself spending the rest of your life with me?" he asked but held up his hand to stop her from speaking. "This is your opportunity to tell me exactly how you feel about me. I need you to be honest."

She smiled, didn't realize that she was crying until the tears ran wet trails along her hot cheeks. She'd loved him since the moment he'd smiled at her. He'd been the man she had waited for, longed for, dreamed of since she was a little girl.

A soft mist started falling, like tiny diamond crystals raining around them.

"Do I see myself spending my life with you?" she repeated, nodding, "A thousand lifetimes...My answer is yes!"

She took a step toward him, and he took a step back. She didn't understand. Why was he moving away from her?

Then he uttered the words that would burn into her soul and never heal.

"And you see, that is the problem," he said. It was as if telling her that he'd discovered why he didn't like the taste of a particular herb or seasoning that had just ruined a wonderful entree.

"I don't see myself spending my life with you..."

# CHAPTER ONE

*Twelve years later…*

"Idiot, fool, masochist," Diana Hunter muttered as she slowed her company car and turned at the ornate, carved wood sign for Mountain Valley Vineyards. She pulled the shiny, red BMW into one of the visitor parking spaces in front of the tasting room and wondered for the hundredth time why she had agreed to take this contract.

"What the hell is wrong with you?" she asked her reflection in the mirror as she applied an even layer of bright red ginger flower lipstick to her heart-shaped lips.

What was she going to do, show up with cookies on Logan's doorstep and tell her first and only true love that she was his next-door neighbor for the next three months? Maybe say hello to his wife, the woman living Diana's life? She sighed and shook her head again. She did not want to be here, wanted to be anywhere but here—in beautiful, lush Yamhill County, with its farms and miles of vineyards on rolling hills in western Oregon.

If she'd wanted to torture herself, she supposed accepting a contract that would put her directly in the path of the man she'd once thought she'd spend the rest of her life with was probably the way to do it. What made it especially hard was how vulnerable she was feeling due to the current state of her pathetic love life. There hadn't been anyone who came close to Logan and Brad, her now ex-fiancé, who had done one better by cheating

7

on her, in her bed—the bed she'd shared with Brad for two years. But that was over, and had been for a couple of painful months, but it hadn't hurt as much as that day with Logan all those years ago.

She hadn't laid eyes on Logan Parrish in years. Twelve to be exact. Not since the day he'd broken her heart. It was a ridiculous waste of time and energy to dredge up old feelings and regrets that she had long ago buried. She'd moved on, and so had Logan.

"For crap's sake, get a grip," she whispered as she stepped from her car and inhaled the clean, country air. It smelled earthy and rich, so unlike the slightly salty sea air of her hometown of Seattle.

"That's right, keep talking to yourself," she said, shaking her head as her heels crunched on the loose gravel. "It is the first step toward insanity."

Mountain Valley Vineyards was paying her company a lot of money to do a spectacular job. It was time to suck it up and get it done. Win this for Mountain Valley, possibly rub a little dirt in Logan's face while she did it. Three months would be over in a flash. It would feel like a couple of days, and she'd be on her way back home. She would deal with the past, and as a side benefit, she'd maybe make partner. There were worse ways to spend the summer.

Today, she'd only had one cup of coffee three and a half hours earlier when she'd left Seattle and taken the boring drive down Interstate Five to Portland.

Her nerves were as frayed as if she had consumed a gallon of the strong caffeine-infused elixir.

Despite Diana Hunter's desire since childhood to blend into the background, she stood out. At thirty-four, she was one of the leading beverage experts in the country. She had a reputation as a force to be reckoned with. And despite her self-deprecating opinion of the woman she'd become, her reputation was beyond reproach. Not bad for a grubby little girl raised in a trailer park by a semi-present alcoholic widower father with an inability to hold a job for any length of time. She wished her father could see her now. It was a bitter pill to lose both parents before you turned twenty-five, but she knew they'd be proud of her.

She had earned her success through hard work and a personal drive to be the best. For her, failure or disappointment was a dead end. A one-way ticket back to the trailer park she'd fought hard to break free from the time she was old enough to understand what it was to be on the wrong side of the tracks. So, she drove the flashy company car, she wore the tailored, expensive designer clothing, and exhibited the perfect manners and social graces. But most of all, she worked her ass off to be the best. Because just as she knew her old life was there if she failed, failure was for everyone who came in after first place.

As Diana made her way to the looming wooden tasting room that was trying to be a Tuscan farmhouse, which it definitely wasn't, she pictured herself running into Logan.

Maybe they'd laugh about running into each other again. Laugh about how they'd once been an item during the last three months of their senior year of college when they'd been twenty-two. Love wasn't supposed to endure when you were that young. But it had endured for Diana.

Logan had ripped her heart into bits and then handed it back to her as if it were nothing but a pile of dry leaves. Still hurt if she allowed herself to think about it.

Diana had at least learned an important life lesson. Life wasn't soft dreams, sweet fairytales, and happily ever afters. Somewhere in her being, she should be a bigger person. She should be happy for Logan. He was living his dream. The pain of losing him only smarted like a never-ending paper cut that he hadn't wanted her to be a part of her life. On that fine point, he'd been quite clear, crystal, in fact.

*"I don't see myself spending my life with you..."*

She felt the full pain of his words, as if the twelve years hadn't passed, as she reached for the large brass handle on the door to the tasting room. Diana did admit to herself her recent breakup probably added some fuel to the memories too, possibly even making them more vivid than ever.

Fortunately, she had a new and exciting project to occupy her time in the here and now. And she hadn't exactly had any choice in the matter. Her boss, Stephan, had assigned the Mountain Valley Vineyards Project to her and hadn't asked if she had any opinion. For if Diana had been asked, she'd have said that she'd suddenly developed a wine allergy. Knowing that Logan was happy was one thing. Having it rubbed in her nose was quite the other. It wasn't something she needed to see firsthand.

Yes, a stronger woman might be over this by now — good God, it's been over a decade. She'd be cordial to Logan and his wife, Juliana. Diana was a professional after all.

The past was past, and Diana's job now was to make D'Salvos vineyard a success. So she'd do what she was paid to do and take Logan down.

Diana had earned an MBA from Wharton and parlayed her career successfully into a lucrative future. She was up for partner at Wave, the cutting-edge marketing company she'd worked for the last three years. She'd made something of herself, exceeded her expectations. It wasn't easy, but she'd made it through, despite her lack of home life and support. But that had always been a constant ever since her mother died. When her father died, she felt the loss, but it was different. She wasn't a little girl. She knew how to earn enough money for food and clean clothes, but still she missed him, the idea of him.

Diana did have something to look forward to when she was done here. After she completed this project successfully, she'd return to Seattle and decorate her new apartment. If all went well, heck, maybe she'd buy a little house or condo. And if she were more lucky than good, she'd be ordering new business

cards that featured a new title under her name. *Vice President /
Partner*. And didn't that just have a lovely ring to it?

Yeah, things were looking up.

*Focus on the good.*

Diana's close friend Bonnie Elder, who had stepped in and
become a mother figure to her, had always encouraged her from
a young age to 'focus on the good,' and that stuck with Diana
ever since. It had become her personal mantra.

Once inside the dark, massive tasting room that felt like a
cool, damp cellar vault despite the large windows, Diana
stopped short, her eyes darting to the three employees attending
to the customers. Each one of the all-male staff had a similar
look. They were good-looking in a chiseled, hard way. Two were
bleached blonds, and a third man was younger, shorter, with
dark hair and olive skin. They were all tanned and wore their
hair shoulder length. The muscles bulged against their Mountain Valley Vineyard black polo shirts. These boys spent some
time in the gym.

Diana made eye contact with the youngest of the three, and
he immediately crossed over to her.

"Welcome to Mountain Valley Vineyard. Would you like to
taste some of our delicious wines?"

"I already have. I'm Diana Hunter from Wave. I'm here to
meet with Salvatore D'Salvo," she replied, glancing at the blond
men. Maybe she'd made a wrong turn and ended up in a job
placement program for aging Chippendale dancers or displaced
pirates.

"I'm Marco. Salvatore is my father," he said as he extended
his hand. He had an eager smile and a firm grip. Diana surmised
he had to be in his late twenties. He was the next generation in
a family business, probably eager to start running the show and
proving himself. Even though she was probably five years older,
she could relate.

"It's nice to meet you. I'm excited to be working with your

family," she said and glanced at the blond men, who were helping customers, more to the point, women who appeared to be enjoying the attention they were getting. "Are they related to you?"

Marco followed her gaze and said, "They are my cousins from Italy, Davide and Antonio. They are here for the summer and fall harvest. We thought we might need them with the contest, and they wanted to see America. Their father, my uncle, has a winery in Tuscany. We hope to do more with them. Possibly, combined wine tours here and in Italy. They do very well with customers. We think it is the accent."

"I'm sure it helps," Diana said.

Diana noticed how the women stared intently and hung on every word they said.

"It was my idea," he said proudly and smiled. For the first time, she could see that he had one tooth that slightly overlapped another. From that moment forward, she would forever think of him as *The Snaggletooth.*

"Very impressive. If you'd like, we can discuss your vision while I'm here," she offered.

"I would like that. It's a date," he said, smiling a little wider, prominently displaying the misaligned tooth. "I suppose I should take you to meet my father before we get completely carried away."

Diana bit back a frown. Little Snaggletooth gave himself a lot of credit. She didn't date clients. After what she had been through with her cheating fiancé, she didn't feel like dating anyone at the moment. She knew she was overly sensitive, but whenever she entered into a new contract, she kept her guard up until she fully understood all the relationships at play.

"Right this way," Marco said, leading her through a door that bore the notice *Employees Only.*

"How was your drive from Seattle?" he asked, smiling at her as they stopped in front of rustic carved wood double doors.

"Long, but uneventful. I'm glad it wasn't raining," Diana replied. "How long have you worked in the family business? I'm guessing your whole life?"

"No, I've been back almost three years. I didn't always work in the vineyard," he replied with another smile. That one tooth that was slightly out of alignment, that otherwise marred his perfect teeth, made him look slightly cruel. She wondered why he'd never had it fixed.

"What did you do before?" she asked.

"I was in the entertainment industry in Las Vegas," he replied vaguely. She wondered if that was a euphemism for porn. He had the look of someone who wasn't much different than his cousins—a little too easy, a little too sexual, a Player with a capital P. He was rough in a way that spoke of addictions and a hard life.

He rapped on the door to Salvatore's office and said, "Father, your lovely Wave consultant is here." He looked over his shoulder and leered at her.

Diana wondered how many men were described as lovely. It was always so hard when you knew you disliked someone on sight. She disliked Marco, and there wasn't anything he could do to improve or change the situation or her first impression.

"Come in," a deep voice answered.

Marco opened the door and waited for Diana to walk ahead of him. Diana recognized Salvatore D'Salvo, the owner and man who'd hired her. They'd spoken on the phone and had Zoom meetings several times, and although he was expecting her, the look the older man gave her was one of doubt. He looked like the traditional stereotype of an old-world vintner. She knew that his parents had come from Italy in the 1930s and that he'd been born in the United States. If she had to guess, she would surmise that he was fluent in both English and Italian, probably referred to marinara as sauce or gravy. And a good deal of the homeland still existed with the man.

He probably was suspicious of her for two reasons—one, she was a woman, and two, she wasn't Italian. Far from it, she had her mother's Swedish coloring and her father's German stubbornness. Possibly it hadn't done her parents any favors, but it had combined in their daughter to make her the driven person she was. Not that this man would show her any mercy. Nor did she want it. She liked to earn her way as long as she was given a fair shot.

Scrutiny, therefore, was just part of the territory. She got it from most of the family businesses she helped, especially if she was dealing with the patriarch. It always triggered her irrational fears of not quite fitting in. She tried to ignore the hypercritical assumptions, but it didn't come easily.

"Mr. D'Salvo, I'm Diana Hunter from Wave. So nice to finally meet you in person," she said, extending her hand and introducing herself.

"I thought you'd be here yesterday," he complained.

Normal posturing, Diana realized. He was concerned, possibly nervous, and the best way to work out some of his aggression was on her.

Salvatore D'Salvo was on the cusp of getting a large hotel contract, and over the next three months, he needed her help to close the deal. He needed the contract because he needed the money it would bring in for some expansion he had planned, and he didn't have the best wine in the competition. His wine was the worst of the competitors. She'd know. She'd tried them all.

It had to be frightening to have so much on the line. This was where she excelled, making the business owner feel as if she had a deep investment in their success that went beyond the financial terms of their business agreement. At the end of many of her projects, she received hugs, not handshakes, and felt like an honorary member of the family.

"I'm sorry, no, I thought my itinerary had been shared with

you. My apologies if you didn't receive it," she said, thinking that it had been quite clear and sent to him. He'd made a comment about the duration of her stay and extended her time by a week to the end of August.

Salvatore D'Salvo, clad in jeans, a western shirt, and cowboy boots, looked her over critically, from her black patent heels to her stylish designer black suit.

"No matter, I'm sure you can catch up," he said with a wave of his hand.

Suddenly, she was getting a bad vibe. By chance, maybe this deal wouldn't be successful. Nope, Diana couldn't think like that. But why had she accepted this job?

Oh yeah: *Partnership.* She had to keep remembering how the title *Vice President* would look on her business card.

Diana took in the surroundings, a big desk, wood paneling, and a large aerial map of the vineyard along with miles of neighboring property. Salvatore caught her looking.

"This is my current land," Salvatore said proudly, standing before the map and adding, "And this is how it is going to look a year from now, almost twice the size."

Pulling his hand away from the aerial map, a clear plastic overlay fell into place, showing an additional chunk of land to the east of where they currently stood.

The land east of them belonged to Logan Parrish and his vineyard, Forget-Me-Not. She knew. Logan had taken her there for a weekend twelve years ago. It had been a magical time.

There had been no mention of a land acquisition, just an expansion when they'd spoken on the phone. She'd done something stupid and made an assumption. She thought he was remodeling or building a new building, starting a new line of product, not taking over his neighbor's land. She was told that her chief responsibility would be to help win a lucrative, three-year contract with the Stark Hotels, a line of luxury hotels headquartered in Portland, Oregon, that wanted to offer Oregon wines at all their hotel restaurants here, in North America, Europe, and the Middle East.

Was Logan selling his land to Salvatore D'Salvo? If there was one thing she remembered about Logan, besides his passion for her, it was how excitedly he used to talk about his family business. He loved this land, which been in his mother's family for several generations. He wouldn't sell it unless something happened.

"That looks like an impressive undertaking," she said as disturbing thoughts flooded her mind. Did Logan still run Forget-Me-Not? If not, what had happened? When had she checked on his website last—what, a week ago? Nothing had changed. The smiling photo of Logan and his wife, Julianna, still graced the bio page as it had for several years. Nine years and six months, to be exact. Not that she'd stalked her ex-love. Well, maybe a little bit.

"I've been planning this for over twenty years," Salvatore D'Salvo announced.

"It has taken a long time, but I've just waiting for the opportunity to present itself, and it has."

"Is the sale in escrow yet?" she asked, thinking if this was moving forward with the speed he was indicating, he was probably well in the development stage. And if it was, Wave had been left in the dark. It could affect the terms of their agreement, which might need to be sorted out with her boss Stephan before she began.

"No. You could say we are in negotiation with the owner, a very troubled vineyard that is struggling. He is underwater, and it is just a matter of time. I'm just waiting for him to announce his bankruptcy, which might come sooner than later with his water rights up for negotiation in September. You see, the spring that supplies water to this vineyard and the one next door belongs to me. Due to some antiquated riparian rights that were in play at the time the Parrish family purchased the land next door, we negotiate the water rights every ten years. And this year, I'm not feeling especially generous. I don't think he'll be able to pay the price I'm going to quote to renew them. Then, his land will be mine."

Diana flinched. As much disdain as she'd felt for Logan, she didn't want to think that he'd lose his business to Salvatore D'Salvo's unfair business practices, and what he had just admitted to involved price gouging. Logan was Mountain Valley's biggest competition for the Stark Hotel contract. And Logan's wine was very good.

The Snaggletooth laughed cruelly and said something to Salvatore in Italian.

How convenient, considering she only spoke a little French.

"Is the land where Forget-Me-Not Winery is currently? I drove by their entrance on my way here," she said, trying to elicit more information.

"Yes, from this valley," Salvatore said, pointing to a natural divide in the land, "to this grove of pine and cypress trees. The land now belongs to a man named Logan Parrish. He's a mean son of a bitch. It will give me great pleasure to relieve him of his land."

The Snaggletooth nodded in agreement and smiled, that crooked tooth almost winking at Diana.

Logan had always had an edge, but she'd never considered him to be mean until the day he'd broken up with her. She'd felt his cruelty then but had considered it to be personal, not universal. Obviously, in the last twelve years, that unpleasant aspect of his personality now dominated...interesting.

"What will you plant on his land when you acquire it?" she asked, her mind trying to make sense of what she was hearing.

"He's got acres of good Pinot Noir grapes. I'll rip out the rest of his plants and plant more Pinot Noir. Because after this summer, after you help us, there had better be an increased demand," he said, looking at her expectantly.

"That's what you're paying me for. Don't you worry, we'll get the Stark Hotel contract," she said, hoping confidence she didn't quite feel would somehow materialize. Over the next three months of summer, Mountain Valley would be in competition with four other wineries for the exclusive, lucrative hotel contract as the grand prize. There were extreme expectations for Diana to make it happen, despite the fact it was supposed to be about the flavor of the wine and the wine alone. But most of all, her reputation was on the line, as was her partnership.

Salvatore reached into his desk and pulled out several papers from the drawer.

"The official kick-off to the contest is this afternoon at a champagne reception. I need you to go to town and hand over my signed documents acknowledging the rules of the contest. It will give you your first glimpse of the competition."

Diana nodded and said, "Will either of you be attending?"

"No," Salvatore answered. "We have a meeting with our distributor that cannot be moved. Besides, we know all the competitors, but they don't know you."

"You want them to wonder who I am?" she asked.

"Precisely," he replied.

"No problem," she said with a smile she didn't quite feel. Logan would recognize her, and she would get to see him for the first time in twelve years, not to mention his wife, the woman he'd chosen over her.

# CHAPTER TWO

T n the last two years, Logan Parrish had learned that sentimentality was not only overrated but a great way to continually torture oneself. Bittersweet memories were skinned knees that never healed, hurting with each painful step into an unknown future. As the embittered man gazed one last time down at the photo of a woman he'd known long before his beloved wife, he fought the ensuing guilt. Despite his conflicted feelings, it appeared he was unable to toss the Oregon State University Alumni magazine in the trash can next to his desk. Not for the first time, he cursed his sentimental self.

Twelve years and a lifetime later, Diana Hunter was still hard to forget. She didn't look any older than she had when they were in school together. Only her hair was different. The mass of blonde curls that he used to twirl around his fingertips no longer floated around her face. Somewhere along the way, the unruly locks had been tamed into long, silky waves. But her high cheekbones were the same. They still gave her face a slightly haughty classiness, which could intimidate with only a glance. And those dark hazel eyes, edged in shadowy jade, even now had the power to haunt him.

He had loved his wife, Julianna, with his whole heart, or at least he tried to convince himself that was true. But Diana would always own a piece of it, and he suspected that Julianna knew that to be true. Was that why she strayed from their marriage?

It was only in the last couple of months that he'd finally started to pull out of his self-executed prison of grief over losing Julianna during their divorce proceedings two years earlier. Would it have been different if he'd fought harder for their marriage? Said different words? Forgiven her for her transgressions? Probably not, but he still had to torture himself. He hadn't gotten the chance to try to save his marriage, and that was what haunted him.

And now here he was, gawking at the one woman who'd always been on the edge of his periphery, just beyond his reach but never completely out of his thoughts. The one woman he had sent away twelve years earlier, ensuring his own broken heart. She would never have done what Julianna did. Diana had loved him in a way that Julianna never had. Diana looked at him as if he were the only man in the world. For three glorious months, he had been the only man in her universe. He had made a huge mistake and had only himself to blame. Fortunately, he and Julianna never had children, even though they'd talked about it; he'd wondered if Julianna prevented it because she thought their future was bleak. Maybe she was right. There was always a part of his heart that would belong to his first love.

Why was fate placing her photo so blatantly in front of him now? What was he supposed to do, call her? Tell her that despite the years and twist and turns his life had taken, he still thought of her, still dreamed of her? It was a ridiculous notion, especially when he saw how far Diana had come. He took a little pride in the knowledge that he'd helped her along, given her a push in the right direction, no matter how painful it had been at the time.

In the photo, which dominated the article, she was dressed in a dark business suit, sitting on a tall chair, her hands in her lap. Her fantastic legs crossed regally. Logan regarded her neatly folded hands for the hundredth time. Her long, elegant fingers held no rings, but several gold bracelets graced her wrists, contrasting to the dark backdrop of her suit. She wasn't married, or if she was, she wasn't announcing it, nor was she using her husband's name. It could be an older photo, he mused, but he thought it was probably taken when she was interviewed for the featured alumni article.

The photo credit suggested it was taken in Seattle, probably at her office.

Now a marketing strategist from a prestigious Seattle firm, she'd made a name for herself as a self-proclaimed 'fixer,' specializing, ironically, in the food and beverage industry. He'd always known she'd make something of herself. As much as it hurt him to admit it, he wasn't sorry for the role he'd played in her success all those years ago.

Logan decided that fate had a nasty sense of humor as he looked out the curved window at the fields of vineyards before him. Land he owned as far as the eye could see, at least for the time being. In a few months, it might be a much different story. Julianna would be so disappointed and yet not surprised that he was in the current mess he was in. She'd always complained that he didn't have the stomach for what must be done when it came to business. He could play dirty when he needed to. He just hoped it wouldn't come to that. His disappointment in himself and what he'd become, combined with his ever-present grief, had all but consumed his once affable personality.

He glanced down again at the paperwork on his desk. The water rights agreement between him and his neighbor, Mountain Valley Vineyards, had never seemed as ominous as it did at this moment. He had until September 30th to renegotiate the irrigation to his land. Only one thing would save him and allow him to continue his business—money, and lots of it. He needed a very large, very important infusion of cash to pay for the renewed water rights. Certainly, Salvatore D'Salvo didn't want him to renew, and Logan knew exactly what Salvatore wanted. And Salvatore wasn't going to get it, no matter what Logan had to do. Salvatore D'Salvo was not taking Forget-Me-Not away from him. The D'Salvos had taken enough from him. Well, one D'Salvo, Marco, had gotten away with murder as far as Logan was concerned. Call it what you may, but he knew the truth. Logan was sure of one thing, he'd die first before selling his land to a D'Salvo, and there were no ifs, ands, or buts about it.

Logan still had two long shots—the contest with the Stark Hotels and his possible ace in the hole, his three-year-old Pinot Noir that was yet to be bottled.

A strange and bewildering thought entered his mind. Diana was a food and beverage specialist. Should he call her and ask for her help?

What was he thinking? If he couldn't think of a way out of his mess, why did he think Diana would be able to show up and save him? He knew his business better than anyone else. Besides, he wasn't sure of the real reason for his agenda. If it had been a different person in the alumni magazine, would he feel the same need to call them? No. It was because the person in question was Diana, and that wasn't a good enough reason.

He doubted he could afford to hire her. Heck, he didn't even know if she would want to talk to him. She might have not looked back when she left after he'd held open the door and asked her to leave.

He picked up the agreement for the Stark Hotels' contest and grabbed his jacket. He was late and had to get downtown.

The movement caught the attention of his dog, a Hungarian Vizsla named Ginger, who had been lounging in one of many overstuffed dog cushions which graced most of the rooms of his large house. At the sound of his keys jingling, the long-legged, velvet-furred copper hound with an overly sweet personality ran to his side, hoping she was about to get a walk.

"When I get back, I promise," he said as he petted Ginger and watched as she cocked her head to the side, as if she had heard him.

Ever since his wife left, the dog, who had been his wife's constant companion, was glued to his side, Ginger's grief matching that of her master. Julianna had indicated that she had wanted Ginger in the divorce. Having Ginger now was the only positive in this otherwise bleak situation.

"I'll be back soon. You guard the house," he said and bent to kiss the top of her velvet-furred head as she wagged her tail. He knew that if people saw him kiss his dog goodbye, they would think he was crazy, but Ginger wasn't just any dog, and she always kissed him back with a tongue lick to his chin.

He drove into the city of Portland, thirty miles away. At the flagship hotel of the Stark Hotels and their corporate office, he left his car with a valet and went inside the elegant hotel. He walked past a crowd of people having what appeared to be afternoon tea in the lobby.

Stepping into the Mt. Hood ballroom, a large party midprogress, he found a quiet corner to stand and observe. A passing waiter offered him a glass of champagne from a silver tray, and he re-thought his choice of apparel.

He had been in the vineyard that morning and hadn't thought he needed to change.

This announcement was just a formality.

He knew he had been accepted into the competition. This was just the public announcement, so he hadn't changed. In a chambray work shirt and jeans, he was at least comfortable.

A woman stepped to the podium and tapped on the microphone. She was in her early thirties, pretty, blonde, dressed immaculately, and had a lovely smile.

"Good afternoon, ladies and gentlemen. I'm Daisy Stark, one of the marketing partners with Stark Hotels. I want to welcome everyone to the start of the Stark Hotels' Wine Vendor Competition! We know this new contest is a bit different and a bit unconventional. Still, we wanted to provide a wonderful marketing opportunity for our local vendors and get a little excitement from the public for everyone involved. Thank you for taking the time to participate in our little competition. I think we are all going to have a lot of fun and hopefully make some good friends by the end of the summer." She went on to explain the contest in detail as members of the news media took hurried notes and then asked her a variety of predictable questions. Logan surmised that it must be a shallow news day.

With the questions out of the way, Daisy Stark announced, "It is now time to meet our participants. I will ask that when I call the name of your vineyard, that you come forward, wave to the reporters, get your photo taken, and present your signed consent form."

"The first of our finalists is Blanc et Noir," she said.

"Forget-Me-Not," Daisy Stark called five minutes later.

Logan uncurled from the wall and made his way to the front.

He shook Daisy Stark's hand, then posed for a photo with the pretty blonde before going back to his corner. Yet, he still didn't see any of the D'Salvos.

This whole "opening ceremony" was a complete waste of time. Logan had other things to do, but he needed to play by the rules of their game. He wasn't a conformist, never had been. But desperate times called for desperate measures. He would have left right after his name was called, but he wanted to get a look at Marco. He had yet to see him in the crowd, but that meant nothing. He knew from experience that Marco didn't like to occupy the same space as Logan for good reason opting for the comfort of dark corners like a cockroach.

"Mountain Valley Vineyards," Daisy Stark announced.

But Marco wasn't who stood and walked forward.

"What the hell?" he muttered under his breath as the woman from the magazine he had been reading earlier that very morning materialized before him. The woman he'd loved and lost.

*Diana.*

For a moment, Logan couldn't believe his eyes. It couldn't be. It just couldn't be.

But after she handed the contract to Daisy Stark, Diana shook her hand and then turned around. He got a good look at her for himself.

*Diana.*

Her beautiful hair was up in some severe style, but her eyes were still just as hazel. From where he leaned against the foyer door frame, he could see them. A familiar tension stirred in his chest. The way he felt, that grip on his heart, that memorable spell she had once cast was still strong and had the ability to hold him close after all these years.

Up until recently, Logan had been under the false delusion that she was just a memory.

What was she doing here?

Was she working for Mountain Valley Vineyards?

His cell phone vibrated in his pocket, causing him to jump ever so slightly. Diana was returning to her chair at a table he'd walked by earlier.

Had he not noticed her sitting there?

He had to take the call; it was his wholesale distributor, Rob Miller. Reluctantly, he stepped outside into the quiet lobby and tried to make sense of what he'd just seen.

"Hey Logan," Rob said by way of greeting.

"Rob, what's up?" he asked.

"We are knocking down the price of the Pinot Gris from two years ago, thinking two bucks a bottle. It isn't moving."

Logan hated phone calls like these.

"Fine, do what you need to do."

"I'm sorry, I know this isn't good news. Listen, how is the three-year-old Pinot? Any chance that will be ready soon?"

"I need to check it," Logan said vacantly as he pictured Diana. She was dressed in a tailored black suit with a long skirt that all but hid what he knew were fantastic legs. Had Salvatore hired her knowing of her past association with Logan? That would be one way to mess further with him. *First Julianna and now...*

"Look, I'm not a winemaker, but when we tried it in March, I thought it was almost there."

"Rob," Logan said but then couldn't find his words. People were flooding out of the ballroom. He searched for Diana in the crowd.

"I know, I know...I just don't want you to lose Forget-Me-Not to that asshole.

I care, you know?"

Logan did know. Rob and everyone he surrounded himself with at Forget-Me-Not cared and had a stake in seeing the winery prosper.

Diana walked by with a crowd of people who she was chatting with. She didn't look his way, and he couldn't catch her eye as she walked rapidly out of the hotel. He could see her speaking through the glass, double doors to the waiting valet, wondering if he should go out and greet her.

Daisy Stark emerged from the room and was greeted by a tall, dark-haired man who Logan recognized as Alex Stark, the owner of the hotel chain. He kissed her quickly on the lips and said, "Nice job, darling." They walked past Logan, and Daisy nodded and smiled.

"I know, Rob. Listen, I've got to go, but I'll try it this week," Logan said, wanting to get off the phone and walking quickly to the front of the hotel.

A flash of red appeared, and before he got a chance to speak to Diana, she was getting into a fire engine red BMW. The valet opened the front hotel door for him, and for a brief moment, his eyes locked with Diana's. She gave a small smile of recognition and then pulled her car into traffic.

# CHAPTER THREE

By late afternoon on her first day at Mountain Valley Vineyards, Diana had moved into her temporary quarters, a picture-perfect guest cottage on the edge of the vineyard.

It was one of four cottages Mountain Valley rented out to tourists from spring to fall for wine tours. Salvatore told her the cottages were completely booked for the fall harvest for the next four years, but the Merlot Cottage was hers until the 1st of September. The cottage was a bit dated, with yellowed, knotty pine walls and a musty, woodsy scent. The furniture was old, but the space was clean. It was spacious for one person and had a nice view of the vineyard. Although there wasn't a television, there was a fridge. In the bathroom, there was a huge, original clawfoot tub. And there was a large table that she could use as a desk in the main room.

Her actions were mechanical. Now and then, she'd drop whatever was in her hands and take several deep breaths of air. She had seen Logan today, after twelve years. He had dressed a little like a gentleman farmer, in faded jeans and a chambray shirt, but she'd recognized him in an instant. His hair was quite long, and she thought he needed a shave. She didn't like the scruffy beard look. There was a general disorder to his appearance that was surprising and uncharacteristic. On anybody else, Diana would be turned off by that look, but on Logan, the outfit made him look just as handsome as the day they had said goodbye all those years ago.

He had looked right at her, under the Stark awning in front of the hotel, and what had she done? Driven off. She never merged into traffic faster in her life. Five minutes later, she pulled off the freeway, got out of her car, and leaned against the hood until the shaking stopped. She had to get a grip, as their first competition was in two weeks, and she would see him again. What was she going to do? Run screaming from the event?

Once inside, she distracted herself by unpacking two of the four suitcases she'd brought with her. The standard pre-arrival Zoom interviews her company insisted on were great, but they lacked the authenticity of an in-person meeting. For Diana, it meant not knowing how to dress in her temporary workplace, which equated to always overpacking. Even though the tasting room staff dressed in uniforms of polo shirts and black trousers, Salvatore D'Salvo dressed in jeans. She' would dress to match the man paying her. And thankfully, she'd brought several pairs of denim.

Her suit was out of place and would need to be hidden away from daily life on the vineyard. There might be another event in town where she would represent the vineyard, and she had a few more suits for the occasion. She had written in her contract that she would receive Mountain Valley Vineyards branded t-shirts and polo shirts for use at the competition events.

The vineyard was quiet, which no doubt was totally normal. There was no noise except for an occasional sprinkler or truck engine and the beating of her own heart. It was so unlike the sounds of Seattle that it made her edgy. She thought she could hear her mind spinning with what had happened that afternoon. Her thoughts went to Logan again. His scruffy appearance surprised her because he lacked a women's touch. He knew who the Starks were and what this competition meant—definitely, his wife would've, and if nothing else, surely she would have prodded him to choose an appropriate outfit.

It had been twelve years since she had seen him, but something seemed different.

The carefree smile she was so used to seeing was gone. The one he sported today was forced. He looked, for lack of a better word, bitter and not put together, unkempt. She would possibly be negotiating with him on the sale of his land at some point, and seeing Logan again made that thought a difficult one. Torn, she wondered if she should call Stephan and tell him not only about the land acquisition but also about the depth of her past personal involvement with Logan Parrish.

In an hour and a half, she would be having dinner with the D'Salvos. After the day she had thus far endured, that seemed like punishment. Marco just had that ick factor you sometimes encountered with people, and not just because of the overlapping tooth. It was something else though Diana couldn't put her finger on it just yet. But one thing was for sure. She needed to stay on her guard around him.

Deciding she needed to recharge in order to make polite dinner conversation, she used the shower attachment in the big claw foot tub for a nice, hot shower and then changed into a creamy yellow silk sheath dress with a pattern of delicate buttercups.

She roamed the cabin like a restless animal and finally decided on a walk to kill time before her dinner. Slipping into a pair of canvas walking shoes, she headed out with purpose, needing to work through the images of the day as she strode toward the valley that divided the land between the D'Salvo and Parrish properties.

The moment she'd seen Logan's vineyard on Salvatore's map, she'd tried to remember everything about the one weekend Logan had brought her up to meet his aunt and uncle when they'd been in college. They'd stayed in a lovely old Victorian on the property and enjoyed walks along Persephone's Creek, which originated on DeSalvo land. She now understood the creek was the source of the water rights Salvatore had mentioned earlier. Funny how she suddenly remembered Logan had told her about it the complex water rights twelve years earlier. It was all coming back to her now. She was curious to see the valley and the small stream that ran in front of it again after all these years.

When she ran out of vineyard land, rich with new foliage and more plants than she could begin to count, she walked down an incline to a lush, green valley. It led to a small, glistening creek, which was just as she remembered. She could hear the water before she saw it, and when she arrived at the water's edge, she couldn't help but think of how beautiful the clear, sparkling water appeared. Logan had been the one to name it Persephone's Creek when he was a kid in honor of his favorite mythological figure. Persephone, the reluctant wife of Hades, who was the king of the underworld.

Persephone was allowed away from the underworld for three months and would stay with her mother, Demeter. When she was on Earth, it was lush and fruitful for the summer months of June, July, and August. And when Persephone was back in the underworld, the Earth experienced fall and winter. Spring began in anticipation of Persephone's return.

Diana couldn't help but to think of the best three months of her life had, now twelve years ago when she and Logan were embroiled in their love affair. She turned away from the view of the creek and stopped.

<hr />

Logan brooded. He reread the article on Diana, and then he sat at his desk and tried to make sense of things that made no sense. Did she work for Mountain Valley? How long had she been there, and in what capacity? He was bothered, irritated, offended, and a little pissed off. Did Marco have to ruin every woman Logan had once cared about? After Marco's affair with Logan's wife prompting Julianna to leave him, Logan had been under the impression Marco couldn't do more harm to him than he'd already did. Apparently he'd been wrong.

Over the next hour, the walls in his perfectly decorated office seemed to tighten, making him feel claustrophobic.

Needing to get some fresh air and in keeping a promise to his loyal companion, Logan whistled to Ginger. He tucked his cell phone into his back pocket and waited until he had the dog's complete attention, and then uttered a single word: "Walk."

The dog lifted off her front feet and made a "rooing" sound that was a part howl, part bark, but meant only one thing, yes, she wanted to go for a walk.

Happily running ahead of him, Ginger began her exploration of the vineyard beyond, hoping to scare up a rabbit to play with. Logan hoped with every step that he would discover a solution to his mounting problems. As he scanned the hills before him, his thoughts drifted to the last two horrible years of his life and then to Diana and the last conversation they had twelve years earlier. He still couldn't get over how easily she had walked away and never looked back. At least when Julianna left him, she'd had a lot of reasons. Some of them, he agreed with, but he never thought she'd be gone for good. He always thought he might win her back, but then the choice had been taken away from both of them. Logan walked with Ginger until something stopped him dead in his tracks.

Diana stood at the edge of Persephone's Creek just like twelve years earlier. He'd only seen her photo that morning, and then she all but ran away from him earlier today. Yet here she stood on his land, in a pale-yellow dress the color of sunshine like some blonde sun nymph.

One thing was for sure; there wasn't a red sports car waiting nearby for her to make a quick getaway. Good. Maybe now he could get some answers.

She took a step toward Ginger, hesitated, and then asked, "Could you please call off your dog? She is scaring me."

Logan observed that those mystical hazel eyes, which had haunted him for years, sparkled in the sunlight. They were more beautiful if that was possible. Pulling his gaze away from his first love, he focused on his dog.

"Ginger, friend!" he yelled, his voice uneven and faltering as he said the words. He wasn't sure he could categorize Diana as a friend if she was working for the D'Salvos, but it was a command Ginger usually respected. "Come!"

Ginger took one look over her shoulder at her master and then charged toward Diana, her butt beginning its familiar tail wiggle that meant nothing but an attack by a soft pink tongue. So much for several years of obedience training. Ginger had a mind of her own, just like all the women in his life.

"Ginger, damn it!" he yelled as he rushed after the dog and added, "Don't worry, she's friendly. Hope you like dog tongue."

"I love dogs. She's pretty," Diana said, her voice sounding raw, as if she were having a hard time finding her words. He could relate.

By the time he got to Ginger, the animal had collapsed to the grass, rolled over on her back, and stuck her paws in the air so that Diana could pet her pink tummy.

"Really?" Logan said in disgust as he regarded his best friend.

"Some guard dog she is," Diana murmured and then looked up at him, meeting his eyes for the first time. "Logan? Is it really you? It's been years."

"You know it's me. You saw me earlier today, Diana. I tried to get to you, but you sped away."

She seemed just as hesitant to acknowledge him as he was to

say her name out loud. He knew he looked much different than he had at twenty-two. If she'd been any other friend from school, he'd have hugged her, but they'd know each other a little too intimately for that kind of familiarity.

She straightened, smiling unsurely as she did so. The years had been kind to her. She was more beautiful, almost glowing with the ethereal peach light of the lowering sun. He couldn't say the same of himself. He looked like he'd ridden the highway to Hell and back. He had.

"I'm sorry, but I was late for another engagement this afternoon. I was in a rush." She wasn't a good liar. Never had been.

"You ran like a scared animal," he replied.

"I wasn't running, and I'm certainly not scared," she fired back.

"You must have been in a rush," he surmised.

She didn't answer, just narrowed her eyes ever so slightly.

"Strange to see you after all this time," he continued. "I just read an article about you in the Oregon Stater Alumni magazine this morning."

"I hated that article. It was a terrible photo," she replied, raising her chin.

"No, it wasn't, but you look better in person," he countered, meaning it.

She was beautiful. "What are you doing here? I can't believe I was just reading about you this morning, and here you are."

Gone was the devotion he used to see in those mysterious hazel eyes. She wasn't the girl who would smile broadly at the sight of him. Not anymore. She was a woman in perfect harmony, with her beauty at its peak from years of maturity and life experience. There was also an underlying something about her, a wariness. He knew she'd had a tough childhood. He had been there to add a little salt to that wound in college at the end of their time together. But he sensed the new wariness in her had more to do with whatever she was doing for the D'Salvos.

"From the article, you probably know I'm a consultant with Wave out of Seattle. I'm doing a project for the Mountain Valley Vineyards this summer. I'm their consultant," she said, her tone a little guarded, formal even, as she leaned down to give Ginger's tummy a rub.

He was a little surprised she admitted it so easily.

"So, you're working for Salvatore and Marco D'Salvo, the two most dishonest men in all of Yamhill County," he said and shook his head, having a hard time tamping down his anger. But after what happened in college, he should have expected a little karmic retaliation that he wouldn't see coming. He'd just never expected this.

"Why would you say that about your neighbor?" she asked, her spine straightening a little as she spoke. If there had been any warmth in her tone, it disappeared. Shaking her head, she gave Ginger a final pat and stood. The dog blinked in surprise at the abrupt loss of attention.

"I have my reasons," he answered, no longer feeling any reminiscent warmth for the woman across from him. Salvatore D'Salvo, arguably the second worst man he'd ever known—next to Marco D'Salvo. Would he ever get a break?

"Anything you care to tell me about?" she asked, her smile now replaced with an edge he didn't remember.

"I hope they are paying you well," he said, shaking his head in disgust. "If they aren't, they should be. And watch out for Marco. He's a real piece of work and is known to every attractive woman in a five-mile radius as the self-proclaimed 'Italian Stallion.'"

"They are paying me quite well," she said, offering him a tight smile and changing the subject. She didn't respond to his comment about Marco. Had she already fallen under his spell?

"How are you, Logan? How are the wife and family?"

He flinched, she didn't know, and now he had to tell her. He

34

was so tired of telling people. He was tired of the stigma of the suffering widower. It drained him.

"My wife died two years ago in a car accident. She was killed by a careless driver in the car with her, and no, it wasn't me," he said, patting his leg to get the dog to move back to his side. Ginger remained on the ground, looking at him with incredulity.

"Logan...I'm so sorry. I didn't know," she managed, her hand reaching out to touch the sleeve of his work shirt but stopping well before it could make contact, as if she was worried contact with him might burn her. It hurt a little considering how close they had once been.

"How would you know anything about my life? It wasn't like we stayed in contact after you left," he said, not meaning to sound as accusing as he sounded.

Her lips moved but she said nothing. Then she asked, "Are you getting along okay?"

"I'm fine. Can't you tell?"

"You're anything but," she said, her words trailing off.

"Thanks a lot," he said sarcastically, knowing he was acting like a jerk.

"I just meant; how could you be fine? Your world changed drastically. You lost your wife, your partner. I don't think you ever get over something like that."

"You don't," he said, examining the creek beyond her. "You just learn to live with it."

"I don't know what to say," Diana said.

"Well, maybe that is a good thing. I'm not sure your employers would think this little conversation with me, the enemy, was a good idea," Logan offered. He'd like nothing more than to invite her back to his house, open a bottle of wine, and fill in the gaps of twelve missing years.

Longing that he hadn't felt in a very long time needled at him, an itch he couldn't quite reach to scratch. Knowing she was out in the world was manageable. Having her in front of him was another feeling all together.

The years away from her had taught him something. His feelings for her had been all-consuming, so strong that when she'd left, it had almost destroyed him. She was like a kind of fever that was potentially fatal. He'd had her and now wasn't he supposed to be immune?

Apparently not.

Logan conveniently forgot that he'd considered hiring her himself only a few hours ago. She was now a very personal kind of enemy. She would try to take him down, and how could he fault her?

Maybe D'Salvo had purposefully sent her to Logan's property with an agenda, or maybe she was just as unscrupulous as the old man. Logan couldn't vouch for what might have happened to her character over the last twelve years, but based on the company she kept, he would have to be careful.

"I don't know how the D'Salvos would feel, and I'm not sure I care. We haven't discussed business, but it would be nice to sit down with a glass of wine and catch up," she managed. He watched as a blush crept up her neck, making its way to her cheeks. He could still inspire a reaction in her, but this time it hadn't been from passion. If he wasn't mistaken, she still cared for him. She was fighting it, barely able to meet his gaze, but when she did, he could see the hurt in her eyes. At that moment, he remembered the first time he saw her. The first time he'd caught her attention and held it. It was not too unlike the way she was looking at him now, wide-eyed and unsure.

"It's just that I don't associate with people who associate with the D'Salvos," he said bluntly.

"If it makes any difference to you, they sought me. I didn't go looking for them," she said.

"Let me guess," he said as he folded his arms and stared down at her. "They want you to win the Stark Hotel contract for them and then put me out of business so that D'Salvo can steal my land. The final nail in my coffin."

The look that crossed her face told him all he needed to know. She recovered quickly, but not quite quick enough for him.

"I thought so," he said and smiled. The smile hurt. He wasn't used to using those particular facial muscles, and the intensity with which he offered the gesture hurt his face, cracking his skin like fissures in marble sculpture.

"You're partially correct. I'm here for the contest, only the contest. I don't know anything about the land," she answered carefully.

"Just like senior year and BA 438 all over again."

That's how they'd met in their strategic marketing class, BA 438, winter term of their senior year at Oregon State University. His presentation had been on tractor company, John Deere. Hers was on Ciba-Geigy, the international pharmaceutical company. They'd gone head-to-head in their final presentations, and the professor gave them the honors of being the best in class with nearly the same grade.

No one else had received an A.

After class, Logan caught up with her and struck up a conversation. They'd ended up back in the attic bedroom he rented in a big old Victorian off campus, making love in his narrow bed with the squeaky springs. Over the next three months, they spent a lot of time in that little bedroom, their own private love nest. He'd never known such passion, such love. Her background was tough, and so was his, but for different reasons.

He'd never known his biological father, and his biological mother had died giving birth to him as a teenager. She had gotten in trouble at the age of sixteen and tried to hide her pregnancy. The lack of prenatal care hadn't hurt him, but it had hurt his mother and contributed to her death. His maternal uncle and aunt were his parents. They had adopted him when he was a baby. He'd grown up on the vineyard and held the family name of his mother and uncle.

Diana was the first person who hadn't acted like he was damaged goods. Far from it. She thought her background made her the damaged goods.

"This time, there won't be two winners," she said, looking pointedly at him.

"Will you get paid less when you lose the contract to me?" he asked.

"You need to prepare yourself. I'm not going to lose, Logan. I'm very good at what I do, and now I get paid for it," she said, the steely determination he remembered so well finally showing up the party that was their banter.

"Let me ask you a pretty basic question. Have you tried all the wines at Mountain Valley, as well as all the other wines in the competition?"

"Yes, of course," she said, matching his stance with one of her own, folding her arms stubbornly over her chest. He remembered this pose. She had used it with him whenever she wanted to appear tough. He had a nearly photographic memory. It might have been years, but he could remember every inch, every curve, and flavor that was Diana Hunter.

"Then I'd suggest you not make any grand declarations. I'm not going to make any judgments about your wine palette, but even to the least sophisticated sommelier, there is something wrong with Mountain Valley Vineyards recent vintages."

"Really?" she said, a little of her bravado turning to curiosity. "What would that be?"

"All that D'Salvo bitterness has finally ruined the flavor of their wine."

"To my way of thinking, if there is someone who supposedly sounds bitter, it isn't the D'Salvos," she replied as she raised one eyebrow and looked at him.

A direct hit. Nice to see she hadn't lost all her fire with her new corporate polish.

"Touché," he said and stopped himself before he had the urge to wink at her.

"Look, Logan, I hope that we can be civil with each other during the contest.

After all, we were once very good friends."

They had been best friends. There was a time that nothing could have separated them. Then Wharton ruined everything.

"I'm very sorry to hear about your wife, which is a truly, horrible thing. But I'd appreciate it if we didn't insult each other. That isn't the memory I want to have of you," Diana said, looking directly at him, her eyes sad and pained. It got to him in ways he didn't want to contemplate, as if he were an errant child, and she was the understanding parent who wanted him to know she still cared despite how much he acted out.

Who had loved her after she'd left him? Had she ever felt as deeply for anyone else? Did she still remember the time they spent in his narrow little bed with the squeaky springs?

"What memory do you want to have of me?" he asked, curious.

"Someday, I might tell you," she answered and then glanced at her watch. "But that day is not today. I've got to get back for dinner with the family."

Of course, the D'Salvos would try to get her entrenched into their family quickly.

It was how they operated. They are your good friend until they want something from you that you don't want to give. Then it was all-out war.

"Wait," he said, not wanting her to leave on a sour note. "You should know something about walking around the vineyards, especially at night. It's not a good idea."

"Why?" she asked as she absently reached down to pet

Ginger. He could tell his disloyal dog was already half in love with Diana. He wanted to warn Ginger not to get too attached.

"There has been a cougar in the area. They aren't shy around humans."

"What?" she asked incredulously. "You can't be serious."

"I am," he said, whistling for Ginger to return to his side. "At night, I walk Ginger on a leash, and I carry a gun. I recommend you do the same."

"I'm not going to get a gun. I'd shoot myself or someone else," she said, her eyes narrowing in on him at the very idea.

"Then get pepper spray, the bear repellent kind, not just the regular strength, and stay alert."

"I'll think about it…"

"Just be careful, and please stay away from Marco," he said.

"Stay away from my client?" she asked. "That's a first."

"He's the most dangerous thing in this area," Logan added. "He makes the cougars look like house pets."

"Thanks for the advice," she said as she reluctantly turned and walked back toward Mountain Valley Vineyard.

He started missing her the moment she turned her back to him. The longing he had once felt for her tickled every cell of his body as it awakened after a deep sleep.

# CHAPTER FOUR

Diana walked away from Logan on shaky legs. When he told her that his wife had died, she didn't know what to say, as nothing seemed appropriate. And in her troubled, guilty mind, she felt a little excited at the knowledge that Logan was single again. It was wrong, and she was a horrible person for allowing such ideas to flood her mind, but she was only human. Under all the bitterness, was Logan still the man she remembered? The man who held her and taught her how to love?

She had been wrong earlier. He wasn't disheveled; he was rough-hewn in a way models strive to be. He hadn't been this handsome in college. He'd been almost gangly then, but she certainly wouldn't call him gangly now. No, all the hard edges had filled out with muscle and the right kind of bulk. He had untucked the blue chambray shirt. It was unbuttoned to form a v where she could see a smattering of dark chest hair. The last time she'd seen him without his shirt, his chest had been baby smooth. His narrow waist was still just as trim, but his body had filled out with lean muscle. He wore faded jeans with a rip on one of his knees. A hint of skin winked through the tear.

Logan's once very short black hair was too long and now streaked with a few strands of gray. She used to love running her fingers through that coal-black smoothness, which tickled her fingertips.

When she'd been with Logan, she hadn't had anyone to

compare him to as he'd been her first lover. And she'd been an apt pupil under his tutelage.

In the relationships she had since, no one had quite compared to Logan. She surmised it was because he was her first. Sure, every man who had come since had been fun, enjoyable, but nothing quite compared to that first love.

By the time they were seniors in college, they both lived off-campus, Diana with a group of girls, six sharing a three-bedroom house with no privacy. Logan, on the other hand, had his own bedroom in a big old Victorian on the edge of campus. He had the corner bedroom on the third floor, which was always a little too warm that spring term, always a bit stuffy and requiring a large fan to blow air over their damp skin.

His old, full-sized bed had a natural dimple in the middle of the mattress, causing them to roll toward the center all night long. They spent hours exploring each other's bodies, learning how to bring pleasure to each other.

*Logan.*

She'd seen Logan, and it was a much different reunion than she'd pictured. Not like she'd spent a lot of time thinking about Logan, but she had fantasized about how a reunion might play out. In each and every one of her stupid little fantasies, he was divorced. Their affair would be rekindled as if no time had passed. For him, just like it was for her, no one had ever come close to the magic, the passion that had so taken them all those years ago. In her fantasy, they questioned why they ever parted, Logan offering apologies for being stupid to not realize what they had. But it didn't matter because they were back together, and all was forgiven.

Maybe they'd meet up at an alumni event or just bump into each other at a wine festival. She'd attended enough of them. And what was the first thing that she always did when she got the program? Search for Logan's name. Search for the name of his winery. She'd had his wine. It was fantastic. She knew firsthand because she had her wine broker send her at least three cases a year from Logan's vineyard. Not that she'd ever tell Logan that little piece of information. From exploring the Forget-Me-Not website, she knew that Logan had inherited the vineyard from his aunt and uncle, soon after he had graduated from Oregon State. They would be proud of his skills as a wine-maker. They had been proud of him when she met them all those years ago. It hurt her heart to know they had both passed.

His wine was better than Mountain Valley Vineyard's—at least it had been. She should have known something had happened. She hadn't cared for his last years' vintage. There was something missing, the magic of love. Just as Logan accused Mountain Valley of adding bitter to their wine, his wine had suffered, and she thought she knew why. As the winemaker, when his wife died, he had lost some of his finesse. A wine-maker had to mix each vintage with a skillful hand and a magical touch. In his pain over the death of his wife, Logan had yet to re-master that touch. It showed in his products.

Wine might be made from organic material, but there is something unseen that converts the grape juice into wine. The same materials, in the same ratios, all balanced, in the same way, should make the same recipe taste the same, but it didn't. And in that magic was what Diana could see. Salvatore D'Salvo was the winemaker at Mountain Valley. She wondered if Marco had been learning that skill and not quite up to par yet. Suffice it to say. Neither vineyard was at the top of their game.

Diana sighed and then took a deep breath of the cool valley air as she walked back to her cottage. She didn't need to solve all the mysteries around Logan this evening, nor did she need to torture herself with what could have been. She had a job to do, and it started with dinner at the D'Salvo family dinner table.

A glance at her watch proved that she was just on time for dinner with the family. She made her way to the large house on the hill beyond the cottage where she was staying with a carefully wrapped bundle in her arms. Thinking it best to take something with her, she'd picked up a bouquet of peonies in pink, white and dark rose after the ceremony that afternoon.

Who didn't love fresh spring flowers, especially peonies?

Salvatore's wife, Sophia, was a curvy Italian woman with olive skin, a sweet Italian accent, and a vibrant smile.

"They are gorgeous," she exclaimed as she took the flowers from Diana and pulled them close.

"Peonies are some of my favorites," Diana said, feeling like she'd earned points with Salvatore's wife. She was as gracious as her husband was weary. "I was getting a bouquet for my cottage and thought you might like to have one as well."

She was introduced to the tasting room staff, the cousins, who had been invited to dinner to meet her.

Marco did the honors. "Diana, I know you saw them earlier, but may I formally introduce my cousins, Davide and Antonio."

Davide and Antonio were almost shy in her presence but quickly opened up when they discussed their love of wine.

"I love everything about the grapes, the way you hold them and feel the juice they will give to make the wine. It is love," Davide gushed, his accent heavy and affected. He and his brother reminded her of Italian Hemsworth brothers with longer bleached blond hair and no doubt half the IQ. Somewhere, romance novels were missing their cover models.

Antonio shared his brother's enthusiasm and heavy accent, "This autumn, we will crush some of the grapes by hand to show the Americans how we used to make the wine at our vineyard in Italy, gently as not to break the skin."

With their accents, "wine" sounded like "vine."

When they weren't speaking to her and telling her about wine, they spoke in Italian. When they found out she had never been to Italy, they spoke of the country in great detail. The conversation took them through the antipasti and her first glass of wine, and then she engaged Sophia in a conversation.

"It must be wonderful to have your son in the business," she said as the second glass of wine appeared before her.

"It is very exciting. He has many new ideas and big dreams like Sal and I did when we were first married. We've integrated several in the last few years, but he has more. I can't wait to see what Marco will do."

They ate outdoors at an oversized picnic table covered with a traditional gingham checkered cloth in red and white, the evening air unusually warm. Sophia lit pink, orange, and red Chinese lanterns and had the tall cousins place them on tree limbs. They illuminated the space while large outdoor space heaters were placed just a few feet away from the four corners of the table.

Diana enjoyed sitting next to Sophia at dinner and getting to know the softer side of the D'Salvo family as Marco and Salvatore spent a lot of time speaking Italian with the cousins.

As the evening progressed and the third and fourth glasses of wine were poured, Diana steered the conversation to several items on her agenda while she was still coherent.

"Who has the winery next door with the red dog?" she asked, playing aloof.

"That is Logan Parrish," the woman began and then took a large sip of her most recent glass of wine. "He is a widower."

"He's pretty young to be a widower," Diana said, thinking again of how that must have affected Logan.

"It was a tragic accident," Salvatore said. "But all was not well in that marriage. They were divorcing. I liked his wife, Julianna, very much."

"Divorcing?" she asked, her head spinning, and not just because of the wine. The news of the divorce was blindsiding, a complete game changer. She needed to know more.

"There was a lot going on behind the scenes, but the accident several years ago put all of that to the side. May Julianna rest in peace," Sophia repeated as she made the sign of the cross over her chest.

Diana could feel the path of the wine she'd drunk burn its way down her throat. Logan's tragedy was much worse than she'd imagined. They were getting a divorce? Based on what Sophia said too, the accident was quite a while ago. What had Logan said? Two years? She'd have to search this on the web to see what took place.

"Ever since Julianna's death, the winery, as well as Logan, has been in disrepair. He appeared to give up on everything that once mattered. The rumor is that he is close to bankruptcy. It is so sad to see," Sophia added in almost a whisper.

"I saw him walking with his dog earlier today. We briefly said hello," she admitted, feeling like the wine had opened her personal vault of secrets. She had to be careful.

"Was he nice to you?" Sophia asked. "He's been known to call the police if we set foot on his land. You didn't get too close to the little valley that dips between the two properties, did you? Salvatore should have warned you." With this last statement, she looked at her husband, who merely shrugged.

"Mr. Parrish was polite enough," Diana said, feeling a little trapped.

"Well, that is a first in a long time. He didn't die with his wife, but he has certainly given up on life and tried to make everyone around him suffer," Sophia said, making Diana wince.

"Salvatore is doing him a great favor. I just hope that Logan comes to his senses and agrees. He needs to move on and get a fresh start somewhere else. Salvatore once offered him a job as a traveling representative for Mountain Valley Vineyards. He took offense to it, but he should've been flattered. It isn't just anyone who can travel around and market for our vineyard."

"Despite our differences, I've always respected Logan," Salvatore offered. "I've watched him grow up next door."

Diana didn't know what to make of Salvatore or Sophia's

comments. Insulting was the word that kept circling back to her again and again at the mere mention of being a traveling salesperson. From what she knew of Logan, even when he was in college, he would have been overqualified for such a tedious position. She felt there was a back story and only hoped she would hear it someday. But for the moment, she'd asked enough questions. She did not want them to get suspicious about her interest in Logan.

The D'Salvos did a good job of distracting her by continuing to pour glass after glass of wine for her to try. She had a fairly good tolerance for wine; it came with the territory of being a beverage specialist. But today had been anything but typical. Somewhere between the fifth and sixth glass, she made her excuses and decided it would be a good idea to call it a night before she passed out or otherwise made a fool of herself. As it was, she could already feel the world spinning at the edges. She needed to leave before the full effect of the wine took hold.

"May I help with the cleaning up?" she asked Sophia.

"Oh dear, no, you are our guest," Sophia protested. "That is why I have all these strong men at my disposal."

"Thank you for a lovely evening. I'll say goodnight," Diana said.

"May I walk you to your cottage?" Marco offered, standing, and reaching for Diana's arm.

"Oh, thank you, but that isn't necessary. We can see the backside of it from here," Diana said. "Besides, Sophia needs your help. I'll be fine."

"As you wish," he said, smiling at her insincerely with his snaggletooth.

She made her goodbyes, aware they were watching her go. At the back edge of her cottage, she waved to them and rounded the corner onto the front porch, where something large moved in the shadows.

"No, no, no," she whispered aloud, remembering Logan's warnings. "I cannot believe this. Damn it, damn cougar!"

Just as she was about to scream, a voice she recognized said, "It's not a cougar, it's me."

"Logan?" she asked as the world gently shifted out of its edges.

"Damn it, are you drunk?" Logan asked with definite disapproval.

She was a little drunk, but she wasn't going to admit it to him. "What are you doing here?"

"I brought you something."

"You what?" she asked, stepping gingerly onto the porch, her eyes adjusting to the face in the darkness.

"You should leave your porch light on if you are going out at night, or you really could get a cougar on your porch," he said, sounding angry. "Maybe you should make it a rule to turn it on every night."

"Thanks for the advice, but you don't have to sound so mean about it," she said. "This is only my first day."

"What if I had been a cougar?" he asked, "By now, you would have been a delectable snack."

"Would you have even cared if I'd been mauled and eaten?" she asked as he stood, the wicker rocking chair he'd been in, groaning with his departure.

"Well, it would've solved a problem or two," he said as he handed her a small canister that looked like hairspray. "Careful with this. Technically it is a weapon. If you use it on a human, there could be consequences."

"What is it?" she asked, holding the bottle tentatively.

"I brought you some bear retardant. It is a very strong pepper spray. I had an extra bottle lying around."

"Well, thanks, I guess. At least it isn't a gun," she replied and then giggled.

"Careful," he warned.

"I still think you might not care if I was attacked," she said.

"Come on, Diana...I wouldn't have wanted you to be eaten by a cougar," he said, his face only inches away from hers. "And I definitely wouldn't want you attacked, especially by Marco or one of those bleached blond creeps employed by the D'Salvos. Feel free to use it on them if they get too close."

"Maybe you do like me still, just a little bit," she teased as she leaned forward, lost her balance, and fell against him. Strong, warm arms wrapped around her, catching her before she could do any real damage, steadying her body as if she weighed nothing. Without thinking, she wrapped her arms around him and sank against him, enjoying the sensation of being held by a man she had once loved, possibly still loved, in a small recess of her heart.

"Whoa...Easy there," he warned as his arms held her.

She heard more than one warning in his words and decided to ignore, unilaterally, each and every one of them.

"I'm glad you wouldn't want to see me mauled by a wild cougar or a D'Salvo," she mused.

"Come on, of course, I wouldn't want to see you mauled," he said. "Maybe a warning nip—but when it comes to those weird blond relatives from Italy or that ass, Marco, use the spray and use it liberally."

"Logan, I still like you...More than I should. It is strange, after all these years and what happened between us, but you're still really handsome, and I've missed you."

"Thank you, I think," he said awkwardly.

"You're welcome," she replied, inhaling the scent of him, cedar, fresh cotton, and a hint of bergamot as her heart hummed in reaction to the sound of his voice.

"We should get you inside, where you can sit down," he suggested, his arms starting to steer her in the direction of the door.

Giggling like a teenager she'd never been, she said, "Maybe

we should stay like this."

"Diana, this is not a good idea," he said, but she could feel his heart beating steady and strong against her ear. She remembered being held like this, remembered him. She had ached for him. She ached for the memory of how it had felt to be in his arms. It was so bittersweet it reminded her of those weeks after they'd broken up. The memory sobered her as she bit back a jolt of pure pain that hit every nerve in her body with shocking speed.

*God, maybe she was drunk.*

"Did you bring a gun?" she asked, summoning up her strength to let go of the one thing she wanted to hold onto more than anything else in the world. She straightened awkwardly, her arms reluctantly relinquishing their hold on him.

"It's leaning against the door frame," he replied, stepping away from her and walking her to the door of her cottage.

Holding up her key, she felt his fingers brush over hers as he snagged it from her hand and used it to open the lock. Her skin felt seared from his touch, as if he'd left permanent fingerprints on her flesh.

"You're going to have such a bad hangover tomorrow."

"Probably, the world is spinning around me. Wine is the worst for hangovers. Have I said anything really embarrassing?" she asked, trying to lighten what had become an awkward situation.

"No, but if the world is spinning, remember to put—"

"My foot on the floor to make the world stop spinning...I know you told me that a hundred times back at school." She'd almost added "when we together," but caught herself.

"That's right," he said, a small smile curling up the corner of his mouth. It refreshed one of her most tender memories. That smile, the "melting" smile she'd always called it.

"Are we trying to be friends now?"

"I'm not sure," he said, the smile dropping from his face like a switch turning off a light and plunging a room into darkness.

"Why not?"

"Because of whom you work for, it makes it very complicated," he said with all seriousness. "You are working for the enemy."

"You must like me a little. You brought me pepper spray," she said, her voice warm and soft.

"I'm serious about how strong that stuff is. Please be careful with it," he said, pointing to the pepper spray she dropped on the nearest table.

"Do you think of me as your enemy too?" she asked, her voice taking on a pathetic edge she didn't like.

"Let me put it to you this way. I keep my friends close and my enemies closer," he said.

"I'm not the enemy. Logan, we were the closest of friends once, doesn't that mean anything to you?"

"Diana, yes, of course," he said, his voice softening. "This is business. Another time, different circumstances, but I'm a much different person than I was twelve years ago. I hardly think you'd like the new Logan Parrish."

"Can I have a chance to find out?"

"I don't know if we can be friends, not now, not with the competition."

"That makes me sad," she said, hoping she wouldn't start crying at the irony of life and how, yet again, fate had decided to punish them.

"It isn't personal."

"Of course, it is personal. And sad. And kind of mean," she managed, feeling that familiar lump in the throat that was a purely emotional reaction she could count on from her body at times like this.

"Then I guess I'm kind of mean," he said, sadness in his voice as he turned, picked up his gun and disappeared into the darkness without a glance back in her direction.

# CHAPTER FIVE

Diana heard a familiar, obnoxious beeping. Her damn alarm clock was fouling the peace and quiet of her restless sleep. For reasons she did not yet comprehend, the noise felt like it was sounding off inside her head. Rolling over on the too soft mattress after her first night in the Merlot Cottage, she grabbed the offending travel alarm and tried to find the button that would make it stop. Staring up at the open beam ceiling, she watched the large beams fade in and out of focus. Forty-eight beams. She had counted them last night when she was wide awake, reliving every nuance of her conversation with Logan. At close to three a.m., she'd dozed off. Somewhere a fly buzzed back and forth, further annoying her. Her mouth tasted like something had died in it, leaving a carpet of debris on her tongue.

The evening before came back to her like a disturbing scene from a violent movie.

The dinner, all the wine, the blond Italian cousins, the conversations about the love of wine, Sophia talking about Logan, the pending divorce, and then more wine. And last, coming back to her cottage and finding Logan waiting with the pepper spray. She'd hugged him, felt his solid body in her arms. What had she done? More importantly, what had she said? She thought she had a pretty accurate idea, but it swam like a nauseating dream.

"Oh, damn," she said aloud. She'd thrown herself at him.

Thankfully, she hadn't tried to kiss him, or had she? No, that felt right. She hadn't done anything to completely embarrass herself. She had called him mean and told him he'd made her sad, and he had walked away without looking back at her.

At the thought of it, tears formed at the corner of her eyes. She refused to let them fall, blinking them away. She was tougher than this.

Any romantic notion she'd had of rekindling their relationship had died in a matter of moments. She'd only been able to enjoy the fantasy for a couple of hours. Maybe that was for the best. If he hadn't shown up the night before, her mind would have lingered on the possibility for days. Built up unrealistic expectations. It would have hurt more to have those dreams shattered in a few days, right? Sure. Then why did it hurt so much now?

Why had he shown up to deliver a gift? Okay, it wasn't flowers or something nice. It was pepper spray, but still a gift you'd give someone you were worried about. What was going on in his head?

He'd said they couldn't be friends. Why it cut her to the quick, she didn't know. It wasn't like she had lost anything, like all those years ago.

Pushing herself out of bed, Diana almost fell back in, the world moving a little too fast.

Finally making it out of bed on the third attempt, she took a cold shower and washed with a lavender scented body wash, hoping it would remove the scent of "old wino" that clung to her body like musky perfume. She brushed her teeth twice and used mouthwash and chewed gum but it still felt the sins of the night before seeping out of her pores. She had to use extra makeup under her eyes to take a little of the darkness away.

Breakfast was dry toast and strong coffee. For several moments, she wasn't sure she'd get it down, especially after she looked to the coffee table and found the pepper spray canister where she'd left it.

And strangely, this gift, coming from Logan, meant more to her than anything that her ex-fiancé had ever given her—including a diamond engagement ring she'd thrown at Brad's head when she'd discovered him in bed with another woman.

"You're not friends. He doesn't want to be your friend," she said to herself as she moved around the cottage.

Ignoring her complex feelings toward the pepper spray, she focused on setting up her office space at the cottage's dining room table. The pine surface was uneven, constructed of reclaimed lumber, which was full of knots and holes. Great, had she known, she would have brought an office blotter with her, so she would have a smooth surface to work on. She didn't like things that were untidy, and this table was going to complicate her sense of order and control.

It wasn't the uneven table messing with her sense of order and control. But she pushed the real reason further to the back of her mind, where hope, rainbows, and thoughts of everlasting happiness liked to poke fun at her in quieter moments.

Her first order of business was to start working on her plans for the first competition for the Stark Hotel contract—a tasting booth at the Portland Waterfront Carnival. It marked the start of the summer on the waterfront in downtown Portland, thirty miles away. From what she'd researched, it sounded like a tacky, low-rent carnival event. She wondered about the level of sophistication. She didn't want to misjudge their audience. Logan would be there, along with three other competitors, and she wanted to make sure they had an impressive first showing.

By ten o'clock, she had a few good ideas in mind, printed out a summary sheet, changed into jeans, a button-down white shirt, and a bunch of chunky silver jewelry. Put together as well as she was ever going to be, she headed to Salvatore's office to discuss her ideas with him.

When she arrived, it wasn't Salvatore who sat behind the patriarch's desk, but Marco. Diana knocked softly on the open door.

"Good morning, Marco. I enjoyed meeting everyone last night. You have a great family," she said, meaning it. When you didn't have a family, you envied anyone who had relatives, good, bad, or indifferent. She'd known she was different from an early age. She didn't have a mother to pick her up at the end of the school day. No one was there to make cookies or make sure she had pencils and other basic school supplies at the beginning of the school year. No one cared if she bathed or had clean clothes.

Sobriety for her father, who was the king of odd jobs, was the exception, not the rule. It is amazing she survived, let alone grew up. Whenever she saw a certain brand of condensed soup in the store that used to sell for sixty-nine cents, it was all she could do not to shake as she relived the memory. Growing up, soup from a can was the closest she came to a homemade meal. It wasn't until she was in college that she learned to cook using recipes her roommates generously shared with her from their own childhood. Now, she made Betsy's mother's stir fry chicken and Lorinda's Aunt Mary's beef thingy, which was an all-time favorite. Each little step she made toward normalcy made her feel better about herself, at least on the days she didn't worry that she was a large fraud.

"Yes, I am very lucky. Good morning, by the way. Are you ready to get started?"

"Yes," she said, "I was just working on an idea for our tasting booth for the first event of the contest. I was thinking about an Italian street scene, paying homage to your heritage."

"I like it," he said. "I've had a few ideas myself."

"Can't wait to hear them. Where is Salvatore?" she asked, instinct telling her to wait until he'd returned than to share the full concept. Marco looked at her in a particular way that made her uncomfortable, definitely checking her out as his smiled with that evil grin.

"He's out walking the vineyard. He does it each morning, picks different sections every day. He should be back at any minute."

"Good," Diana said, wondering why the heir apparent didn't go along. "Maybe I'll have a look around until he gets back, and then I can share the full vision."

"Sounds great. Get to know the place," Marco said. Then he added, "Why don't you allow me to show you around?"

Diana agreed with his offer, not that she felt keen about being in his presence. The D'Salvos had a large operation with a lot of people. Marco tried to impress her, and she let him to a certain point, but mainly she wanted to keep her distance from the man Logan had referred to as the "Italian Stallion." With his smile and creepy ways, he definitely had a lewd vibe about him.

Over the next few days, she worked hard planning for the Waterfront Carnival event. Salvatore liked her ideas, thought she was creative, and he complimented her profusely. Marco showed his father his ideas, and when placed in a position between the two sides, Salvatore gave into his family. Diana smiled and agreed, but on the inside she made note of the first signs of disaster. If this was the way it was going to be over the next three months, there had been no need to hire her.

When she wasn't thinking of the mess she'd just stepped into, her thoughts lingered on the man in the next vineyard over. After the visit that first night, Logan hadn't made another appearance. She knew she'd see him in a week at their first competition. They were slated to have booths next to each other, competing head-to-head. Would they chat? Be friendly? Sometimes when you didn't know what to do, the best action was to do nothing. For Diana, who liked to take action, it was an incredibly bad position to be forced into.

# CHAPTER SIX

Diana walked around the charming town of Dundee. She'd had little postcards printed up to let the locals know where they could see their favorite local winery compete.

News flash, she hadn't gotten a very positive reaction from the last five businesses she'd visited, as she proclaimed that Mountain Valley was a local favorite. They had a lot of unflattering gossip to share. No wonder Logan despised Marco. She hadn't liked him on sight, but now she despised him more. Poor Logan.

She stopped in at a little bookstore that had wonderful displays in the front bay window focusing on summer reading. What went better with wine than books? Okay, cheese, but still she thought she'd find likeminded individuals at the local bookstore.

Wearing her biggest smile and business casual attire, she'd found a couple of novels by one of her favorite authors that she had yet to read.

Walking them up to the front counter, she added two pieces of handmade fudge. She needed the calories like a hole in the head, and fudge was a weakness. This chocolate-walnut variety and butterscotch looked especially good.

"Welcome to Merlot-to-Love-Books," an older gentleman offered as he set down a pipe that smelled sweet. Diana bit her lip. She didn't need to lecture him about the cancer club. His pipe completed his look.

"Thank you. I needed some books to read before bed," she said. "I'm staying here for a few months, and my cabin doesn't have a television. I just love this author."

"A few months, you say? Writing a novel that has always been inside of you or fulfilling a childhood dream by working at a vineyard?" he asked.

"You're good! I'm working at Mountain Valley," she said and held up a card. "I'm a beverage specialist, and they are in a contest for a contract with Stark Hotels."

"Ah yes the D'Salvos. Sophia D'Salvo is a nice lady, but her son...Well, you watch out for that Marco D'Salvo. You look like a nice girl. He isn't a nice man," the man said with disgust. She was getting the feeling *no one* in town liked Marco.

"Thank you. Trust me, I've met him," she said conspiratorially. "I do like Sophia. She is a sweet person."

"It is unfortunate her only son is trouble. That boy is trouble for our whole valley. Hell, he should be in jail after that accident he caused a couple of years ago. A lot of us don't drink their wine after that happened, despite how much we like Sophia."

Feigning surprise, Diana said, "I heard rumors about a bad car accident. Is that what you're talking about? I've heard snippets here and there, but I didn't get the details. Do you have a moment? Would you please fill me in? I want to know the truth." Diana was the only one in the store, and if she was predicting correctly, this was one of those older men, like many of his generation, who liked to chat. She leaned against the counter and tried to look interested. Actually, she was fascinated.

"Well, now, let me get the details correct in my mind," he said, seeming to ponder for a few moments. "Okay, now I remember. It was June, no May, two years ago. We think Marco was drunk when he was in a terrible car accident on Highway

20, on the way to the beach that killed that Parrish girl. His daddy, Salvatore, who is just like him when he was young, paid off the local law or some such so the heir apparent wouldn't go to jail. Marco didn't even get a ticket. He did get a broken arm, but it hardly sounds fair when that Parrish girl died."

"Logan Parrish's wife? Julianna Parrish? Why was she with him? Or was she in another car?" she asked.

"Yeah, that was her name. No, she was Marco's passenger. Rumor is, Marco had met her along the fence that divides their vineyards. He made it his mission to seduce her because he didn't, and still doesn't like Logan Parish, his neighbor. Marco had designs on forcing Parrish out of business. Like that would ever happen. Logan knows how to make wine, Marco does not. And seduce Mrs. Parrish, that little jerk did. And the price she paid for the dalliance was death."

"How awful! That might be the most awful story I've ever heard," Diana said.

"Rumor was when Logan found out about the affair, he threatened to kill Marco, but his own people stopped him from confronting Marco. He did go a little berserk, broke a bunch of empty wine bottles, but no real damage. But the wife, she got a little vicious and used it as a reason to move out. Or maybe she wanted Logan to know she was serious, or she wanted to get his attention. Anyway, she moved in with Marco."

"Marco for Logan? Was she crazy?" Diana asked.

"Naw, she wasn't meant for this life if you ask me. She was a Keary girl from the Keary family of bakers in town. A little wild, always wanted to get out of here for bigger and better things. Not cut out to be a vintner's wife. I think she was bored, tired of the vineyard life from what I hear. I don't think Marco would have ever married her. Probably promised her a ticket out of here, a bigger city, more excitement. I would bet her accommodations at Mountain Valley were a bit of a shock. Forget-Me-Not is a much nicer vineyard. It has been in the valley for a bunch of generations. Heck, Logan built her a big house for her when they got married.

"She was just a conquest for Marco, like a lot of women in this valley. Heck, two weeks after the accident, he'd moved on to someone else. Aside from the cast on his arm, he acted like nothing had happened."

"Wow," Diana said. No wonder Logan hated Marco, and she couldn't blame him.

"That is the most scandal this little town has had in thirty years since the Priest at the Catholic church ran off with one of the high school girls. I hear they made a happy life in California."

Diana had thanked the man, paid for her books and fudge, and felt the puzzle pieces all come together. Marco was a jerk. Julianna must have been very desperate to ever get near Marco. What a waste.

Diana walked around a bit to clear her mind. Eventually, she happened on a little boutique and decided to reward her efforts of the day by trying on outfits and not mentioning her affiliation to Mountain Valley Vineyards. She seemed to get better service when she did.

Forty-five minutes later, she had a new Eileen West nightgown and matching robe in white with a soft blue rose pattern. The shop owner was almost as excited as Diana was with the purchase. It was the first new sleepwear she'd bought in several years, and she thought it was well past time. The tee shirts and shorts she'd favored after her breakup with Brad were getting a little old. She wanted something feminine that didn't have any memories associated with it.

"I love this nightgown and robe!" the woman exclaimed as she carefully folded each piece and wrapped them in crisp rose-petal pink tissue.

"I like it. I can't say no," Diana said, nodding, loving the ritual of the packaging that came with purchasing delicate things.

"It just feels like the area. I picture you wearing it as you drink a glass of wine and watch the sunset over one of our beautiful vineyards."

"That is a lovely vision. I'll try to make it come true," Diana promised.

"May our little town become one of your sweetest memories."

As much as Diana appreciated the well wishes, she had a sneaking feeling that that may not be the case...

# CHAPTER SEVEN

The Waterfront Carnival was situated on a mile-long park next to the Willamette River in downtown Portland. The grassy park had been transformed into a colorful carnival with a Ferris Wheel and carny rides and booths bringing a cortege of families and onlookers. The air smelled of tired and faded plastic play equipment, burnt caramel popcorn, and steaming hot dogs that were sure to cause stomach distress.

Toward the south end of the festivities, with a view of the port-a-potties, where the grownups tended to congeal and commiserate about their ride-hopping kids, the five Yamhill Valley wineries were given booths for the Stark Hotel competition on the beat down grass pathway.

Logan, who even as a child hadn't liked The Waterfront Carnival, arrived early to set up his booth. He stared in disbelief at the Mountain Valley Vineyards space next to his. He'd shown up with cases of wine and everything he'd need for his wine tastings and thought he had everything in order. That was until he'd walked up and found out that his booth was the equivalent of the worst house on the best street. This was Diana's work, no doubt about it.

His little white table was adorned with a banner, which read: Forget-Me-Not Winery. There were several little potted forget-me-nots he'd arranged as décor. The delicate blue flowers seemed to whither in their pots as they were completely overshadowed by the space next door he could only describe as "Little Venice."

How Diana had achieved it and what it had cost, he didn't know. At the back of the booth was a huge, curved panel television running a street scene from the canals of Venice. It was large enough that you felt that you were standing next to the actual canal in Venice. If you stared long enough, it threatened to make you motion sick. How she'd gotten the power to the tent, he could only imagine.

Diana had set up six small café tables with red checkered cloths and wrought iron chairs on a flat platform that was painted with fake cobblestones to resemble a real Italian street. Soft, subtle Italian dinner music wafted his way. Above the booth, a sign proclaimed: Mountain Valley Vineyards: *A Taste of Italy*. Then her staff arrived, and Logan reconsidered that the booth should be entitled: *The Best Little Whore House in Italy*.

"What the fuck?" he murmured as he watched the large staff of six young twenty-something women, all dressed in crisp white shirts with black lace bras underneath, arrange themselves. They proudly displayed the Mountain Valley Vineyard monogram in black lettering across the right pocket of their blouses, which strained tightly against their breasts. They hardly looked old enough to serve alcohol. They wore black miniskirts and black nylons tucked into high-heeled patent leather boots that should easily hobble them within a couple of hours. They all looked strangely alike, with slicked back hair.

The word 'Fembots' came to mind, and Logan was a little surprised that Diana would stoop so low as to target solely males to her booth. But just when he thought he'd seen it all, she surprised him again.

"Double fuck," he murmured as the two men he'd thought of as "The Blond Idiots" arrived. Their puffy bleached hair was styled into what could only be described as manes. Their black silk shirts were unbuttoned to mid-chest, displaying a lot of tan, smooth, hairless chests. Somewhere, a pirate ship had a couple of deserters. Then he recognized the man he hated with every ounce of his being, Marco D'Salvo.

"The Blonds" manned an ornate Gelato cart, which quickly became a draw for wide-eyed mothers toting bewildered children. It was a carnival inside a carnival and wrong on every level.

Logan just saw red.

He wanted to pick up one of his insipid pots of forget-me-nots and toss it through the screen of Venice or, better yet, directly at Marco's head. He'd have to add that particular idea to the list of ways he'd like to kill Marco.

The whole experience made him feel stupid and inadequate. He'd brought a slingshot to a machine gun battle. And most of all, Diana had bested him. He was mad at himself most of all for underestimating her.

Salvatore wandered over to Logan's booth and offered, "Hello, Logan. Good to see you here."

"Salvatore."

"You know, it doesn't have to go on like this. You don't need to be in this competition. I've always liked you, Logan. You have a drive so like my own. We can help you. You could make a new start, get away from the bad memories of this place."

"And why would I need your help or a new start?" Logan asked, feeling his fingernails dig into his palms.

"It might be better for everyone."

"Don't you mean it would be better for you and your murdering, philandering son?" Logan asked.

"Logan, you know it wasn't like that. It was an accident, and what happened with Julianna was not something that could be predicted."

"In your mind," Logan fired back.

"I can see I can't talk to you about this. Maybe another time," he said and turned to leave.

The Mountain Valley booth was jammed with people from the start. Diana had quietly arrived shortly before the gates opened, dressed like a freaking lion tamer. All in black, her hair was pulled back into a severe bun. She wore knee high boots like the girls serving wine and even had a short, tight black skirt, which showed off the curves he remembered so well. Logan wouldn't have been surprised to see her carrying a whip. Considering the company she was keeping, carrying a weapon wasn't a bad idea.

She moved efficiently, giving instructions to the staff assembled and encouraging people to fill out their ballots to vote for the best booth. They were supposed to be voting for the best wine.

From his quiet space next door, Logan observed the happenings and made a few mental notes for their next event, the Hot Air Balloon Festival, in two weeks. Occasionally, he'd catch the eye of one of his neighbors from one of the other wineries in the competition. They'd give a nod toward Mountain Valley's booth and just shake their heads in mutual frustration.

As Logan watched, several people placed ballots in the secured box at the guard station without giving his booth or his wines a second glance. At this rate, he would be dead in the water in no time at all. His tasting room managers—Ben, along with his wife, Tess—arrived shortly before noon. Ben studied the booth next to them before turning to Logan.

"Damn," Ben muttered under his breath as he reached out to shake Logan's hand.

"We have a problem," Logan agreed.

"Any idea what to do about it?"

"No. Everything I've thought of is illegal. I'm thinking we give this one to them, but for the next event, we bring it."

"So, you're just going to give up on today?" Ben asked.

"No, but I haven't thought of something that will save us.

Not *yet*," Logan empathized, watching as Diana's hazel eyes locked with his. She smiled, a smile of assumed victory.

That did it.

That smile was exactly the catalyst he needed. It was time to get down and dirty within the rules of the competition. He'd read them carefully and didn't remember seeing anything about bribery.

"I just got the idea I needed," he said to Ben and Tess. "Hold down the booth. I'll be back."

He walked away from the wine tasting with one last, long glance at Diana, which caught and held her attention. A man on a mission, once he was out of her sightline, he started to run. He didn't have a moment to lose.

# CHAPTER EIGHT

Logan looked better today than he had the day she'd seen him down by the creek, Diana thought as she stole glances at him. He wore a simple black polo with a pair of faded, comfortable jeans. He still needed a decent haircut. The black of his shirt set off the traces of premature gray in his hair. At least he'd shaved. Seeing his clean, strong jaw did strange things to her, reminding her there was a space low in her abdomen that liked to beat to its own rhythm whenever she was close to this man. Especially when she'd been making love with him. Memories of those intimate times in his hot attic room rolled over her, heating her cheeks. Now was not the time or the place, but she couldn't help that her stubborn mind kept flashing images before her eyes.

*Remember, he doesn't want to be your friend.*

Looking away, she regarded her booth once more.

Logan made the blond cousins in her booth look fake. He was the sexiest man within ten miles of this event. Why the women weren't clamoring to his booth, she didn't know. If she'd happened upon this wine tasting, she wouldn't have given the Mountain Valley Vineyard booth a second glance. All her attention would have been reserved for the good-looking man at Forget-Me-Not.

Despite the fact that they were winning this event, she felt bad for Logan. She wished he wasn't in this competition. It made it hard for her to concentrate on winning. After hearing

Logan's story, she didn't want to compete with him. She wanted him to be okay. She only wished circumstances were different.

If he'd called her instead of Mountain Valley, maybe she could have helped him and found a way to save his business.

She watched as Logan spoke with the others in his booth and then sped away from the wine tasting area. What was he up to? Something that was not good. She was sure of it. She was also sure that she had the winning booth for the day. What could he possibly do to catch up to her?

She didn't have to wait long to find out.

Logan returned an hour after he'd left, carrying three large panels wrapped in butcher paper. On his second trip, he returned with three large easels and several boxes from a local seed company, Lily Miller. On the side of each box, in big letters, someone had written: *2,000 qty*.

*Forget-Me-Not*.

Placing her large sunglasses on her face to cover her eyes, she watched Logan without really watching him. She could have been looking anywhere; he at least wouldn't be able to see how intently she observed him.

"What is he up to?" Marco asked from behind her.

"He's getting into the game," she replied as she glanced toward the women Marco had hired for the booth against her advice. Davide and Antonio were charming women with their accent as they worked their gelato scoops. Marco had taken her idea about an Italian street side café and modified it to be the equivalent of one-stop wine tasting and porn shop. She wondered where he'd found all the women. They had food handler licenses, but she'd bet their "day" jobs involved poles and black lace, crotchless panties. And the way they were flirting with patrons was starting to get on her nerves.

As she pondered all these things, Logan unveiled his first poster, and Diana felt the twist in her gut. A large, tasteful sign read: "Vote for Forget-Me-Not Winery and Ensure that No Child is ever Forgotten." The next poster read: "A Vote Equals a Donation to Support Local Foster Children in Need." And a third: "Forget-Me-Not Understands That Not Everyone Can Be a Foster Parent, But Everyone Can Help a Foster Child in Need."

"Damn it," she murmured under her breath, but secretly she had to hand it to him.

He'd found a way around the rules.

Marco exclaimed, "He can't do that!"

"Yes," she said, quietly as she seethed, "he can."

"Then why didn't we do something like that?"

"Are you serious?" she asked, lowering her sunglasses as she turned to look at him. "Our display drips of money and sex. If we did something like that, well, let's just say being next to all those sweet little pots of forget-me-nots and all that white space make us look dirty and more than a little creepy."

"You thought it was a good idea a week ago."

"Marco, I liked my idea. I'm not crazy how you embellished it with these freakish women. We've probably won today, but I'm not sure I like how we did it."

"I understand," Marco said. "It is a little over the top."

"That's one way to put it."

Turning her attention back to Logan, she watched as a woman approached Logan's booth and sampled his wines. She then asked him for a pen, which she quickly used to fill out her ballot. She showed it to Logan and received one of his gorgeous smiles and a packet of forget-me-not seeds.

Damn it! That woman hadn't even stopped by the Mountain Valley booth!

---

Logan smiled brightly. When was the last time he'd felt the drive to succeed? To win? It had been a long time. But he could see the reaction he was causing in Diana next door, and it was

73

highly satisfying. Ben and Tess had already high-fived him twice, and he'd counted twenty-five ballots going into the ballot box for Forget-Me-Not. Now all the other wineries were looking at him the same way he'd been looking at Diana earlier.

Within three hours, two other wineries—The Honey Bee Winery and Blanc et Noir Vineyards—had similar signs to his, one to help soldiers in need and the other to help battered women. The fifth winery, Five Star, just shot daggers in his direction. They were all shameless, Logan included, but he couldn't care less. By his count, he was slowly narrowing the lead with Mountain Valley Vineyards.

During an afternoon lull in activity, Diana sauntered over to his booth, her sunglasses hiding her beautiful eyes, her red lips pursed in an expression he recognized as a mix of anger and envy. He'd gotten under her skin, and it bothered her. *Good.*

He couldn't help it, when she stopped in front of him, he started laughing. The sound was strange to his ears, and he wondered how long it had been since anything had amused him as much as Diana's pouty lip. There was a time when he'd have pulled her into his arms and kissed that look right off her face. But that was a lifetime ago.

"What's so damn funny?" she asked as she fingered a flower from his pot of forget-me-nots.

"Your booth, of course. Where did you find those servers? And did you have to remind them not to tuck their tips in their underwear? Or maybe they aren't wearing underwear?"

"Haha," she said, her lips pulling into a tight grimace. "Just how much money are you donating to charity, might I ask?"

"Two dollars a vote," he said proudly.

"Good for you. I don't think you can catch up, but it is nice that you're trying."

Logan smiled and laughed again.

"I remember this about you," he said and tapped her on the tip of her nose.

"What?" she asked as she pulled back in surprise. He hadn't wanted to touch a woman since he'd lost Julianna. The action was instantly sobering, but he didn't regret touching Diana.

"You were always the most competitive woman I ever knew. Remember what Prof. Bekker said about you?"

"Vaguely," she replied, blushing, the color of her cheeks striking against her black ensemble.

"You remember exactly what he said. You tried to expose the weaknesses in my presentation by pointing out what we'd missed. You were downright feral."

Diana's eyes narrowed. "I don't think that is what I did. It didn't bother you at the time. You still bought me a sophomore cheeseburger."

"Bekker likened you to a shark that could smell blood in the water. I liked that about you. Your spirit. I figured you'd be just as driven in all areas. Feral."

"Well, you would be the one to know," she said, her cheeks turning a bright crimson.

"And what did it matter? We both got As."

"I scored three points higher," she said.

"That's my girl."

"Damn it, I came over to wish you luck today," she said.

"Thank you, but I'm afraid I can't invite you out for a cheeseburger later."

"That's okay. I don't think there are any sophomore bacon burgers within fifty miles of here," she said, a slight smile showing on her face.

He shouldn't have said that. It evoked a memory that was almost too powerful. He'd bought her a cheeseburger, and they had ended up in his bedroom apartment making love. It had been her first time. He hadn't meant to seduce her on their first date, but the passion they felt carried them away. Being her first meant a lot to Logan, even to this day. He ground his teeth at the thought of who might have come after him.

Just as the sun was setting in his little attic apartment, he was amazed that she was in his arms. She'd admitted that she'd had a crush on him all year. Ironically, he'd had a crush on her since the first moment he had laid eyes on her at the beginning of their first trimester. After that night, they were inseparable for three months.

He stepped out from behind the booth and indicated for her to follow him out of earshot of the others. They stood away from the crowds along the esplanade, looking out over the river.

"Diana…. Back then, I liked the way you came after me. I liked your fire, the anger I saw in you. It made me want you. I wanted to seduce you and see if you brought that fire with you to bed. You did, you know."

"I thought we had something special," she said, the tears pooling in her eyes.

"Do you know what your problem is?" he asked, his tone no longer friendly.

"No, Logan, obviously I don't. Please, do tell me, what is my problem?" she asked as she wiped away a tear.

"You don't like that I'm fighting back. When we were in school, I didn't fight you as I could have. If I'd unleashed my full fury, you wouldn't have gotten those three points on me, but I had a hidden agenda. I wanted you in my bed, so I let you off easy. I planned it. That will not be the case in this competition."

"Are you serious? How can you say this to me?" she asked, touching her fingertips to her chest as if he'd speared her heart. More than anything, he wanted to pull her to him and tell her that he'd loved her. It hadn't just been about the seduction. It didn't end because he grew tired of her, but when she got the Wharton Fellowship, he had to make sure she took it. She'd needed to see that she was more than her past. But he couldn't tell her that, not now.

"This time, the stakes are a lot higher, and I'm playing for keeps," he warned. "You almost bested me today because, for a moment, I forgot and underestimated you. I won't do that again."

"Gee, thanks for telling me how it will be. I'm so glad you held back before. Here is a little advice for you, Logan. You better start trying a little harder because I'm not impressed with gimmicks and potted plants. I haven't even got started, so you give it your best shot," she said and then turned her back and walked away from him.

# CHAPTER NINE

Diana seethed for two days after the Waterfront Carnival event. She knew she'd won it for Mountain Valley. Although she wouldn't know until the last ballot was cast in August, that wasn't the point. The three judges from the Stark Hotel—Daisy Stark; her sister-in-law, Rebecca Wilder; and her cousin-in-law, the artist Laura Hokensen Stark—appeared to like their booth.

Well, all except Rebecca Wilder's one comment. She'd quipped, "This has turned into a popularity contest, not just a wine tasting." Diana couldn't blame the woman. She wasn't proud of her work on the booth. It felt sleazy. She was going to have to have a talk with Salvatore and Marco about the level of sophistication she wanted at the next event. She needed to tread lightly, as she now understood that Marco was using the competition as a way to prove himself. He was falling short in her estimation, but the need to help him look good in front of his father was now another agenda item to add to her list. It wasn't one she wanted to prioritize.

But what bothered her much more than the booth was what Logan had said to her. When she said that what they had was special, he'd dismissed it. That hurt. She'd thought right up to the offer from Wharton that they had a chance at forever. Even when he'd shattered that dream, she hadn't given up on the idea that he'd change his mind and come back for her. On Valentine's Day, on her birthday, on *every* holiday, and the days in-between, she hoped beyond hope that he'd call her, send her a card, show up on her doorstep. Proclaim his love and tell her that he was sorry, that he'd made a mistake. That he wanted her back. She'd been so naïve, but she'd never given up on the dream. Not for several years after their breakup. Not when she moved back to the Pacific Northwest and taken her first job in Seattle as a media consultant with an ad agency. Then she had discovered he was married. But the silence since that rainy day twelve years earlier had been the sharpest dagger to her heart.

There was only one person who'd made a mistake: *her*. How stupid of her to have pined for so long for someone who could care less about her. He'd only wanted her for an affair, and she'd delivered. It made her question much of her past. Those creeping little thoughts whispered that he didn't think she was good enough. That he thought she was still the girl who spent her holidays with her drunken father at the trashiest trailer park on the outskirts of Salem. She had even trusted Logan enough to tell him about her mother and how she had died of cancer when Diana was ten.

Logan hurt her feelings in a way no one else ever had. In a little over two months, she'd be back in Seattle and away from Logan for good. She would only need to see him a couple more times, and then the torture of being so close to what she most wanted would be over.

At least one man was very happy with her. Salvatore D'Salvo was ecstatic. And she couldn't blame him. Mountain Valley Vineyards was ahead and in good shape for the next event as long as Marco didn't have any more "ideas."

To get to know more about Mountain Valley Vineyards, Diana asked to shadow several different workers around the vineyard, everyone from the assistant winemakers to Antonio and Davide in the tasting room. And Salvatore had given her the green light to start redesigning the Mountain Valley label to give it a newer, more sophisticated look. She had a design team at

Wave, but she'd wanted something a little more regional and authentic. Marco wanted to head this up, so they'd agreed to start interviewing local artists together. She hoped it would be a good learning experience for him.

Her mind circled back to Logan, always back to Logan. It was a tidal wave of different, conflicting emotions pushing and pulling her in different directions. She hadn't mulled over her ex-fiancé Brad's betrayal as much as she thought about Logan's last words to her.

*"I don't see myself spending my life with you..."*

What was wrong with her? After twelve years, she'd have thought it would be easier, but with Logan right next door, the hurt raged within her anew.

Diana walked over the hills and valleys of the vineyard, trying to clear her mind before sunset several days after the first phase of the Stark Hotel competition. With every step she took, she thought of Logan. The very setting of a vineyard in Yamhill County was incredibly romantic, and she wondered how Logan had survived living here after his wife died.

She wondered endlessly about the state of his marriage. What, aside from Marco, would make any sane woman leave a man like Logan? Or were they both to blame? Diana may never know, but focusing on it would drive her crazy.

Diana felt restless and lonely. She didn't miss her ex. True, it had only been a couple months, but there had been relief finally getting to the bottom of something that had always felt wrong.

It made Diana wonder if she ever loved Brad. She had never felt for Brad the way she had felt for Logan. In retrospect, she couldn't honestly say that she had ever loved Brad. And that thought was disturbing on a whole other level. Brad had just been there at the right time, the time she'd begun to wonder if she would ever get married or have children. She always felt her relationship with Brad was safe, that if they ever broke up, it wouldn't hurt as bad as it had with Logan, and she was right.

Now she felt a new freedom. If she was meant to have children, she would. If not, she'd find a way to be okay.

She'd try to be like Bonnie, her Language Arts teacher in junior high school, who had made such a difference to a needy kid. Diana didn't want to think of what would have become of her if Bonnie hadn't stepped in. She hadn't needed to. It would have been so much easier to ignore Diana like everyone else did. But Diana knew what would have happened if she hadn't had the positive influence of Bonnie. She'd be living in her father's trailer, probably becoming an alcoholic just like her father, or worse. College, Logan, Wharton, and now Wave—none of it would have happened without Bonnie.

As she walked along the perimeter of the vineyard property, her loneliness grew.

How much longer could she keep moving from place to place, fixing other businesses like some nomad? Just how much was this partnership worth to her? It had been the thing she'd always wanted, so she thought. Security was her most basic of needs. But what about love and family?

If she was made a partner at Wave, it was no guarantee she'd be able to settle down and grow roots in Seattle. She was pretty sure that the only things that would change in her life were her title and her pay grade. Did she even want to settle in Seattle? Did it feel like home? Would she know what home felt like if she ever found it?

Logan had made a life for himself in sleepy Yamhill County a home.

She walked until she was at the edge of his property. The lush, green valley lay between them. If she listened carefully, she could hear Persephone's Creek just below. Curiosity stirred as she climbed over the low fence that separated the properties.

It took another fifteen minutes of walking before she could see Logan's operation clearly. She'd walked along the rows of lush, green leaved plants that looked healthy and happy.

Eventually, she could make out the tasting room, the processing plant, and several other large buildings that housed his operation. Two houses looked down from the top of a hill. A modern house with large glass windows that looked new and impressive, as well as an elegant older dwelling—the large Victorian farmhouse that she had been a guest in so many years ago.

She didn't like the way their last conversation had gone. It had made light of what they shared, and that wasn't right. She wanted to tell Logan how she felt to his face.

A movement caught Logan's attention from where he was analyzing figures at his desk. He held up his binoculars and stared out his office window to the view of his vineyard below. He couldn't believe who he saw walking through the rows of vines.

What the hell was Diana doing on his land? Snooping for D'Salvo? That took some nerve, but he couldn't say he was surprised. Not after they'd finally shown their cards to each other at the first competition.

He was having a particularly bad day. He had just come from a meeting with his bank and was concerned that they wouldn't give him the loan he so desperately needed to extend his water rights for another ten years. The loan was going before the loan committee, and if he didn't get it, the only immediate thing that would save him would be winning the Stark Hotel contract. There was a Pinot Noir he was currently aging in The Vault, the largest warehouse, but he needed to wait a little longer before bottling it. If his hand were forced, he'd have no other choice. And even if he did bottle it, he wasn't sure it would generate enough income to get him out of the mess he was in.

Grabbing the phone from his desk, he hit a number on his

speed dial. He was connected to his summer intern, a horticulture student from his and Diana's alma mater. Peter had practically begged to work for Logan, showing up several times and asking if Logan had an internship program. He didn't but hadn't had the heart to turn the kid down. So, within a matter of days, Forget-Me-Not had an internship program, and it was even blessed by Oregon State University. The kid would get six hours of elective credits for being at Forget-Me-Not this summer.

"Peter, I've decided that zone six needs some extra water. Could you turn the sprinklers on for me right now?" he asked and waited.

"Sure, Logan, no problem," Peter said and got off the line to complete the request.

Logan raised the binoculars once again and watched as Diana cut through one of the rows in the center of zone six. She paused and looked around as the irrigation system engaged with the sound of pressurized, rushing water filling pipes, followed by hissing release. As if knowing what was about to happen, she picked up her pace, but it was too late. Within thirty seconds, she was thoroughly soaked from head to toe with cold water from the underground spring that he leased from the D'Salvos. As she stopped, hands on hips, and looked up at his house, he wondered if she could see his silhouette in the window. Considering that he could see her scowl, he thought she probably could. That would teach her to visit without calling first.

He watched as she ran for the nearest open land. It appeared to take three times as long as it should. Her expression growing angrier with each step.

By the time she was free of the aggressive sprinklers, she stood at the edge of the vineyard and seethed, her sleek blonde hair clinging to her skin like cold seaweed. Mascara ran down her cheeks, streaking them with black tears. She looked like she was melting.

Logan laughed as he watched her rub at her eyes and pull off her drenched fleece.

As she squeezed out the sleeves of the absorbent material, Logan's attention landed on the wet t-shirt that molded to her apple-shaped breasts. The laughter died a quick death as he remembered just how much he'd loved kissing those firm, rosy-tipped mounds. Shaking his head, he tried to clear the image of her lush, naked body lying in his bed twelve years earlier. Even as he pictured it in exact detail, he felt the first stirrings of something long dead. *Pure animal lust.*

The hostility came off Diana in waves as she made her way up the incline toward his house. By the time she got the end of his driveway, she was panting and shivering.

Logan picked up the phone and spoke to Peter again. "I think section six has had just about enough. Why don't you go ahead and turn that water off?"

"Sure, Logan, whatever you say," Peter responded eagerly.

He was chuckling as he walked out to his front porch and looked down at her, toasted her with the glass of Pinot Noir in his hand.

"You did that on purpose!" Diana yelled up at him.

"Of course, I did," he said, enjoying the fire he saw in those tiger eyes of hers.

"You're a real ass. You know that?"

"And you don't belong on my property. By chance, did you walk past one of a dozen 'No Trespassing' signs about a half-mile back the way you came?" he asked as he tried not to laugh. "They are meant for people like you. To keep you out in case you didn't know."

As if to illustrate her master's point, Ginger joined Logan on the deck, raised her nose, caught Diana's scent, growled, and let out one fierce bark.

"I'm your neighbor, and I was coming to talk to you. Do you

always treat your neighbors this way?" she asked from the bottom of the steps that led to his porch.

"Only the ones you choose to work with."

"Logan, damn it!"

She looked like she wanted to stomp her foot in frustration. This was the girl he remembered; he thought as he looked down at the dripping mess that was still incredibly beautiful despite the water damage.

"Would you like to come up for a glass of wine?" Even as he said it, he knew it was a bad idea.

"Wine? Are you kidding? I'm freezing, thanks to you," Diana replied.

She looked so adorable that Logan thought about setting down his glass and meeting her halfway on the steps. He was having a hard time forgetting how it felt to have her in his arms the night he'd taken her the pepper spray.

At the time, he thought it was only because he hadn't held a woman since his wife.

He missed his wife... Rather, more to the point, he missed the feel of a woman. It was as simple as that. Diana was familiar, so she awakened familiar feelings. He wasn't falling for her, not again. She could have been any attractive female. But she wasn't. She was Diana. The Diana who had always been in the corner of his mind, always there, always haunting his dreams.

"Would you prefer some warmed brandy? I made a small batch a few years ago. It's pretty damn spectacular."

"How can I be sure you didn't poison it?" she asked, now six steps away from the top of his porch.

"The only thing that will poison you is that crap you're drinking next door. Come on up, and I'll treat you to some good wine."

"Do you have a *really* expensive couch I can sit on and ruin?"

Despite her tone, he laughed. An angry Diana was just more

fun, especially when he had the advantage. And at the moment, she was definitely in check.

"Wait right there," he said, holding up his hand and offering, "I'll see if I can find you a towel."

"I'm drenched. A little towel isn't going to do it," she complained.

Logan nodded in agreement as he thought of a way to irritate her further. "You're right. Tell you what, meet me by the garage. I'll take you in through the mudroom. I wouldn't want you to ruin any of my furniture."

He could hear her sigh, but after he and Ginger had stepped inside, he shut and locked the front door, leaving her no choice. A walk all the way back to Mountain Valley would be torture in her current condition. Those wet jeans would chafe something awful.

Logan stopped by the master bedroom, grabbed his white terry cloth robe and a couple of large towels for her. He shouldn't be so...what? Happy? He wasn't happy. Was he intrigued? Curious...Maybe. Old ghosts from long ago reminding him what they'd once shared? Taunting him?

He'd give her a couple glasses of wine and see if he could get some information out of her. She worked for the D'Salvos. That put her on the wrong side of the war between them. And from what he observed on her first night at the vineyard, she had a very low tolerance for alcohol. Nothing had changed since her college days.

Opening one of the four garage doors, he met her just inside. Up close, he could see her shivering, noticed the way she looked at him, part indignant, partly drowned feline. Without fanfare, he handed her one of the towels, which she promptly used on her face as she followed him through the oversized garage.

At the door to the mudroom, he looked at her over his shoulder and said, "There's a powder room just to the left where you can get out of your wet clothes. I'll toss them in the dryer for you."

Saying nothing, she followed him quietly. When he heard the door shut with a little more force than was necessary, he smiled. She was angry. *Good.*

# CHAPTER TEN

Diana stepped inside the bathroom at Logan's house and slammed the door behind her.

So much for an elegant entrance that involved a civilized conversation. He'd turned the water on her! She didn't know when, she didn't know how, but she would get even with him.

When she flipped the light switch, in the little half bath, an elegant, petite crystal chandelier-lit over her head, and she felt an odd tug at her heart. This room had obviously been decorated by a woman, Logan's Julianna. Fancy, floral wine labels from an early vintage of a Forget-Me-Not Pinot Gris decorated the walls like wallpaper, creating an eggplant, light lavender, pink, and powder blue floral pattern that, on close inspection, gave up its whimsical origins. It was a little like an optical illusion but so artfully done that it spoke volumes to the creativity and design acumen of the person who had chosen such an interesting idea of using leftover labels.

The small, octagon black-and-white tile floor and white pedestal sink brought a classic edge to the space. Guest soaps in coordinating pastel colors in the shape of hearts adorned a small basket. Diana felt like she had stolen someone else's dance card.

The soaps and everything in the bathroom looked brand new. Had no one been here since Julianna?

Diana looked at her reflection in a large, oval mirror that was gilded tastefully with platinum and gold accents and felt embarrassment ripple throughout her body. She looked like a drowned rat. Whatever damage the sprinkler had done, she'd enhanced it with a careless swipe to her face, which had managed to smear her dark mascara, eye shadow, and lipstick.

Looking at the pristine white towels, which hung on gilded racks, Diana rejected the idea of using them and opted for tissue instead. With a little warm soap and water, she was able to remove most of the offending makeup and expose her rosy cheeks.

Next, she stripped out of her wet clothing. The water-laden fabric slipped over her skin like cool, slimy fingers and took more effort than it should to peel away from her chilled skin. Diana couldn't bring herself to strip out of her hot pink bra and panties. She'd felt too vulnerable. Hadn't the purpose of her walk been to get to see Logan? Hope he would invite her to his house for a drink? Well, now here she was in the house he'd shared with his dead wife. Mission accomplished. Good for her.

It felt wrong.

It felt wrong to slip into his robe, which smelled faintly of citrus soap and fresh cotton. It felt wrong to be in another woman's house using her heart-shaped soaps and pretty white towels despite what Diana knew about the state of her marriage.

She could hear noise coming from the other side of the door. Not pots and pans banging, exactly, but something was happening in the kitchen.

Ignoring how she was shaking from the cold, she contemplated slipping back into her clothing and walking back to Mountain Valley. She was starting to doubt herself and her motivations. No good could come of her being here. Besides, how angry would the D'Salvos be if they knew she was cavorting with Logan? How angry would her boss at Wave be? She knew the answer. Everyone would be mad at her. Hell, she might even get fired from the contract, from her job.

Was it worth it? What did she hope to accomplish? Prove to

Logan that he still had feelings for her? Show him that she still had feelings for him? It hadn't started out that way. Not when she'd originally thought of confronting him, but something had changed. Was it worth putting her career in jeopardy?

After she towel-dried her hair and ran trembling fingers through the icy cold blonde streaks, she slipped into the bathrobe that had the monogram "LBP" on the pocket. In a New York minute, she understood the meaning of those letters. *Logan Burke Parrish.* The Burke was a family name on his mother and uncle's side, his grandmother's maiden name, and from whom he received his black hair and blue eyes. She was wearing his robe. Something that he probably wore every day.

His aunt and uncle, who raised him, would be proud of what he'd accomplished.

She wondered how he had coped with the loss of his aunt and uncle. Everyone close to him had died. He was alone. What did he do during the holidays? Who was there for him? It was something she could easily relate to.

Diana had done all she could do without benefit of a hairdryer, styling products, and a lot of makeup. She made sure the belt of the robe was secured with a square knot. As she turned the doorknob, she wondered just what Logan had been up to on the other side of the door.

Logan looked comfortable in his kitchen, appeared not to notice her reappearance until she had emerged from the hallway. He paused then, a long piece of string in his hand. He was trussing up a chicken carcass's legs. Wedges of lemon and sprigs of rosemary were barely visible at the cavity end of the bird. She'd caught him in the middle of dinner preparation. Maybe he was having guests over, maybe a date. Wouldn't that just be her luck?

A motion distracted Diana, and then Ginger wiggled over to her, stuffed animal in her mouth, her nails making click-clack music on the terra cotta tile floor as she greeted Diana.

"Ginger, jeez, at least sit," Logan said, his gaze never leaving the chicken he was manipulating.

"I didn't mean to disturb your dinner," Diana said. "I should go."

"I usually don't feed trespassers, but in your case, I've decided to make an exception," he replied, his soft blue eyes meeting hers for the first time.

"You don't need to feed me," she protested, her tone a bit edgy, as she bent to pet the wiggling dog. "I think you've done enough."

"Let me start over. An old friend stopped by, so I asked her to dinner."

She gave him a suspicious look. "Okay, continue."

"We are having three courses, so you can try three of my wines. I know you've tried some of them in the past, but these are rare vintner's pick. You can see for yourself how much better they are than the slop hey serve you next door. Besides, you walked all the way over here to see me. Now we both get that chance to catch up."

Diana sighed. He hadn't exactly called her up and asked her to dinner. He'd told her she was staying, and for some reason, it irritated her even though it was better than she'd hoped for when she'd decided on a visit. There was no winning with this man. Not that there ever had been. The rules, her rules when it came to him, kept changing.

Logan was now heaping new potato halves into a roasting pan and adding seasonings. As she watched, he placed the chicken carcass on top of the potatoes and then washed his hands.

"I take it that I don't have a choice."

"Why, are you a vegetarian?" he asked.

"No," she said, her stomach starting to growl.

"If you had other plans tonight, you probably shouldn't have stopped by."

"I didn't have any other plans," she admitted.

"So, you're free?"

"Yes," she answered unconvincingly. "Where's your clothes dryer?"

Logan pointed back to the hallway she'd just come down and said, "Second door on the left. And try not to sound so tortured. It isn't every day that someone makes you dinner. Unless the D'Salvos make you dinner every night."

"They don't," she replied too quickly.

"There you go," he said, holding his hands out as if she'd made his point for him.

Diana seethed for no good reason all the way to the laundry room, which proved to be decorated much as the bathroom had been, professionally with a slight bend to the feminine. No way had Logan designed this space by himself, of course not. He'd shared his life with another woman, married her, and planned a future with her. He might still be having a life with her if she hadn't died. She still couldn't quite believe the divorce rumors. Who would divorce Logan?

Not that she'd ever get a chance to prove she never would. Diana was, after all, someplace in line after his second choice.

Shaking her head, she thought she was giving herself too much credit in his world. She thought she ranked. It was kind of ridiculous that she thought so highly of herself.

As she tossed her clothes in the dryer and turned it on, she wondered how Logan could continue to live in this house that was so filled with his wife's memory. The house was more Julianna's than Logan's. Heck, he'd built it for his wife, so she was told. Diana felt like an intruder. She had no business being here, no business contemplating past regrets or possible futures.

Returning to the kitchen, she sat on an upholstered bar stool and watched as Logan, now working on a different cutting board, assembled a beet and goat cheese salad with arugula. He'd never cooked when they were in college. She'd been the one to try and cook for him to impress him. She had wanted to prove that although she might have been raised in a trailer park, she could set a dinner table and knew how to cook. Her nerves had gotten the better of her, and she had tried too hard to impress. The result had been a tearful disaster, Thai peppers instead of sweet peppers. She had almost killed them both with the first forkful. Logan had understood so much more than she'd been able to tell him. Through her tears, he had comforted her, reassured her, and told her that none of it mattered to him. He didn't care if she could cook or where she'd come from.

It appeared that it had mattered after all.

She thought of her ex-fiancé and how cooking at home meant ordering takeout, having it delivered, and then serving it on her good china. One of the excesses of having money—other people cook for you. Her life of only two months ago felt like a world away.

When the salad was done, Logan carefully covered an elegant crystal bowl with plastic wrap and placed it in the refrigerator. He returned with a bottle of champagne and two chilled glasses. Placing one in front of her, he opened the bottle and then filled her flute.

"Champagne?" she asked.

"Sparkling Chardonnay," he said, correcting her.

"Oh great," she said without enthusiasm. It didn't take much for her to get tipsy on sparkling alcohol, which was a fact he knew about her. Possibly he was trying to get her drunk and pump her for information.

"It is a special vintage."

"I've had sparkling Chardonnay many times."

"I made this vintage three years ago. I've dabbled on and off with the idea of making sparkling wines," he said, his voice trailing off as he returned to the kitchen. He started shaving shards of Parmigiano-Reggiano from a large wedge of cheese and then placed them in a small silver bowl that he set before her.

"It brings out the flavor of the wine," he said, indicating the cheese.

"I know, but does the cheese count as one of the courses?" she asked.

"Sure, I've decided we're having four courses, so you can sample a few more of my vintages."

"Great," she said.

"Stop saying that," he said, reading her mind. "I'm not trying to get you drunk."

She'd forgotten this about him. He'd always been able to read her mind like some crazy parlor trick. Maybe she should try to being nicer to him. That was her reason for appearing on his doorstep.

"Well, it is surprisingly good," she admitted and wondered what happened to his idea about sparkling wine.

When had he'd decided to serve her dinner instead of the warmed brandy he'd suggested while he was on the front steps?

And why was he being nice to her?

She wondered how they could be so formal with each other, yet she could feel the shared intimacy just below the surface.

She wondered, most of all, how she would keep from falling, hopelessly, completely in love with him again.

And finally, she wondered if she'd ever fallen out of love with him.

In that split second, she realized she never had.

"Why did you stop making it?" she asked.

"Lots of things, I lost interest in it for one. My wife died suddenly, and the world seemed to flip. And I got distracted by a rare vintage of Pinot Noir that is currently aging and could be very spectacular when it is ready," he said and looked at her for a long moment. He was such a man now, no longer the slightly gangly boy he'd been at twenty-two. He was solid, the years etching into fine lines around his mouth and eyes when he smiled. She'd bet that he hadn't smiled much, certainly not in the last two years.

"I'd suggest you pick back up on this," she said, holding up her flute. "That is just a comment from a friend, not my being a consultant in any way."

Logan studied her, leaning back against the black granite countertop and folding his arms. There was no smile on that face, and Diana felt no warmth emitting from the man across from her.

"What do you want, Diana?" he asked. "Why did you come here today?"

She finished nibbling on the small wedge of rich cheese and thought for a moment. "What? No polite dinner conversation?"

"I can see the little wheels turning in your head. What made you walk two miles to get to me today?"

"I don't know, Logan. I'm restless and bothered. I work for your neighbor, and we are in a competition. Does that mean we can't talk? Did you have to turn the sprinklers on me? We used to care about each other. At the least, we were friends. Can't we try to be friends again?"

Logan slowly unfolded his arms, leaned forward, and got his feet under him. Walking around the counter, he stepped up beside her and leaned close.

"Is that it then, you want to be my friend?" he asked, his lips just inches from hers.

She swallowed and tried to find simple words in a confused brain. He was so handsome, his blazing blue eyes warmed her from the inside out, yet the shivers remained.

"Yes."

His eyes searched hers before they moved on to her lips, where they lingered and narrowed.

"Really?"

"Sure," she whispered.

"There is something else," he said, his voice low and dark in the muted kitchen light.

"If you think I'm going to pass information—"

Logan silenced her by cupping her face in his large, rough hands, his fingers weaving into her wet hair, locking her head in place. And then, as she gazed up at him in stupid confusion, he leaned down and kissed her. The moment his lips touched hers, time rewound for Diana. She remembered Logan in a way you remember the taste of your favorite dessert or the smell of your favorite perfume. He was familiar, and until the moment his warm lips pressed to hers, she hadn't remembered how much she missed kissing him, kissing Logan.

The kiss rose like a bird spreading its wings for flight. It deepened and lingered, grew and intensified. And when at last, to her disappointment, he broke away, he was the first to recover enough to speak.

"I thought I wanted to get you drunk and get every bit of information out of you, but I don't. I don't want you to compromise yourself. I don't want to know what you can tell me about the D'Salvos. The only thing I want from you is to hold you in my arms again and forget the last two years of my life."

He wanted to use her to forget his pain. Well, she wanted to forget hers too, and maybe this was quite possibly *not* the smartest move she's made in her life. It was one she wanted. She wanted to make love with Logan, no matter how ridiculous that was.

It didn't stop her from having hope that someday he might want more from her than just a warm body to hold.

Slowly, Diana reached down and untied the belt of her borrowed robe. Logan's eyes followed the action of her fingertips with studied patience. When she finished unknotting the belt, his hands slipped under the terrycloth, tracing her collar bones with his fingertips. He pushed the robe from her shoulders and then pointedly looked down at her pink lace bra and panties. With gentle hands, he cupped her breasts in his warm palms and then bent his head to kiss the delicate sensitive skin between them. Diana leaned back in her chair and bit back a moan. This is what she always remembered about Logan. He was so tactile. He used everything in his arsenal to drive her crazy. She'd been too young to appreciate his close attention to detail.

Her hands gripped the edge of the barstool. She wanted to touch him. But the moment her arms reached for him, he pulled back from her. He stopped the sensual assault as quickly as it started. Logan wouldn't look at her, which made all the tenderness that he'd evoked in the last few moments crumble into fetid dust around them.

She was no longer cold. A feeling akin to shame spread across her cheeks, warming her with embarrassment.

"I'm sorry," she said, realizing as she did that she wasn't sorry to have touched him, to have kissed him back. She was only sorry that it hadn't lasted longer, that for whatever reason, he'd stopped, hadn't been about her. No, she could see it in his eyes. He was thinking about his dead wife, not wanting to offend her memory in her home. Diana quickly closed her robe, felt incredibly stupid for arriving on his doorstep without her own transportation home.

Logan turned away, grabbed his wine flute, and downed the sparkling contents with one swallow. Then, in a low, tortured voice, he said, "You're not the one who should be apologizing."

"You miss her," she said, thinking that with each word she said, she sounded more and more like a fool.

"Terribly," he said, his voice husky and pained as he used the trump card that could provide no other answer.

What could she say to that? The best thing to do would be to leave. Grab the damp clothing out of the dryer, slip into her ruined shoes, and retreat. Retreat just as he had. She didn't belong here. Not in the house he'd built for his wife. She wasn't even sure she belonged next door, but she didn't have a choice in the matter.

"You were happy," she murmured and slowly eased herself off the barstool.

"In the beginning, but we had hit a rough patch I'd do anything to try to fix now," he murmured.

"Listen," she said, trying to make her voice sound soft and low. "I should go.

I didn't mean to upset you. I just wanted to talk to you, to see you."

This time he met her eyes with his own deeply penetrating azure gaze, which displayed a mixture of torture and regret.

"I thought I was ready," he said, "but I'm not."

"I understand," she said, but she didn't. Diana would always be ready for him. She realized that now.

"Please, won't you stay for dinner? I'd feel worse if you left."

"Are you sure you want me to?" she asked, still feeling the pangs of rejection. Shouldn't she just leave?

"I haven't cooked dinner for anyone in a very long time. As you were changing, I got to thinking how much I enjoy cooking, sharing dinner with someone," he added, his half smile edged with a little reluctance.

When she didn't reply, he added, "Please, I really don't want you to go."

She looked around the kitchen. He was making an effort to try and impress her. She'd always been the one trying to impress him when they were in school.

"Well, it isn't as if my clothes are dry yet. And I'm definitely not looking forward to putting on my wet shoes. Besides, the chicken already smells great."

Her words had the desired effect on him. The tension relaxed from his face. He topped off her champagne glass with a generous dollop and only poured a splash into his glass, explaining, "I need to be able to drive you home later."

What if he hadn't stopped kissing her a few minutes ago? Her lips could still feel his touch, missed the intimacy with painful awareness.

If he hadn't stopped, would they already be in his bedroom? Or would he have taken her to another room, one he hadn't shared with his wife? She swallowed down the unpleasant thought that she was in another woman's house with another woman's husband. Julianna might be gone, but her ghost was very much with them in this cozy space.

It wouldn't have gone well. As she watched him gauging her reaction, she felt the pain of love lost. They were both wrecked and damaged with the knowledge that love does not last. Love is cruel. It is not kind. Were they both walking advertisements for that fact?

"I guess it all depends," she said, adding a quizzical look to her face.

"On what?" he asked, picking up on her attempt at humor.

Her thoughts drifted to the awkward after. Would he have let her sleepover? When they were in college, he always wrapped his arms around her, spooned her from behind, and held her close throughout the night. It was something that wasn't a negotiation; it was an expectation.

"What are we having for dessert?" she asked, smiling so broadly it hurt her lips. "I mean, there had better be dessert!"

She needed to let him know that she wasn't wounded or hurt. What were a few stolen kisses between ex-lovers? Her smile faltered a little bit, but then he smiled back at her, and she was able to put a little meaning behind her intention. They were older now. They were adults and mature. It isn't the way she felt, but she was a businesswoman. She was used to high stakes, and she wasn't sure if she'd ever presented anything that had cost her so dearly in the past. She physically hurt from the loss of Logan's touch, but he didn't need to see that. They were friends, and that was all. She could do it.

# CHAPTER ELEVEN

As Logan opened a young, crisp Sauvignon Blanc to go with their first course of salad, his hands were shaking. He'd basically attacked Diana. What was wrong with him? Was it because she was the first woman he'd been this close to in two years, or was it because it was her? In college, he had easily fallen in love with her; it had almost been love at first sight. His heart had beat faster, still did, when in her presence. It had always been quick and reckless with her. Much like their relationship.

He'd fallen in love with Julianna in a much different way. It had taken time, months, and months of working together in the vineyard, where she was a part-time employee. They'd grown on each other comfortably. First, she'd had to help him with his pain over losing Diana. They'd never spoken of it in detail, but she had known that someone had come before her, and it hadn't ended well.

There was nothing he could say to Diana. He couldn't turn back time and redo what he'd done. How many times had he thought of that very thing? The ability to turn back time was a very familiar dream in his darker moments. But just which reality would he change?

Would he redo the day his wife died? Stop her from leaving him in the first place to go live with Marco two weeks before she died? Before that even happened, would he have been a better husband so she would never have gone with Marco? How many times had he replayed that last day, the day she'd left him? If only he hadn't been angry. If only he had begged her to stay and forgiven her for the affair. If only he could go back in time.... Would she have still been alive if he'd begged her to stay?

Time to face facts. Even if all could have been reconciled, Julianna was no longer here. Diana was. Her warm flesh was standing right in front of him, and he turned away. Why... Maybe he wasn't quite the confident man he thought he was. Maybe he was scared he'd mess it up again.

He stood in Julianna's kitchen now. For as much as he had the vineyard around him, she owned the house. She'd become the master decorator she was, and every inch of the place exuded his deceased wife. They didn't cross each other's territories despite his deepest wishes that she would somehow want to be a part of the business that meant so much to him, to his family. Shortly after they married, she confided that she didn't enjoy working in the vineyard and had only done it to get close to him. He'd felt disappointed, a little misled, but had dealt with his feelings and moved on. But in his heart, he wasn't sure he'd ever forgiven her for changing so drastically. It made him feel as though he'd been manipulated. Because of that, the marriage had been off to a rocky start. And he was never quite sure that he had fully trusted her from that point on.

Regardless, nothing he did was good enough, and in the end, she had wanted to be part of the D'Salvo's world. Part of Marco's world. Marco had done what he hadn't been able to do, convince her to be part of a family business, the D'Salvo's. He didn't know what other promises Marco made her, but he doubted Julianna would have agreed to vineyard life forever.

And as if his mind wasn't done with the self-torture, Logan began to think of the day he broke up with Diana. What if he'd married Diana instead of Julianna? Would Julianna be happily married to someone else, far away, and still alive, maybe with several children?

What might have been was always nagging at him, playing a game of truth or dare. What an incredibly effective way to drive yourself insane.

Logan pulled two white wine glasses from the overhead rack and poured the Sauvignon Blanc.

"Oh my, not another wine?" Diana asked uneasily. She was trying to sound light after he'd made a complete fool of himself. She was far more gracious than he. This was nothing new. She had always been far too good for him, but ironically, she was the only one who never realized it.

He'd started the evening by trying to drown her like a wet cat. It had been impulsive and mean. But having her work for his worst enemy cut him to the core. It felt a little too personal, and he was mad at her. How could she? If D'Salvo had wanted to punish him, to make him suffer, to pour salt in his already tender wounds, he'd found the perfect way to do it. He'd hired Diana. And she'd taken the job *knowing* that she'd be in competition with him. She'd visited Forget-Me-Not with him while they were in college. Had she forgotten who the next-door neighbor was? No, he had a feeling she knew exactly the lay of the land. So why had she done it? He hoped to get that very answer out of her.

He stole a glance at her as he pondered the question. Her hair had started to dry into the wild blonde curls he remembered. It seemed only fitting considering how much he wanted to pull her into his arms, run his fingers through her hair, and finish what they'd started earlier.

"Just enough to get you drunk and talking, three or four glasses if I remember correctly. Let's see how it is working. What are you serving at the Hot Air Balloon Festival next weekend?" he asked, smiling a little wickedly so she'd know there was an edge of a tease to his words.

"I didn't think you cared about my business dealings next door," she said this with a prim tone, raising her shoulders a little.

"I don't. This is just a mild curiosity, and I'm not stupid. If you want to tell me things, I'll listen."

"Uh-huh," she said, "I thought so. I'll never be that drunk."

He liked having her in this light, teasing mood, so he continued, "At the first event, they served a really bad Pinot Gris. I was kind of surprised. I take it that you are not the one who chooses what they serve because I can't imagine you letting them pour that swill. The label should be changed from Pinot Gris to white wine vinegar. When I harvest my cucumbers this year, I'll use it for pickling liquid. Can you offer me a neighborly discount? I'm talking to you because I don't think those boys with their hair and their blouses can do simple math. They appeared to even have an issue with the gelato scoops at your booth."

"Davide and Antonio are absolute sweethearts. They are from Italy, cousins of Marco's. I can admit, they spend some time in the gym, but they've never been anything but kind to me, very professional."

"In an 'I've used too many steroids to know what to do with a beautiful woman when I see one' kind of way?"

She gave him a look that was both amused and knowing. "They do well with the ladies, so I'm told."

"Really?"

"Yes."

"You haven't had enough to drink yet. I'll ask you more questions in a few minutes."

"Good luck with that," she said and grabbed another bite of cheese.

Logan decided that eating in the kitchen felt too intimate, too much like what he and Julianna used to do most evenings as they looked over the gorgeous rows of grapes, their land as far as the eye could see. He didn't like the memories, so he suggested they move out to the front deck to a small wrought iron cafe table where they could look out over his vineyard and watch the sunset. He turned on his two al fresco heat lanterns to ward off the chill. They looked like big metal Tiki touches but allowed him to use the outdoor deck all year round. Ginger settled in, lying on a plush cushion next to the table and regally anticipating the scraps to come.

They settled across from each other, enjoying an older, private reserve Pinot Noir as they ate the chicken and roast potatoes. He finally asked the question that had been on his mind since the day he'd read the article in the alumni magazine.

"So, Diana, what is your story? Ever been married? Children?" He asked as the lowering sun cast a golden light on her skin, making her look radiant.

She took a long sip of wine and carefully set her glass down on the table.

"You're asking me this after you already kissed me? Isn't that a tad reckless? What if my incredibly jealous husband wants to now beat you up?"

She was playing with him, getting in her jabs where she could. He hoped she was enjoying herself.

"I didn't sense that you were married. You don't wear a ring. And you appear to be the kind of woman who enjoys accessories."

Grimacing, she said, "Why on Earth would you say something like that to me?"

"You are always perfectly put together. When we were in college, I couldn't get over it. You were always perfect. The right hair, the right clothes, the right look."

"That is such crap, and you know it. I was the most insecure woman in the room. Always. I didn't have any money, my clothes were always worn and second hand from Goodwill, and the jewelry was junk. I even cut my own hair back then."

"I never noticed any of that," he said. "I always thought you had it all."

"Well, at one time, I thought I had it all too," she said and looked beyond him to the horizon. She had managed another well-placed dig.

"Maybe I just kissed you for old times' sake. Besides, you could have slapped me."

"I didn't want to slap you. Besides, it would have been more likely for me to punch you."

"Somehow, I don't think you'd have done either," he mused.

"It's always so damn complicated when it comes to you," she said, clenching her jaw. A part of him was very pleased to know that she was single or at least conflicted, which meant there was an issue with the men in her life. Glad he wasn't the only one whose life was complicated.

"What aren't you telling me?" he asked, knowing he was treading on thin ice.

At any moment, she'd tell him to mind his own business or just to go fuck himself. Either way, she was probably right to say it.

"I broke off an engagement a couple of months ago. It was the closest I've come to getting married," she said almost without emotion.

"So, what happened?" he asked, leaning back in his chair, hands clasped in his lap.

"We weren't right for each other. Sometimes you just know you're not meant to share the rest of your life with someone," she said and looked at him pointedly as she set down her fork.

He'd used the same words when he'd broken up with her twelve years earlier, and it appeared she hadn't forgotten.

Ignoring this rather direct hit, even though she'd already seen his reaction and acknowledged it, he said, "Something happened. You are too careful to have gotten involved with someone who wasn't right for you."

"How would you know?" she asked. Not waiting for an answer, she added, "I thought I was right for you, and look at what a mistake that turned out to be."

"Was he like me?" he asked, ignoring her question.

"No, he was quite your opposite in every way. Where your coloring resembles dark, swarthy Sardinians, he was more of a Viking, with blond hair and pale skin. Brad has a very lucrative law practice."

"How many ex-wives?" he asked, and she seemed to tense at the question.

"He didn't believe in marriage, so imagine my surprise when he proposed. Because I'm that one special woman who makes men do things they would never do," she said and looked pointedly at him.

Logan toyed with his fork and set it on the edge of the colorful Italian Deruta dinner plate. He hated having such a crazily good memory. Time passed, but for Logan, some things were as fresh as if they had happened yesterday. He remembered details almost as clearly as he could remember his reasons and what he'd said to Diana on the last day they'd seen each other.

She was wearing a red V-neck sweater that he'd given her for her birthday. She had on lipstick that matched the sweater exactly. He remembered that it clung just tight enough to enhance her natural curves.

"I didn't break up with you because you weren't right for me," he said and watched as her fork fell to the table with a clatter that she didn't seem to notice. "I broke up with you so that you would go to Wharton. It was too important of an opportunity for you to have passed on. It was life-changing, and I couldn't let you miss it because of some emotional entanglement to me. I would have thought you'd have figured that out by now. It was one of the most painful things I've ever had to live through."

But until he'd said those words, she hadn't figured that out, and he could tell by the way she was looking at him. She looked away, out at the vineyard, her face contorting in pain. Why had he said anything? Why couldn't he keep his big mouth shut? By more importantly, why hadn't she figured it out?

He would never be stupid enough to say he understood women. But watching as Diana swallowed hard, fighting down what she really wanted to say to him, he understood that he'd possibly made a very large mistake.

Her hand, the one that was calmly resting on the table next to the abandoned fork, tightened into a fist.

He started to open his mouth to speak, but she held up her hand to stop him.

"No," she said, her voice turning feral. "My turn! So, you made a major life decision for me without even consulting me? Is that what I just heard? You made a decision that I'd better go to Wharton, so you broke up with me with some lie to force me to go? Did you ever think that maybe you were more important to me than school? Did you even ask me what I wanted to do?"

"Diana—"

"I was *so* in love with you. And it wasn't a crush or my imagination. It was real, the realest love I've ever felt. I've never felt for any man the way I felt for you. I would know, I've compared everyone to *you*, you bastard!"

The alcohol had finally taken effect. He just hadn't expected her to say what she had.

Logan took her words like water from a sneaker wave, rolling over him, throwing him off balance, and slamming him into the hard sand. By the time he was ready to speak, she'd had enough and was on the move.

Her chair shot back with a groan, and then she was gone, her feet pounding on the outdoor deck and then the hardwood floors inside. Logan stood, his chair falling and hitting the wooden deck with an awful splitting crack. Then he was following her into the living room and down the hall to the laundry room with Ginger's paws clicking rhythmically behind them.

Diana flung her robe at him the minute he crossed the threshold, the belt hitting him in the face hard enough that the whiplash stung his cheek. Tossing the robe to the floor, he watched Diana in her hot pink bra and panties pulling open the dryer door and wrestling into her jeans. Watching her with that body that he knew so well but no longer could touch, his jeans tightened uncomfortably. She was making a lovely spectacle of herself, and it brought on the first erection he could remember at the sight of a woman not his wife in over ten years.

"Diana, please," he said, as the dirtier part of his mind observed that her body had grown lusher with time. She'd always been a little too skinny, ribs showing, hip bones prominent.

But now, as she wrestled with the still damp jeans, he couldn't pull his eyes away from all well-proportioned curves she now had. Every bend and twist had just the right amount of padding. He wanted to lose himself in her curves, bury himself in the warmth of her.

She stopped hands on hips, breasts heaving against the lacy cups. "For years and years, I've wondered what I could have possibly done that made you change your mind about us. I tried to recall every conversation we ever had. I cried for days...for weeks, for months over you! It hurt for *years*. It still hurts! And now, you tell me it was all for my own good? It was my choice, Logan! Mine! Not yours to make, never *yours* to make."

It was hard to think with her standing before him, her nipples puckering against the lace of her tight bra.

"Wouldn't you agree that it all turned out for the best?" he managed as the full weight of her words took hold. *She'd been in love with him.* There was no doubt now. She'd told him, and he knew. He'd known it for years. She'd loved him. He'd loved her equally, if not more. And he'd thrown it away. He couldn't think of the consequences of this truth. He'd have never known his wife, but he'd have had Diana.

She'd have never forgiven him for missing Wharton. She didn't understand that at the moment. She was too angry. But in time, she'd realize he made the best decision for both of them.

"Turned out for the best? Are you serious? We will never really know that, will we? We don't know what would've happened if we'd stayed together. I've never met anyone that I cared as much about. When you broke up with me, you broke something inside of me, Logan. I haven't picked anyone worthy of me since. You did that to me. You ruined me for anyone else," she said, the tears streaming down her cheeks. "And for that, I'll hate you to my dying day."

He wanted to go to her, pull her close, and tell her he was sorry, but he knew instinctively that she wouldn't let him within striking distance. Her words swirled around him like a tornado.

"I'm sorry," he said, hands raised in surrender.

Marching past him, she shoved him out of the way and stomped into the kitchen, where her shoes were drying over a heater vent. Following after her like an ashamed animal, Logan didn't know what else to say. They were in uncharted territory, and her words were still sinking in. He couldn't let her leave. Not like this.

"Diana, please sit down. Let's talk about this," he said, coming up behind her, reaching out to touch her but pulling back at the last moment.

She whirled on him. "No! Not one more word out of you tonight."

"Please—"

"Shut up! Shut up! Shut up! I don't want to talk to you!" She yelled and pushed past him, running now to the door that led to the garage while Ginger started barking in frustration at the raised voices around her.

"I'll drive you home," he said, his voice cutting through the tension.

"The hell you will," she said, looking back at him through the open door.

"I remember what you said, and this time, I believe it. We're on opposite sides. Now, I believe you. Stay away from me!"

After she had slammed the door, he watched as she ran down his driveway and back through the rows of grapes, the setting sun casting a shadow on her figure as she went.

Diana ran as if fueled by unending anger. Despite the pain in her lungs, the stitch at her side, she didn't stop until the Merlot Cottage came into view. If anyone witnessed her near Olympic stride, they were unable to draw her attention or get her to stop.

As soon as she was inside Merlot, she collapsed into the nearest chair and finally released all the pent-up tears that had been stored in her body for the last twelve years. She cried for the naïve girl she'd been that spring, who fell so hopelessly, incredibly in love with a man incapable of loving her back. She cried for the broken heart that had ruined a part of her beyond repair.

She cried for all she'd lost in the years Logan had chosen to be with someone else. She cried for all that could have been between them. For despite what she had said, she was still hopelessly in love with a man who would never belong to her.

After an hour or two, she stripped out of her damp clothes and stood under a hot shower until the water ran cold. She felt numb. Numb and emotionally drained. Looking down at her leg, she noticed a large bruise and barely remembered the piece of fencing that had caught her in her rapid spree and been responsible for the angry mark.

That was the funny thing about bruises. They looked

painful and had the ability to bring on sympathetic comments from complete strangers. But the bruises on the inside, the ones that no one could see—now, those were the very definition of pain.

Emotionally exhausted, physically spent, she fell into bed and then couldn't sleep. Was it better to know why Logan had done what he'd done? Or would it have been better always to wonder? Her logical, business-minded brain couldn't make sense of everything. Had she run through his house in her underwear? Yes. And then she'd lost it, and admitted what she said she'd never, ever admit. She'd told him exactly how much he'd meant to her. He was probably really enjoying all those wild declarations she'd felt beyond compelled to share.

Why couldn't she stop? Why had she said so much?

She wanted to blame the wine. But she hadn't had enough of it to let it be the combination to her personal vault of deep, dark secrets.

And where did they go from here? He hadn't declared his undying love for her. And if he still had feelings, why didn't he tell her? He obviously didn't have those feelings, if he ever had, not anymore.

When it came to Logan Parrish, she was the very definition of a fool. The opportunity to give herself a break and let go of the largest disappointment in her life had come and gone. She'd given that humiliation a refresher, least she forgot the unending pain.

She pictured Brad. A brief glimpse. She'd caught him making love to another woman, her *neighbor*, in her bed, which at that time was *their* bed. She'd given *that* bed, the sheets and pillows, custom cherry headboard, matching nightstands, dresser, and designer duvet to Goodwill that same day. Yet aside from tossing her very large, very impressive, and what turned out to be very *sharp* ring at Brad's smug face—and getting rid of Brad by throwing his possessions from the third-story window of her condo—she hadn't considered it a humiliation worth her pain beyond the initial shock and betrayal...

"That is all kinds of sick," she said aloud and took a long sip of the hot peppermint tea she brewed herself after her shower, hoping to ward off a chill.

The moment she'd first been told about this project, she should have turned it down, partnership be damned.

Growing up, all she ever wanted was a loving family. And when it hadn't materialized, after Logan shattered her image of what a future could be, she'd done what she could for herself.

"You always want what you can't have," she murmured, willing the tea to warm her and take her pain away.

When her mother died of cancer when she was ten, Diana's grief-stricken father might as well have died right along with his wife. Diana was an afterthought to her father, always coming in second to his dead wife. It wasn't easy to compete with an angel. As a result, she didn't take relationships for granted. She never let people into her life easily. But she had let Logan in and letting him go had changed her. She could admit now that Logan would always be in her heart.

If it hadn't been for the generosity of others in the trailer park, she would have gone hungry a lot more often than she had. Her father could forget about his daughter for days on end. She knew what it felt like to go to the local food bank. She knew how it felt to listen to her stomach growl as she lay in bed, wondering when and if her father would come home. If tears were dollars, she'd have been a millionaire by the time she was fifteen. She'd never had nice things. Just getting clothes or a pair of shoes that fit felt like Christmas. Today, child services would have no doubt snatched her from her alcoholic father and placed her with a foster family. She didn't know how she felt about that. She could have ended up so much worse. But, as it was, trust did not come easy to the girl who wasn't wanted.

Bonnie had literally become that surrogate mother figure she so desperately needed. Diana knew if she hadn't met Bonnie, she'd still be living in her father's trailer—or worse, married to a man like her father.

Bonnie had seen something in Diana, possibly the first time anyone had seen beyond the ragamuffin exterior.

Diana never forgot Bonnie's kindness.

One afternoon, Bonnie asked Diana to stay after class and told her she was a bright girl with an unlimited future. She offered to help Diana and helped she had. She'd helped tutor her not only in school but life. By the time Diana got to high school, she had a part-time job, solid grades, and no longer had to worry about some of her basic necessities. And for her father's participation, he seemed to not even notice, obsessed as he was with his drinking. Sometimes he held a job, but most times, he had issues with his employers, who were always "out to get him."

With the help of Bonnie Elder, Diana applied for and received a scholarship to attend Oregon State University. The Wharton Fellowship hadn't even been on the horizon.

With nothing to come back to in Oregon, Diana had thrown herself into the fellowship. It led to a second scholarship, and this time, the degree was an MBA from Wharton. At least her father knew she'd made it to Wharton. Unfortunately, he died between the first and second year of her master's program, the alcohol and pain of losing his wife finally catching up with him. There had been scant phone calls with him while she'd been on the East Coast, but to be honest, he didn't seem to care about her—not like Logan once had, not how Bonnie did.

After Wharton, the measure of success in Diana's life shifted to money, which led to security. Anyone who said that money couldn't buy happiness was only half right. Diana was extremely comfortable by most peoples' standards, but she would never quite embrace the idea that a dirty trailer park wasn't in her future if she ever let up, even for a moment, despite what people like Bonnie told her. Bonnie was proud of her, and that meant the world to Diana. She'd see Bonnie at Thanksgiving in Texas, where Bonnie had moved with her husband after retirement. Diana and Bonnie talked every other week, but she wasn't sure she wanted to tell her mentor about this latest debacle. One thing was very important, she wanted her own security, and that meant money.

That was why her partnership was so valuable. It represented security, the kind of security that meant you'd never know hunger or had to be ashamed of how you looked.

But Logan messed with her world. He messed with everything she thought was important because the truth was when she'd been with Logan, those sweet three months, it was the closest she'd ever come to happy ever after. The missing, undefinable part of her that had never forgotten what it felt like to be in love.

Hearing his words tonight had only broken her heart all over again. With him, she might have had the happily ever after. Maybe she wouldn't be at Wave, maybe she wouldn't have any money, but she would have had him. And that would have been priceless.

# CHAPTER TWELVE

Diana followed the wild hand gestures of the kid who was directing traffic. She hated parking the BMW on a dusty plowed field. It felt like she was driving on four flat tires. As she parked in a roughly assembled row of Hot Air Balloon Festival participants, she tried to give herself a little pep talk.

"Balloons don't bite," she said as she looked out the moon roof of the Beemer, when a shadow passed overhead, causing her to duck involuntarily. She didn't get it. Who wanted to fill a silk sack with hot air, step into some rickety wicker basket made of twigs and soar into the sky? Yeah, that sounded rational. Hot Air Balloon people were just a little whack in the head. They loved this festival. They were insane.

The heart of the matter was simple. Diana didn't like hot air balloons because they combined two of her greatest fears: flying and falling. Since she'd been a little girl, she hadn't liked heights and had done everything in her power to avoid them, along with an unnatural fear that she would free fall to her death. Still, in her early thirties, she had to medicate herself to fly. If she didn't, she was overcome with paralyzing panic. Thankfully, any business travel that involved flying, she insisted she arrive the day before. All the better to medicate, no one the wiser. She would arrive at the job bright-eyed and drug-free. Still, there was always a moment or two of panic that she had to deal with when she flew, but she liked to think she was getting better.

She'd discovered her fear the hard way on her first flight back to Wharton. Her dreams had almost disappeared before her eyes twenty minutes into that memorable flight. Thankfully, the woman in the seat next to her gave her half a Xanax. That was all it had taken to calm her down and get her to forget she was traveling through the sky in a jet-fueled rocket. More than once, she had looked skyward and thanked that sweet angel, wherever she was, for giving her a happy pill, which saved her future from being a total catastrophe.

Getting out of the car, Diana kept looking overhead at the balloons filling the sky. She felt like an extra on a remake of *The Birds*. Only the birds were colorful balloons. And the skeptical townspeople, who couldn't see the tragedy before them, held cell phones in front of their faces snapping pictures. Naïve idiots.

She couldn't wait for this event to be over. The very thought of those balloons in the sky made her palms sweat.

She carried a box of Mountain Valley cheese stick crackers, which would hopefully confuse the palette of everyone tasting the wine that Marco had insisted they serve today, as she went in search of her booth. Ironically, she was more concerned about what everyone else was doing after the tasteless display of flesh they'd offered at the first event. Everyone would no doubt step up their game.

From the preliminary schematic, she knew the next few hours wouldn't be easy. Logan, who she hadn't seen since she'd run away from his house in her still damp clothing, was going to be directly across from her. The chaffing she'd received from the wet jeans after her run home that night was still a little visible on her inner thighs. What a disaster that night had been. Not only was it embarrassing because she was willing to have him ravish her body, but then to find out *he* thought he was saving her by ending their relationship all those years ago. *Blindsided.*

The angry rash was just a painful reminder of what happened when she made rash decisions.

"Hey guys," she said in greeting to the team assembled. In the aftermath of the Waterfront Festival, she had put her foot down and asked for a refined booth with regular people as the servers. No black bras with white cotton shirts, no models. It wasn't lost on her that all the judges from the Stark Hotel were women. She only hoped they hadn't offended them. Marco has reluctantly agreed.

Antonio and Davide were trying to blow up two one-sixteenth scale Mountain Valley Vineyard balloons that would flank the booth. The specialty vinyl pieces had been an expensive addition but necessary. Each balloon had the Mountain Valley Vineyard logo in gold wrapped with lush green metallic vines dangling with bunches of reddish-purple grapes on a black background. If balloons could be sexy, they were smokin' hot.

As she watched the cousins fight with each other over the proper way to inflate the balloons, children curiously meandered around the booth waiting for them to open the gelato stand. And their parents watched as well. But they weren't checking out the brightly colored gelato cart, they were watching the Italian imports with amusement. Possibly, they just needed a good glass of wine or the excuse for a wine they were serving at their booth today.

"Rhonda," she called to one of the servers, whom she had personally hired. "Could you start uncorking six bottles of the red?"

Turning to Davide and Antonio, she said, "Here, guys, let me show you." Then she tightened the nozzle on the compressor and switched it on. A gentle hum began to inflate the first balloon. Both of them seemed completely mystified by her easy finesse of the machine.

"I got this. Why don't you make sure the gelato doesn't melt," she warned and bit her tongue before adding, "this time" to the end of her statement. Surely, this time, they would remember to keep the dry ice replenished.

Halfway in at the Waterfront Carnival event, right about the time Logan had begun his charity push, children had been disappointed when the gelato was too mushy to scoop onto cones. The cousins had spent a little too much time flirting with the mothers and other females in general and not paying enough attention to the children. It might seem like a little thing, but she knew it had cost them some votes.

Logan watched her as she filled and secured the first balloon and then moved to the second inflatable. She could feel his laser beam blue eyes penetrating the back of her head.

"Fine," she wanted to yell. "Look all you want…" Eventually, she'd have to stop fussing with the bottles and decor, turn, and face him. Considering everything she had said the night at his house, that would not be fun.

The minutes passed, and eventually, Daisy Stark announced that it was officially time to open their booths and start serving.

Diana thought she showed real strength by completely ignoring Logan. He was doing his best to make eye contact, but she'd focused on the growing crowd, forcing herself to smile and make light conversation with everyone she could. But that isn't to say that she didn't look across at Logan's booth and give it a scrutinizing comparison.

She was surprised to find it was a very similar theme to his last event. Lots of potted forget-me-nots, and this time his charity was for Pet Advocacy. He had several people from a local non-kill shelters with a surprising large variety of cute dogs who all needed homes. Even though it offered no reference to wine and was a blatant attempt to jerk the heartstrings of wine-tasting parents, it still bested her. A soft, cuddly puppy in the makeshift petting zoo was far more appealing to a kid than gelato any day of the week.

She'd hoped they'd stop with all the gimmicks. She wanted

this particular leg of the competition to be a clean fight. They were serving their samples in nice quality plastic wine glasses with stems, and there were mini appetizers. She'd made sure that every member of the staff had food handler licenses. Aside from the cheese stick crackers, they'd partnered with a local dairy farmer who made local artisan cheeses. Half of their booth held the crackers, cheese, and a selection of mini wine-friendly finger foods. They had pre-prepared little red and white paper baskets that held just the right amount of food. They had four gelato flavors for the kids, and hopefully, the cousins would remember to add the damn dry ice.

Several other booths had signs out for charitable events, but nothing compared to the damn puppies right across from her.

The flood of people was fairly even between their booth and Logan's. The other three competitors shot daggers in her direction at every chance they got.

"How do you think we are doing?" Marco asked.

"I've been watching where people put their ballots after trying all the wines. I have a clear view of the ballot station. I think we are neck-and-neck," Diana replied.

"I wish we had thought of puppies."

"It is gimmicky. I thought more of them than to pull at heartstrings."

"I'll be back. I'm going to try to hunt something up for us," he said, and before she could inquire as to what that might be, he was gone. She saw him chatting up with a buxom blonde reporter. Maybe he could get some coverage for them, or maybe he could get lucky. Either might improve his mood.

There was an increasing desperation about Marco that she didn't like. She only hoped he could keep it together through the end of the competition.

Diana made the mistake of looking up and meeting Logan's gaze from across the walkway. He smiled at her as if letting her know he knew exactly what she was thinking. It was unnerving.

She wasn't eating well; she was distracted and lay awake thinking about that night at his house. She was tired and irritable. All of the anger she'd stored away had unleashed now, knowing he done it purposefully, supposedly broke it off for her, and this should have tainted the sight of him forever...sadly, it only made her want him more.

Had he really kissed her? She longed for his touch.

As she watched, a pattern emerged. Women were flocking to Logan's booth. Every time she looked his way, he was pouring a taste for a woman, or women as the case may be. They'd finally awakened to the idea that there was a good-looking man in their midst. He still wore his wedding ring, but it wasn't distracting any of them. She wondered how long he would keep wearing it. What an odd thing it must be to have a spouse you'd been married to, seeking to divorce, and now no longer here. The significance of the band—the commitment, everything it meant—gone in an instant.

Marco returned to her side, smiling that snaggletooth grin that always meant trouble for her. "I just got us something so amazing, so wonderful. You are going to be so excited," he said, mimicking one of the puppies across the way. She wouldn't have been surprised to find that he'd grown a tail and was now wagging it.

"What have you done?" she asked with a smile, trying to share in his excitement.

"I got us a ride on the Sunset Balloon in a half-hour with two news anchors from Channel Five. We are going to be on the eleven o'clock news," Marco said and added, "That little blonde kinda likes me."

"Great! Have a good time," Diana replied and thought it would be good to get him out of her hair for a few minutes as long as he didn't say anything incredibly stupid. Or hit on the news anchor while on camera.

"I can't go by myself," Marco said.

"Well, I'm not going," she said firmly.

"Diana, you have to go," Marco pleaded.

"We don't need to go for an actual ride. Why couldn't you have just got them to come over to our booth? Our décor is fabulous," she said.

Marco hissed out his snaggletooth and said, "I don't know how to say this without hurting your feelings, but our booth is boring. In a balloon, we can serve them our wine when we are two thousand feet in the air overlooking the valley."

"Enjoy yourself in that balloon," she fired back, adding a little steel to her words. No way, no, how she was getting into one of those things.

"You have to go," Marco said.

"I have a very real, very traumatic fear of heights," she replied. "I'm telling you; you do not want me in that balloon. I cannot be responsible for my actions."

"Please, please, Diana! I just told the reporters all about you. They asked to interview you specifically."

"Are you kidding me?" she asked. Marco showed a real talent for playing all the angles, the little jerk.

"You're the best. We wouldn't have hired you if you weren't."

She didn't know what to make of all this sudden, shallow flattery.

When she'd started this project, it was her understanding that Salvatore D'Salvo was her boss. Now, a little over four weeks in, she was finding that wasn't the case.

She was a glorified babysitter to the headstrong kid who wanted to run his daddy's business, the entitled ass.

She knew how much Wave charged for her services. Her boss had reminded her anytime she had ever complained. If it hadn't been for that, she'd have told Marco where he could take his little balloon ride. This could end so badly.

"I'm telling you; you don't want me to," she said.

"Please, Diana, I'll do anything you want. I'll take you to dinner at the best restaurant in town. I'll be your slave for a day. Anything you want. Please..."

"Um, no, thank you. I warned you," she said.

Logan was deep in conversation with three women when she left the booth with her little basket filled with wine and glasses for the balloon ride. He didn't even look her way.

Following Marco to the launching area, she felt little pinpricks of panic start at her feet and work their way up her legs. She was shivering in the near eighty-degree heat.

The Sunset Balloon was striped with red, orange, and yellow. It was already getting outfitted with a camera to record the spot Marco had persuaded them to film. As they waited, her pre-flight shaking got out of hand. The wine glasses bumped in her basket and made sounds akin to crystalline wind chimes.

Marco said, "It's going to be great. You are going to be great."

Under her breath, she whispered, "Stop talking."

Glancing over her shoulder, she saw Logan step from behind his booth to watch the happenings at their balloon. This was all she needed. He knew she was scared of heights. They'd once gone on a hike up Mary's Peak, just a few miles from campus. As the terrain got steeper, so had her anxiety. At one point, she'd gotten on all fours and grabbed the ground to keep from falling. It had taken Logan over an hour to coax her down off that mountain. The look he gave her now was one of questioning curiosity. He obviously remembered the Mary's Peak incident.

She couldn't let him see her fear. She wasn't that girl anymore, but unfortunately, her body didn't understand the need to look cool in front of the old lover who'd dumped her.

And it only got worse from there. She was helped into the basket, which felt much less sturdy to Diana than it appeared. And how could it be solid? It was a basket made of twigs that was going to hold all of them as it soared thousands of feet into the sky? What if strong wind tipped them and she fell out? She felt overcrowded in elevators made of metal. Now that basket was going to hold how many of them? Six people and all their equipment? No seat belts to keep them from falling out. What about the propane tank? What kept it from catching the twig basket on fire? Or the fabric balloon? Were they all crazy?

Marco gave her a reassuring wink as familiar little needles of terror started wreaking havoc with her breathing, and her lungs seemed to shrink painfully.

Within five minutes, the rest of the crew joined them, the balloon pilot, who looked all of sixteen, and the two reporters. There was the cocky blonde with the perfectly pointed eyebrows that had been plucked and penciled to perfection, who Marco thought was hot. There was a character who reported on all the festivals and happenings in the area, known simply as "The Fun Guy," and a stressed out, sweating cameraman. Maybe he didn't like heights either.

Before they started filming, Diana was calm enough to ask "The Fun Guy" just how old he was. She didn't need to get seen serving a minor on camera.

"Geez, lady, I'm twenty-six, but The Fun Guy gig works. The audience loves the young and stupid act. Yes, I can drink your wine. I'm legal."

"Well...that's good," she murmured and put a death grip on the edge of the basket.

Marco laughed and shook his head as if it was the funniest thing he had ever heard.

Before she could get out, the balloon was lifting off the ground. Or the bottom was falling away from them.

Diana tried to calm herself, regulate her breathing, and ignore the stabbing needles of panic. They were all talking around her, Marco hitting on the eyebrow blonde, The Fun Guy, and pilot talking about open flames and the propane tank.

"Wow, like, so does the fabric ever catch on fire?" The Fun Guy asked.

"Well, if it does, we are all like s'mores," the pilot sarcastically replied.

"I get it, 'toasted'…" The Fun Guy said with a laugh.

"And a big, gooey mess once we'd fall from the sky," the pilot added.

There was nothing funny about getting burned like marshmallows! And it sure wasn't funny to talk about it enough that she could picture it in her head!

Their ridiculous banter was giving her a full-blown panic attack, so Diana tried to tune them out. She didn't want to hear anything else, especially about the propane tank.

Meanwhile, she gripped the edge of the basket, looking down at the ground where Logan had moved closer, his arms folded as he looked up at her. Even from a distance, she could see that he wasn't smiling. He looked upset, even concerned. And how should she feel about that particular detail? At one point, he unfolded his arms and gave her a reassuring wave. She almost started to cry.

"Well, why don't we get started?" the hot blonde, whose name was Tiffany, asked.

"That sounds good. Hey Diana, time for your starring role," Marco said, looking pointedly at Diana.

Did he expect her to let go of the edge of the basket? She couldn't do that! The look she gave him must have conveyed as much because she saw his own fear start to rise. Then, having made some sort of decision, he reached for the bottle himself and started talking.

"Diana is a bit of a hothouse flower. She's a little scared of heights. Luckily, this is my winery, so I can talk about it," he said and laughed. He was quickly joined by Tiffany and The Fun Guy.

What was worse than being in a twig basket thousands of

feet over the ground with a flame being shot into a fabric container? Diana had the easy answer: Being in a twig basket thousands of feet over the ground with a flame being shot into a fabric container while people laughed at you. Aside from jumping out of the basket, there weren't many places she could go to get away from them.

She turned so that she was facing her hostile audience, but then she couldn't see Logan. And for reasons she didn't want to examine too closely, she needed to see Logan. He'd been her last remaining hold on the solid ground, a familiar anchor in an otherwise rolling storm.

She managed to hold a couple of glasses in one hand while Marco poured. He and The Fun Guy took the glasses from her, and they began to film.

Diana smiled for the camera, but she couldn't speak when she was asked a question.

After a long pause, Marco cut in and answered for her.

When they'd finished what could be called a semi-disastrous segment about how great Mountain Valley Vineyards was, Diana looked at the pilot and said, "Okay, time to land."

The pilot said, "Jeez, lady, the ride hasn't even begun."

"We need some aerial shots," the cameraman complained.

Marco and Tiffany had sidled up next to each other, and Diana made the mistake of looking down. Logan was there, but he looked tiny, and she could no longer read the expression on his face.

The Fun Guy asked, "Hey lady, you okay? You don't look so good."

Marco broke away from Tiffany to whisper in her ear, "Wow, Diana, you look kinda green."

Diana started to hyperventilate, a strange wheezing sound emitting from her throat as she dropped to the floor of the basket, an invisible elephant sitting on her chest.

Things happened quickly after that. The balloon descended

rapidly as Diana tried to curl into a fetal position. Despite the thunderous ringing in her ears and the black sparkles in front of her eyes, she could hear Marco telling them he had never seen her lose it before. No one touched her or tried to reassure her. They all got as far away from her as they could in the small basket. As if what she had a disease that might be catching.

"Hey, everybody spread out, take a corner. You are causing a crooked descent," the pilot warned. "She won't bite. At least I don't think she will." This was followed by more laughter at her expense.

As soon as the basket hit the ground with a solid jarring thud, everyone but the pilot dove to freedom, and then Diana was alone, shaking, barely aware of her surroundings.

And then, above all the noise, she heard a familiar voice say, "I'm a volunteer fireman. Let me see her."

"We don't need your help, Parrish," Marco said.

Logan's voice cut through her haze. He was angry but authoritative in a way that suggested he wouldn't be ignored. "I'm not asking for your permission. Get out of my way, or I'll move you out of the way, which would be my preference."

Marco must have moved because a moment later, she felt the basket move as someone got onboard. She recognized his scent, cedar and cotton and then strong arms enfolded her. She didn't think of how angry she was at Logan or even her need to punish him for their last conversation. She just wanted someone to be kind to her, to hold her, to make it all better. And he was there.

"Diana, honey, it's Logan. You're safe. It's going to be okay. I've got you."

She lifted her head, saw the concern in his deep blue eyes, and didn't hesitate.

She reached for him, clung to him, and buried her face in his shoulder. She was vaguely aware that he had checked her pulse and then looked into her eyes to make sure she hadn't had a complete break with reality.

"Still scared of heights, I see," he whispered with a small smile.

She nodded but didn't say anything as terror gave way to embarrassment. Tears now streamed down her face, and the hardcore businesswoman she'd fought so fiercely to become dissolved into a soft, warm puddle.

"This is so embarrassing," she murmured as he pulled a pristine, folded white cotton hankie from his pocket and began to wipe away her tears.

"No, it's not. You're fine. It's going to be okay. I just couldn't believe it when I saw you get in this balloon. You've always been so scared of heights. That wasn't a good idea."

She glanced around, made sure Marco wasn't close enough to hear, and whispered, "I didn't volunteer to go. He made me go."

"Let me guess, that little ass, Marco?"

She nodded and dried her eyes.

"How are you feeling now?" he asked, looking at her so tenderly that it brought more tears to her eyes. Why did he have to be so good-looking? His hair still long, but he was clean-shaven, and she was close enough to smell the lingering odor of his shaving cream. He was using the same brand he'd used in college.

"A little better," she managed, a sob escaping her throat as she bit down hard on her lip. It was taking everything ounce of strength she had not to crawl into his lap.

"Liar," he said and then pulled away from her and stood. Holding out his hand to her, he offered, "You're going to be okay, but you're still shaking like a leaf."

She didn't want to leave the cocoon of the balloon's basket, scared for what waited beyond. But Logan quickly and authoritatively led her away from the questioning reporters, the slightly shaken pilot, and even offered excuses on her behalf that painted her in a much more positive light than she deserved.

"She had quick onset motion sickness with vertigo. It is very frightening," he offered and glanced menacingly at the pilot as he added, "It is just amazing she isn't much worse after that ride."

"Hey," the pilot complained, but Logan ignored him.

It was such a lie; she thought she should correct him, but then she saw Marco, saw the anger on his face, and she decided that a sudden vertigo was the lesser of many evils.

The reporters asked him about the cause and symptoms of vertigo as they began filming him. He briefly offered more lies that seemed to satisfy their questions.

The evening news blurb had suddenly taken on an exciting edge. It was now breaking news. Diana could hear the opening line in her head. *A simple wine tasting segment turned disastrous tonight at the Balloon Festival after the woman in charge of the alcohol panicked and almost had to be restrained several thousand feet off the ground. Thankfully, none of our Channel Six reporters were injured. The cause was later blamed on a lame excuse of vertigo…*"

By now, the Hot Air Balloon Festival was winding down. Diana headed back toward their booths as it was time to start breaking things down, but Logan wouldn't let her go. He grabbed her arm and pulling her back to his side.

"You're done for tonight. How did you get here?" he asked.

"I'm fine," she lied. Diana still felt dizzy and lightheaded. The nausea was just beginning to subside, but she was still shaking.

"Did you hitch a ride with Marco?"

"No, I drove, but I can't leave right now. I've got to help break down the booth," Or try, she thought.

"Marco has more than enough people to help him."

"I can help with the booth," she protested, though her resolve was waning.

"And you aren't driving yourself home."

"Logan, I'll be fine."

Marco appeared and tried to interject, but Logan completely ignored him, turning his body so that he was blocking the other man from Diana.

"Hey Ben," Logan called toward his booth. A man Diana recognized from the event at the Waterfront Carnival walked up to them.

"Ben, this is Diana."

She looked uneasily at Ben but managed to nod and shake his hand.

"I don't want her to drive after that balloon ride. I'm taking her home. Will you take care of my car?"

"Sure," Ben said with a nod and gave Diana a long look that she didn't like.

Turning to her, he asked, "Now, where are your car keys?"

"In my purse in the booth." She wasn't going to argue, she needed his help, and he was willing—something she needed to think about later after the ill feelings subsided.

They walked to the edge of her booth, and Marco reappeared.

Logan asked, "Who has Diana's purse?"

Marco shook his head, pointed at the center of Logan's chest, and said, "Whoa, whoa, you're not—"

"I'm a medical professional, Marco. I'm taking her home. Close down your own damn booth." Logan answered, somehow knowing what the snaggletooth was getting at.

Marco said, "Listen, Parrish—"

"No, you listen to me," Logan said, getting in Marco's face and illustrating that he was at least six inches taller than the shorter man. "Diana is in my care. Back off."

Diana watched the standoff between the two men, as did everyone in her booth. Marco looked like a little bull, getting angrier and angrier.

"You can't talk to me like that," Marco said.

"I'll talk to you any damn way I want. Just give me a reason, and we can finish this once and for all," Logan said.

This was an old vendetta. Diana knew that although the smoke was rising, there had been a fire between the two men. And with all that she knew now, Diana was sure it had to do with Julianna's accident. She remembered the way Sal and Sophia had talked about it not being anyone's fault as they looked at Marco. But the townspeople said otherwise.

"This isn't over, Parrish. I'm only going easy on you because the day I evict you from our new land will be the sweetest day of my life," Marco said with an arrogance Diana had come to despise.

"You'll never own Forget-Me-Not. I'd poison the land before giving it to you."

Marco started to speak, but two of Logan's employees, Ben and another equally large and imposing man flanked either side of him, showing Marco that they outnumbered him.

"This isn't over," Marco said. Then he turned and walked away.

One of the Mountain Valley temporary lady sommeliers Diana had hired grabbed Diana's purse, handed it to her, and whispered, "Wish I'd known he was a fireman. I'd have set a fire."

The woman then looked past her to Logan and smiled. Diana ignored the look and let Logan steady her on the way to her car. She was still feeling like she could hurl any minute, and the grass was tripping her every step, or maybe her sure-footedness had something to be desired after that flight from hell. Glancing at Logan's profile, she could see the hatred he had for the D'Salvos. Thankfully, the altercation had ended peacefully—well as peacefully as it could, all things considered.

Now she had a better idea of the magnitude with which the two families disliked each other. She so wished she was playing for the other team—the one who was caring for her.

# CHAPTER THIRTEEN

I nside the passenger side of her BMW, Diana stole looks at Logan's striking profile as he drove them off the plowed field that had acted as a parking lot.

"You remembered Mary's Peak?" she asked.

"I don't think I could ever forget that. You scared the hell out of me that day. I still don't know how I coaxed you off that mountain." He was calmer now coming off the scene with Marco. How quickly he recovered, Diana thought. His cool was impressive and a little unnerving.

"Well, it was good practice for what happened today," she said and asked, "So you're a fireman now?"

"Only a volunteer," he said. "It is one of my childhood dreams that I made a reality."

"You were good with me that day at Mary's Peak. Good with me today."

When they turned into the drive that took them to Forget-Me-Not, she asked, "Why are we going here? Oh, right. I'm dropping you off."

"No, you're coming inside and relaxing for a few minutes. I don't think you should be alone after what you've just been through, and I doubt that any D'Salvo will come here looking for you. On the bright side, if they do, I'll have them arrested for trespassing."

"You *really* don't like Marco?"

"You could say that," he replied.

"I don't like him either," she admitted.

"Really? Don't tell me that you're immune to all that Italian Stallion charm?" he asked with a sarcastic bend to his voice.

"Ew, I don't like to think of him like that. I consider him to be the little brother who tries hard but just doesn't quite get it right. He's a liability."

"Well, little boys often get into a lot of trouble," he said, and his words were so controlled, so guarded, she knew that he was holding a host of information back from her.

He asked, "Have you ever thought about quitting?"

"I can't quit. We signed a contract. I'm theirs until September 1st."

"That is unfortunate."

"You also know that I don't quit things."

Logan didn't respond but walked around to her side of the car and opened the passenger door. She got out unaided, and he looked ready to grab her at the slightest indication that she might need help.

But when he held out his hand to her at the bottom of the steps that led to his front door, she shook her head.

"I'm fine."

"Humor me," he said, taking her arm, walking so closely beside her that their bodies brushed as they took each step together.

"What happened at the Victorian after your Aunt and Uncle died? Is it just empty? It was such a beautiful house."

"It has been empty since my uncle died three years ago. It wasn't easy for him living there after my aunt died, but he did. I haven't decided what to do with it. Holds a lot of memories. I grew up in that house."

He'd lost his beloved aunt and then uncle, who had raised him as their own after his mother died, Diana remembered. Then he lost his wife within a year of his uncle. No wonder he was so heartbroken. She wanted to ask more but thought it best not to pry. They were on thin ice with each other, and she didn't want to press her luck.

"It is a shame to see it go empty. Maybe, and this is only if you'd be okay with it, you should turn it into a bed and breakfast. It would be filled, especially during the fall harvest. Charge tourists, heck, charge them to crush grapes and help with the wine making process," she suggested treading lightly. Maybe she shouldn't have said a word. Logan was as close to a hermit as she could have imagined. He wouldn't encourage people to stay on his land.

"This may be a business, but it is also a home. I don't want strangers on my land or in my uncle and aunt's house. I'd be more likely to rent this place out," he said with a nod of his head to indicate the house whose porch they were standing on.

Ginger greeted them with a stuffed animal in her mouth. She danced around as if she hadn't seen her master in years. Diana could relate to the energy pouring off the copper animal. Once they'd both petted her and lavished her with attention, she ran outside to do her business.

"You know what you need?" he asked as he waited for the dog to return.

What she needed was for him to tell her he'd made a mistake all those years ago and still loved her. She wanted him to tell her that there hadn't been a day since that he hadn't regretted his decision to let her go.

"Do you want to ply me with more wine?" she asked.

"No, sugar."

Diana immediately thought of the southern term for kisses as the dog stormed back inside and danced around them. "Pardon me. What?"

"Sugar, after a shock or fear, you need something like sugar after your adrenaline rush to restore your body. You burned a lot of calories in those ten minutes," he said, bending down to pet his dog.

"Was I only in that balloon for ten minutes? It felt like ten hours."

He laughed, and it was a sound she remembered like the sound of her own voice. He led her to an oversized leather couch in the living room. Ginger jumped up next to her and lay down, putting her head on Diana's lap, which was somehow very comforting.

"You're a sweet girl, aren't you?" she asked as she rubbed the dog's velvet ears.

Logan lit the fire in the fireplace and then turned toward her, pausing as he did a double-take at the sight of the dog. Shaking his head, he stepped from the room. She heard his footfalls into the kitchen, where he washed his hands, and then she heard ice clinking into a glass. When he returned a minute later with the ice-filled glass and her absolute most favorite beverage on the planet, she questioned why he would have something he didn't like on hand at short notice. Did he have it in his fridge just in case? It was a ludicrous idea.

"Coca-Cola? You hate Coke," she said as she continued to pet the contented dog. She'd always wanted to have a pet but had never had a lifestyle that allowed for one.

"I'm not a fan of the stuff, but it has its uses, like now," he replied and handed her the glass. Then he covered her with a soft blanket. It might be July, but she had to admit, there was a little chill in the evening's high valley air.

He sat across from her in a matching chair, watching her with his dog.

"Thank you for what you did today," she said. Why was she here?

"I'm sorry I turned the sprinkler on you last week," he said, reading her mind.

Taking a long sip of her drink, she watched him over the edge of the glass and replied, "No, you're not."

Leaning forward in his chair, his knees almost touching hers, he said, "I am sorry, Diana."

"Well, if we are trying to apologize for everything we've ever done to each other, I'm sorry you didn't tell me the truth all those years ago."

"I see now that you thought that was a mistake."

As if it were her problem.

"But you don't?" she asked incredulously.

"No, because it made you the woman you are today. Think of everything you've accomplished that you wouldn't have if you'd have turned down that fellowship."

It was the wrong thing to say to her.

She lived a lonely life full of regrets. He was the regret that haunted her the most.

"I might have been a much happier person," she said.

"You might have resented me until your dying day. I'd have been the reason you didn't get to experience the world beyond Oregon," he said. And when she didn't respond, he kept it up. "If that hadn't happened, I wouldn't have met Julianna, and I can't imagine my life without knowing her..."

But Diana could. She could have seen their life together without Julianna. But it was too late now. He was still in love with his dead wife. She couldn't fault him. She couldn't blame him. And she recognized that Logan would never be hers, not now, not ever. Because when you cleared away all the platitudes and cobwebs of the past, one truth lived strong: Logan Parrish hadn't loved her enough, and he never would.

• — ⟨⊙⟩ — •

Logan was an idiot. Why he said the things he did to Diana, he didn't know. His mouth was like a leaking faucet he couldn't stop, and everything he said not only fell out; it fell out wrong. He liked to think it was a result of all that was happening with the vineyard. He was distracted and pulled in too many directions. His frustration, his anger at the thought of losing what had been in his family for the last four generations was too overwhelming to comprehend.

It made him lash out, and like or not, Diana was the closest thing to him right now, the easiest target.

And she was helping his enemy, the man directly responsible for Julianna's death. They'd declared it an accident. The truth was quite simple. If Julianna hadn't chosen Marco over him, she wouldn't have been in Marco's car that night, and she would still be alive.

Just when he thought it couldn't get any worse, the D'Salvos had decided on trying to take his land, and they'd hired his first love to do it. How much more salt could they pour into his wounds?

"I'm sorry your life turned out the way it has, Logan."

"You don't need to be sorry for me," he said, watching her as she stared at the glass in her hand. "I've been very lucky in a lot of things in my life."

He knew she didn't want to hear his reasons or his excuses.

She wanted something he couldn't give her. She wanted to go back to where they'd been all those years ago. He was attracted to her. Hell, his body wanted her even as his brain sent out warning after warning to look but not touch.

But they couldn't go back.

"Listen," she said, "I don't know what is going on with you, with your vineyard. I wish I weren't involved with Mountain Valley because if I wasn't, you must know that I'd help you any way I could. But my agreement with them doesn't allow me to do anything beyond their interests."

"Don't you think I know that?" he asked, much more sharply than he'd meant to.

"Then why did you bring me here tonight?" she asked. "You should have just stepped away. I'd have been fine."

"You were shaking and coming off a shock. I wanted to help you," he said defensively. "I don't need *your* help, not with my vineyard."

"You could have just taken me home."

"I know, but I couldn't. I didn't want to. I wanted you here," he said, looking away from her.

"Why? It isn't because you wanted to pick up where we left off twelve years ago. Is it that you're horny and know that I can scratch the itch? Or is the best revenge letting the D'Salvos know that I'm spending time with you? Well, the only person that is going to hurt is me. I'm going to tell them we went to school together. I'll be vague, say we talked about where we went to school and discovered, surprise, surprise we were in the same class at Oregon State. I knew your name was familiar when I heard it. I bet we had a class or two together and never knew it. If I'm lucky, they won't fire me."

What was she saying? Was she trying to provoke him? Trying to make him mad? Well, he was already mad at her.

"Diana—

"Hey, and don't worry, I know you aren't attracted to me. You tried to kiss me last week to see if any of those old feelings lingered. Guess they weren't strong enough to survive because it didn't go so well for either of us. Remember? You certainly acted as if I was quite repulsive. I haven't forgotten. Your virtue is safe with me, Mr. Parrish. My goodness, maybe I should schedule a makeover the next time I go to the big city. I'm losing my touch."

"That's enough, Diana," he whispered.

"Oh, don't worry," she said mockingly. "I'm used to not being your first choice. I just didn't think I'd come in second to someone who's been dead for two years. What does that say about me? I mean, really...I'm a living, breathing woman."

Logan saw red. How could she be so completely insensitive?

"How dare you? How can you be so cruel?"

Setting her drink on the glass-topped coffee table before her, she looked at him, those hazel eyes smoldering with green ice crystals at the edges. "Maybe I learned it from you."

Diana stood, hands on her hips, waiting for him to respond. The only sound was a groan from Ginger, who'd been disturbed in the process. She jumped off the couch and shook her ears in frustration, and then wandered off to her dog bed in the other room.

Logan didn't like the way she was standing over him. He stood so that they were facing each other.

Pointing at her, he said, "You don't—"

"I don't what, Logan? Don't know how it feels to lose someone? Yes, I do. I know how it felt to lose you. So, if you'll excuse me, I'm going to go home now, or what home is for the next two months. Because sitting here, being this close to you...It's breaking my heart all over again, and quite frankly, I don't need a repeat performance. Because I'm not sure I'm over the first breakage yet."

She kicked free of the blanket, which had fallen to the floor around her ankles, picked up her car keys off the end table, and headed for the door.

He couldn't let her go, not like this, maybe not ever. He realized he couldn't lose her again. Emotion overrode logic, and he reached for her.

Wrapping his arms around her, he pulled her to him. She wrapped her arms around him in the same tight hold, hoping to make the moment last. They held each other tightly, almost painfully. He was much taller than she, but their bodies still fit together in that old familiar way. And in her eyes, he saw the passion that matched his own. In the moment, he just wanted to make up for all the years he'd wondered about her, the years there had always been a little doubt in his heart, and missed her

She softened in his arms as if she could read his thoughts. He kissed her then, watched her eyes widen in surprise, and then close as his lips touched hers. She leaned in, letting him support her weight, and then her arms tightened around him, reaching for him, rubbing each lush curve along his body.

It had been so long since he'd been touched, since he'd felt the curves of a woman in his arms. His body responded like a lightning rod, pulling in her energy and feeding off it, letting it course through him. He didn't speak, didn't utter a word, just lowered her back into the soft leather couch and stopped denying himself the pleasure of Diana.

# CHAPTER FOURTEEN

Diana couldn't think with Logan kissing her. It had been a long time since any man had awakened such passion in her body. What started off as a couple of quick, hot kisses degenerated into pure lust. Logan kissed her deeply, tasting her, his tongue lingering as he nipped and played with her lips. She remembered this sweet torture, the delicious anticipation that had little tingles racing along her skin. This had always been his power over her, his ability to evoke pure surrender.

Logan pulled away her Mountain Valley Vineyards t-shirt, cool air hitting her skin as the fabric was removed. Then Logan's warm lips trailed kisses from her neck to her belly button, lingering along the way.

"Red," he said admiringly as he ran his finger along the lace edge of her bra.

"I couldn't afford the good stuff back in college," she murmured as he smiled down at her. "That is no longer a problem."

"It didn't matter. You always managed to look beautiful in everything you wore."

She bit back the need to thank him for his cliché. He hadn't earned her thanks. Then his hand slipped between her back and the leather couch cushion. He found the clasp on her bra and released it. Whatever she had wanted to say no longer seemed important.

Slowly, he pulled away the red lace as she shivered, an involuntary reaction to the cold leather couch and warm man hovering over her.

Logan freed himself of his Forget-Me-Not white polo and tossed it away.

As Diana gazed up at his chest, now kissed with a smattering of dark hair, she drew in a raspy breath and tried to calm down. How would it feel to have him rub against her skin, her bare breasts? She couldn't wait to find out as she reached up and pulled him down to her. He settled his lips against hers for another deep kiss that had tongues dancing and exploring. Little cries of desire emitted from Diana as his chest hair tickled her sensitive nipples.

Logan's mouth traveled lower, kissing her breasts, using his tongue on the crested pink nipples. He suckled her, used his teeth with just enough pressure to make her back arch, and push off the soft couch. She was unable to vocalize her need, but he knew what she wanted.

With a quick motion, he lowered the zipper on her shorts, pulled the fabric away from her body that was both chilled and burning. Then he stopped. "Do we need to worry about protection?"

"My purse," she said.

She always had been prepared. Quickly, she pulled out what she needed. When she handed him three condoms in a row, he could only smile.

"I'm not twenty-two anymore."

"I have faith in you," she said and held out her arms.

When at last she was naked, Logan freed himself of his remaining clothes and lowered himself to her. Her arms reached out and pulled him close. He quickly sheathed himself. She was panting, couldn't think of anything but Logan. All those coal-black locks fell forward, framing his face. And when he next bent to suck her nipples, she felt the tickle of his hair and thought she might climax from the sheer overload of sensation.

"Logan," she murmured. "Please...

Logan's hand slid between her legs and gently massaged her throbbing clitoris. When she groaned, he grabbed her ankle, placed it on his shoulder, and opened her body to him. Slowly, he guided his erection into her warmth.

He slowly pushed into her and then pulled out. The fifth time he repeated the motion, she climaxed, throwing her head back and screaming in delight. No one had ever felt as good as Logan. No one had ever come close. Her body not only remembered him; it welcomed him home.

He rode her through her orgasm, feeding the fire until it slowed and smoldered. Then his breath hitched, Diana, watching his intense expression in the flickering firelight as he was carried away.

Together they used each other, their bodies slamming together in the most primal of mating. It was both familiar and different for Diana. Her body reacted to Logan in the same way that it always had, but there was a different undertone to their actions. It was perchance less delicate, lacking the deep love they'd once felt but still evoking the passion that was as familiar to each of them as the taste of a favorite meal. Time and life's experiences had left a mark on each of them, but the past had not been forgotten.

Raw and spent, they lay together afterward, the blanket now lightly covering them.

Logan was the first to break the guarded silence.

"We were always good together, Di," he said as he kissed her cheek and then her ear, a familiar intimacy she hadn't forgotten.

"I haven't forgotten," she responded.

"It seemed even better than it was before. Time has improved performance."

"Lots of years in-between, and like a good wine, we've grown better with time," she said. "You know, when we were in school, I used to be so scared that I'd get pregnant. Funny, as the years have passed, the idea of children doesn't scare me as much as it used to." Her fingertips ran along his shoulder, relearning the feel of his body against hers, savoring the intimacy while she had it.

"Really? Well, it still scares the hell out of me," he replied.

"Do you ever want to have children?" she asked, remembering how she used to fantasize about what their children would look like one day. The thought that he didn't want to have children hurt her.

"Probably not," he said. "It's not like I plan ever to get married again."

A little ember in Diana's hearted spurted and died. Of course, he'd never want to marry again, not after Julianna. Diana would always be the leftover. How quickly she had forgotten.

One thing was for sure. It was time for her to get up and out of Logan's house. They'd both gotten what they needed. A reunion of the most intimate kind. And she didn't want him to ask her to leave.

Diana scooted away from Logan and reached for her red lace panties, only to have him grab her wrist.

"What's your hurry?" he asked.

"I'm still feeling a little off from the balloon ride," she lied, but he knew her too well.

"Diana, do you regret what just happened?"

"I don't know..." she said, her voice trailing off. It all depended on how bad she felt tomorrow morning after she'd relived the memory of what they'd just done a few hundred times in her mind.

"You do, don't you?"

"We aren't twenty-two anymore, Logan. Life, as you've pointed out, is complicated. I've just put my career in jeopardy for a little...Whatever this was."

146

Logan looked offended. "Diana, what happened between us is between us. I won't tell anyone about this."

"Don't you think Marco will be able to figure it out?"

Logan shook his head. "I don't care what he thinks."

"Well, I do. I have to sell the lie that I barely knew you in school. Besides," she said, choosing her words carefully. "You're still in love with your wife despite what you two were going through."

Logan looked away from her into the fire. He didn't need to answer. She knew the truth and had guessed it perfectly.

"My life is just complicated. I thought Julianna and I would be together forever, but she had other ideas. It really shattered me. And now I'm about to lose my business. Maybe all I want is to hold you and make love to you. Maybe that is all I can give to you right now, Diana.

But it is a hell of a lot more than I'm giving anyone else. And who knows what will happen over the next few months?"

"So, I should settle for what? What you have left to offer?" she asked, feeling both anger and hurtfulness bubbling inside.

"Diana, you just called off your engagement. Aren't you in mourning for your relationship?"

"He did me a big favor. If I were still engaged to him, I'd be cheating on him with you right now."

"No, you wouldn't."

"Yes, I would."

"That isn't true."

"Stop selling yourself short," she said. "Besides, we were talking about your availability, not mine."

"Can we just see where this goes? Be the adults we are and not the lovesick kids we were? Do we have to read more into it than that?"

Diana relented. If she thought she could stay away from him, she was only kidding herself. She wanted him and would continue to want him, but she wasn't about to share the depth of her neediness with him. This was new, and after what happened the first go-around, it was better to take it slow. Diana admitted to herself he was the sensible one right now. She decided to lighten it up and not scare him.

"Mr. Parrish are you suggesting a clandestine arrangement?" she asked with a small smile.

"Here's the truth, I miss you. I like being with you, but I have to be very honest. I don't know what happens after the contest." Diana felt like there was something else deeper in his words. What happens to the vineyards, his life overall? He was on the cusp of very large life changes; changes he didn't want.

"So, we see each other and see what happens over the next few months."

"Yes."

It was all she was going to get from him, something told her it was the best he could offer, and there was no way that she would turn it down. Besides, he needed her just as much as she needed him, and sooner than later, he'd figure it out.

Diana drove home a little after midnight. She didn't want to be seen coming home the next morning and have to answer questions that would no doubt embarrass her or put her job in further jeopardy. As it was, she wasn't sure that she was going to keep her position as a consultant.

Too many things had happened to put her on unsure footing with both the D'Salvos. This might be the first contract she had ever lost for Wave. There would be a lot of explaining to do, and it might endanger her partnership—a partnership that a few weeks ago meant everything in the world to her. Funny, at the moment, she was having a hard time remembering why.

One drama at a time, she reminded herself.

Right now, she just wanted to reflect on her evening with

Logan. Her body felt soft and limp; completely relaxed in a way she hadn't felt in years since the last time they were together. To be as scared and tense as she was earlier in the day and then to feel like she did now...she couldn't wrap her mind around it. She didn't want to. She enjoyed feeling the way she did, like she was floating with each step she made as she parked the BMW in front of the Merlot Cottage and made her way up the path to her front door.

"So. You're finally home," Marco said from the rocking chair on her porch.

And damn it, she hadn't left the porch light on again. What was it with men and her darkened porch? At least in the dark she couldn't see Marco's snarky snaggletooth.

"Last time I looked, a curfew wasn't in my contract."

"Where have you been? I was worried," he asked as he stood.

"I've been recovering from my panic attack," she said, with a serious *don't fuck with me tone* she had never used with anyone at Mountain Valley Vineyards, especially Marco.

"You'd better not have been with Logan Parrish," he said as he stood and blocked her path.

"You know I was with him. He drove me home after that horrible balloon ride. That you forced me on, may I remind you." She should actually thank him because she wouldn't have had awesome sex with Logan had little Marco not pushed her over the edge.

"That doesn't explain where you've been for the last four hours."

"Excuse me," Diana said as she sidestepped past Marco.

"Did you hear me? What are you doing with him? Are you sleeping with him? Is that it?" he asked.

Diana turned and pushed a finger into his chest to illustrate her next words. Now, the *don't fuck with me* tone had a little more bite behind it. "You're out of line. Especially after what you pulled today. I told you that I didn't want to go in the balloon, but you insisted."

"I don't want you talking to him," Marco said, sounding like a little kid.

"Well, that is just too bad. You should be encouraging me to get friendly with everyone in the competition."

"I don't like the way he looks at you. If I find out—"

"What?" she interrupted in a tone just as menacing as his as she took a step toward him. How dare he. "If you find out what, Marco?"

"If you are telling him about our family—"

"Here's a newsflash for you, Marco. Your wine isn't the best one in the contest. I'd have to say, of the five vineyards represented, it is probably one of the bottom two. If not the very bottom. So, every time you open your mouth and boast about how great it is or how easily we're going to win, you remember that. You should wish that I was getting close to Logan Parrish. Maybe I could find out why his wines are so much better than yours when they are virtually coming from the same land. And if you ever ask me about my personal relationships again, you'll be talking to my company's attorney. This bullshit ends now."

He stepped back, his unnaturally blue eyes glowing in warning as he tried to think of the next thing to say. Diana didn't wait for his retort. She took the opportunity to slam the door in his face. She had no time for punks. She needed to obsess over what she'd shared with Logan for the next hour or two.

Once she'd shut and locked the door, she leaned back against it and felt the heavy burden of all she'd done that day take its toll.

Her life was a blissful mess.

Her career, her personal safety net, was on the line. Up until she'd seen Logan again, the most important thing in her life had been to make partner. But he'd reminded her of something else—her desire for love—and she did love him. And she was sure he felt something for her too, even if it was just a little bit.

◆————— ◦⬡◦ —————◆

Logan took a long, hot shower and then sat in his front room, holding a brandy snifter in one hand and petting Ginger with the other.

Diana filled his thoughts. From the moment he'd seen her again, nothing had been the same. And now there would be no going back. They'd made love in the house he'd built for Julianna. The house Julianna had painstakingly decorated to an interior decorator's idea of perfection because having a big house and a family had been one of her dreams until it hadn't. One day, they were talking about having kids, and the next, she wanted to travel and explore the world. It wasn't easy to make time for such things, as he explained to her. Then Julianna had taken the dream and herself away, taken it to Marco, and it had all gone to hell. Would she have gone through with the divorce? He had a feeling she would have; she had figured out his heart was still with someone else. Only a few people knew the truth when she died. Most people thought it was as *his* wife, not the woman having an affair with Marco and threatening divorce, who had died.

How many women in nearby Dundee had shown up with dinner and cookies and heartfelt messages in the months after Julianna died? It had been a parade, and he'd done nothing except thank them and retreat. Most of them had finally given up. A few still tried, but he hadn't shown them any warmth or encouragement.

But Diana was unlike any of the women in town and very different from Julianna. Diana had been his first love. Nothing had been sweeter. Up until Julianna left, nothing had ever hurt

151

worse than the day he'd said goodbye to Diana. Then he got the news that Julianna had died.

Maybe fate was giving him a second chance. It was an impossible situation. How could it ever be fair to Diana? What kind of life could he give her now? She was a corporate bigwig. She probably made a hell of a lot more money than he did. Hell, what was he but a washed-up winemaker about to lose everything he and his family had built? He'd been on a downward spiral since his wife had left him. He'd seen it coming and yet did nothing to prevent it from happening. He could have saved himself a hundred times over, but instead, he'd stared out this same window night after night, trying to make sense of what was senseless.

Was Diana there to offer the final twist of the knife in his pain or to show him that maybe his life wasn't over?

Without touching a drop of the brandy he'd poured, he retreated to the master bedroom with Ginger at his heels. He sat on the edge of the bed and stared at the photo of Julianna that was closest to him. One of several that adorned his nightstand. He'd loved her, but it hadn't been enough. Even tonight, the ache in his heart was still there, but on this night, the pain wasn't quite as sharp.

Julianna had made her choices, and they weren't his fault. Maybe it was time to let go of a bit of the guilt that he couldn't love Julianna the way she should be loved. Guilt that maybe, if Dian hadn't always been in his mind and heart, he could have loved Julianna more completely, and she would never have strayed. He needed to stop punishing himself over everything that happened. Maybe it was time to join the living again... Damn, he didn't know. He was wallowing in his own self-pity, and that needed to stop.

He wondered if Diana was sleeping well tonight. He should have asked her to stay, but he hadn't. He wouldn't make that mistake again. Logan needed to decide what he wanted first, otherwise, none of this was fair to her. First things first, the photos of his dead wife needed to go, along with her clothing which still hung in the closet. If he wanted Diana back in his life, he needed to make room for her.

It was long past time to make a few changes.

# CHAPTER FIFTEEN

On Monday morning, Diana made sure she looked wide-eyed and professional as she made her way into Salvatore's office. The patriarch and Marco were deep in conversation, no doubt about her as she knocked on the partially opened door.

"Diana, come in," Salvatore said as Marco scowled at her. "I understand there was a little problem at the balloon festival yesterday."

Diana decided that the only proper course of action was a quick response that got to the heart of the matter.

"What exactly are you referring to? Our turnout was impressive. The booth was a success."

"The balloon interview wasn't great," Marco stated primly. He had a lot of nerve.

"Maybe next time you'll listen to your consultant when she advises you not to do something," she said. "If you'll remember, I asked you not to make me do that segment more than once. You chose not to listen to me."

"It was unfortunate that you had a panic attack. But to be honest, Diana, our booth lacked pizzazz. It was staffed with old ladies," Marco added. "That's why I went out and procured an interview to try to make up the ground we lost."

Addressing Salvatore, she said, "Our booth was staffed with knowledgeable sommeliers who know many people in the community. It was fun. Parents and children were entertained and fed. The ladies from Stark Hotel seemed to like and respect the more knowledgeable team. As for the balloon ride, I told Marco I was afraid of heights, and when he made me get in a balloon for a news segment, I had a full-on panic attack. I'm not happy about it, but I did warn him it could happen, and it did. Next time he should listen to me when I tell him something."

When neither of them said a word, she asked, "Anything else?"

Marco shook his head and added, "You left with our competitor."

Fucking tattletale.

"Your neighbor, Logan Parrish, is a medically trained volunteer fireman. He was doing what he gave an oath to do, render aid."

"Maybe in your weakened condition, you shouldn't have spent time with him. You might have unwittingly shared strategy with him," Marco said.

"Oh please, discussing strategy was the furthest thing from my mind. I was trying not to throw up on him. He took care of me, got my panic attack under control, which is more than I can say for you," she said. Marco was becoming a pain in her side now, and this was going to pose a problem going forward. She was sure of it.

"I guess we didn't realize that you were such a delicate flower," Salvatore said with a laugh. "You act like you have it together, but when the pressure gets hot, you maybe can't stand it."

"Really? This is the second time a D'Salvo has called me a hothouse flower. This is the direction you want to go? Trying to infer somehow I can't handle the pressure?" she asked, no longer even mildly concerned about what she might say. "You're in a competition that could be worth millions of dollars for you, and you want to exploit something that I told you I'd have an issue with? You want to focus on your hired consultant's weakness that has nothing to do with business. You don't want to focus on the fact that we are neck-and-neck with at least one of the other wineries and what this could mean? You'd like to share a chuckle over a weak moment? I'd suggest that if you're worried about reputations, you should check on your own. This vineyard is not well-liked in the community. I walked around Dundee and handed out flyers. Do you know how many people warned me about Marco?"

She looked at The Snaggletooth for emphasis and said, "Several couldn't wait to tell me the gossip of affairs and all about the accident that killed Julianna Parish. I don't need to know the details, but I'm going to have to work extra hard to show that this vineyard wants to support the community. And that is on you." She pointed at Marco.

Marco's face tightened in anger as he took three menacing steps toward her. Salvatore D'Salvo intervened in the nick of time, slamming his fist on his desk to get his son's attention.

"Marco!"

"You ever take a step toward me like that again, I'll quit. I will not cave to intimidation, and it has no place in my world, professional or personal," Diana said and turned her back to leave. She thought of the contract she'd signed along with Salvatore D'Salvo. The only way out for her personally was to quit, but not this job. She'd have to quit Wave. Showing fear wasn't something she could do. One thing she'd learned from growing up as she had, sometimes the only way to get rid of a bully was to stand up to him. And if all else failed, let him get in the first punch but hit him back, harder.

"Diana," Salvatore began, "The car accident was just that, an accident. It was proven that Marco wasn't to blame. It is old news, two years ago, to be exact. But Marco is very territorial. He doesn't like thinking of you talking with Logan. He might be our neighbor, but he is our enemy. You are our asset."

"It might interest you to know that over our discussion

yesterday, I discovered that Logan Parrish and I were both undergrads at Oregon State University at the same time. His name sounded familiar. Now, I can dig a little into his background. Now that he knows we are alumni, it may make his guard slip. That could be an advantage," Diana said, taking in every word they said about Julianna's accident. She knew it wasn't "old news" to Logan. Still, she had to add, "My loyalty is to this winery. Don't forget it."

"Do you remember him?" Salvatore asked.

"It's a big school, and it was a long time ago. It was just an interesting coincidence I wanted to tell you about," she said and thought she'd handled the information in the best way that she could. She was under no obligation to share the rest of the information. She'd re-read the contract that morning. Personal connections were addressed in vague terms. She would keep it that way.

"Oh, I almost forgot. Those 'old ladies' are actually from the Ladies' Sommelier Society of Yamhill County. For reasons I don't want to investigate too deeply, they said really nice things about your wine to all the festival goers who stopped by our booth. All we had to do was pay them. That seems like a pretty good trade-off.

"Will there be anything else? I want to see how much wine we poured, write up a report for Wave. We only have two weeks until the Luxury Home Tour. I want to start working on ideas for the booth."

"No," Salvatore said, "I'm pleased with what I'm hearing from you. If you can remember anything about Parrish, let me know. Is there anyone you could call?"

"I was just thinking about that myself," she said.

With those final words, she walked away from D'Salvo's office with her head held high. She contemplated buying a lottery ticket, for she was feeling very lucky to have gotten out of that conversation so lightly.

She had thought she knew Marco, thought she had a good enough working relationship with him, but last night and today, he had thrown her under the bus and driven over her. It was a new complication she didn't need. Fine, she could handle a bully like him. It might get ugly, but it was nothing she couldn't handle.

On Wednesday night, Diana lay in bed, wearing her new cotton nightie and staring at the tongue and groove ceiling. This raw, needy feeling that she couldn't shake was the result of her nocturnal adventure with Logan and her own damn fault. They'd made love three days earlier, and since then, nothing. Not a word from Logan. Had that ever happened when they were in college? No, because after the first night they'd spent together, they'd spent every night together for three months until it ended with his abrupt and brutal honesty about how he felt about her.

Now she didn't know what she expected exactly, but if they were only using each other for sex, didn't he want to get at least a repeat performance? She didn't even have his phone number, nor did he have hers. She had the general number to Forget-Me-Not, and her desk number that rang to her cell when she was out of the office was on the website. They hadn't exchanged business cards. They had been too busy being mad at each other, then ripping each other's clothes off. Not like she'd call him and ask for a booty call, but it might be nice to get a call.

Grabbing a book from her nightstand, she read the same page three times and gave up on it. There was too much on her mind. First, she'd compromised her position by being with Logan, and then there was the contest, and now her job, her future, and the growing animosity with the D'Salvos. All the things in her life were intertwined in a tight knot. There was no way this was going to end well.

In two weeks, the heat would be on. They would be holding a wine tasting at the Luxury Home Tour, situated among nine luxury homes that were on tour and for sale in the old-moneyed town of Lake Oswego. The homes were all priced between three and five million dollars. She had to hand it to the marketing people at the Stark Hotels. They had picked very public events for their competition. Great exposure for their hotels, great exposure for the wineries.

The event usually received three thousand people a day. However, the day they had their contest was also Realtor Day. All the thirteen thousand licensed real estate agents in Portland Metro Area would be given free admittance. As a special twist, there was going to be a special ballot just for agents. The contest title: "Which wine are you most likely to give a client as a Holiday gift?"

In addition to the already chaotic nature of the event, the Stark Hotels were onto the creative ways the wineries were trying to elicit votes. A list had arrived that morning, and it was seriously messing with Diana's plans. Unfortunately, as much as she didn't like it, she thought it leveled the playing field. And hopefully, it would get to the heart of the matter when it came to who had the best wine. Too bad that wasn't Mountain Valley.

- *No charitable donations or fundraisers of any kind. No food items or beverages other than the wine from the winery represented.*
- *No giveaways. No gift cards. No animals.*
- *No music or audiovisual equipment of any kind.*
- *No more than four staff members in any booth at any time.*

She knew the "no animal" part was for Logan, and it made her happy. He had to have received the same memo that morning. She could bet how unhappy he'd been to open that email. Her fellow contest goers had to stop with their Starbucks gift cards, and she had to stop feeding gelato to everyone's kid.

Logan would be there, and she couldn't help but wonder

how seeing him again would go. As far as Diana was concerned, the ball was in his court.

Diana needed to remember her priorities, and they didn't involve sleeping with an ex-boyfriend.

Just as she decided to get out of bed and work on her ideas for the luxury homes challenge, there was a knock on her door. If it was a D'Salvo, specifically one with a snaggletooth, she was going to have a fit and maybe try her new bear spray.

But it wasn't a D'Salvo who waited on the other side of the door. Logan stood before her, dressed in jeans and a black t-shirt, holding a shotgun in his hand. Diana stepped aside so that he could get off her porch. He leaned his gun against her wall and then pulled her into his arms.

"Took you long enough," she said, looping her arms around his neck.

"As I told you, I'm not twenty-two. With maturity comes a certain amount of restraint," he replied as he lifted her into his arms and headed straight for the bedroom. So much for small talk. "Besides, you never left me your phone number."

"You could have found it on the website. Anyway, I happen to think that maturity is overrated," she said as he deposited her on the edge of the mattress. Remembering back to how they used to be with each other, Diana quickly tossed off her nightie and leaned back against her pillows, waiting for him to get rid of his offensive clothing.

As Logan tore away his clothing, Diana's focus fell to the impressive, immediate erection as she reached into her nightstand drawer and pulled out a condom.

"I was hoping you might stop by," she said with a smile as she held up the foil-wrapped condom. Suddenly the three days that had passed seemed insignificant; apparently, he needed the time to figure out his next move — regardless, she was glad he was here.

He gave her a roughish smile and grabbed the condom from her raised hand.

His reaction to her had certainly not changed. When he slid into her arms, covering her nakedness with his own, she sighed contently. How quickly they fell into their old patterns.

He kissed every inch of her body returning again and again to her lips until her mouth was swollen and her body throbbed with need. When she tried to turn the tables on him and torture him in the same, exquisite way, he had none of it, holding her wrists above her head until she squirmed with desire.

"Logan, please," she whimpered as she spread her legs and tried to capture him.

"Let me—"

"Patience," he said as he released her wrists.

Reaching up, she touched his hair and ran her fingers along the planes of his face.

Why did he have to better looking now than he'd been at twenty-two?

"I just want to be on top," she said.

"Maybe later, if you're good," he said as his hands moved lower, gripped her hips, slid beneath them, and lifted.

"Logannnn....." she murmured as his shoulders pushed her knees apart.

"Just as I remembered..." he said, his eyes sparkling as he smiled down at her. Then, he dipped his mouth to her intimacy and feasted, using his tongue on her, just the way he had when they were young lovers.

Diana threw her head back and tried to suppress her cry of pleasure as her body moved like an instrument under Logan's fine expertise. While she was still panting from her first climax, he slid inside her with slow, intense control. When he was fully encased in her warmth, he drew a deep breath, steadying himself. Their eyes met, and he began to seduce her all over again, gently sliding all the way out of her tight heat and then filling her again.

All the slow intimacy that had been missing from their first coupling now clouded the air between them. Logan wouldn't be rushed. Diana wasn't sure if she was grateful or frustrated. He met her eyes and held her gaze as his body did wonderful things to her. Diana fell under his spell, just as she had at twenty-two. This was what had been missing with every man who'd come after Logan.

Long after he had fallen asleep, Diana lay awake listening to his even, steady breathing. His arms wrapped around her, his hand gently cupping her breast as he spooned her body from behind. How she had missed this, this sweet intimacy that had little to do with what they had previously shared in the night. She felt safe with him holding her in this way. Gently, she let the tips of her fingers graze along the smooth skin of his arms. Carefully, she touched his fingers, searching for and finding the ring finger of his left hand. When she had seen him on that first day, he was wearing a wedding ring. As recently as Sunday, it had been there.

But tonight, it was gone. She could feel the groove in his skin where it had once rested. He'd worn it long enough that his body had accommodated the fit of the band. What it must feel like to have any man love you enough to display it with a ring for the world to see. She could only hope his bare hand meant something good, something positive for them both.

A tear leaked from the corner of her eye as she tried not to get too used to the feel of Logan's body, the closeness of him. He wasn't hers to keep. He never had been. And if she thought he'd suddenly come to his senses and ask her to be a part of his life, she was kidding herself. But maybe she could believe it might be possible, maybe for a little while.

# CHAPTER SIXTEEN

D iana heard her alarm and ignored it. She rolled over and reached for Logan, but he'd left well before first light. The last four nights, he'd appeared on her doorstep, and they'd spent the night wrapped in each other's arms. She was getting used to him again, used to the way he would hold her after they made love, spooning her against him as he ran his hands over her skin. And when he'd leave, he'd gently kiss the back of her neck, then her cheek, and tell her to have a good day.

They'd talk after making love — talk about the day, the past, college, and everything in between. It was cathartic. Diana guessed he needed to revisit those memories as much as she did, and she could only hope he was remembering how solid they were before he sent her away.

Fortunately, they didn't argue, didn't waste the time they had with negativity, nor did they discuss the competition, and she was thankful for that. At least she didn't have to lie about it if asked by the D'Salvos.

During the day, she mourned the loss of his body, his warmth, his presence, and the growing need to have him inside her. She missed what she couldn't have: Logan in the daylight hours. They used to make love in the afternoons when the light was bright, and there were no contests or wineries or D'Salvos. They had wonderful conversations and solved all of the world's problems and fought over who made better coffee. They watched movies under the cover of an old blanket and played pool at the local bar. They had fun and enjoyed each other, in and out of bed. Circumstances didn't allow that, and she was frustrated for not being able to have their relationship out in the open.

As she awakened by degrees, she realized the noise was her ringing cell phone.

One glance had her groaning. Stephan, her boss, the man she would be partners with if she played her cards right, was on the line. They had a standing meeting to talk on Mondays and Thursdays at ten in the morning. The fact he was calling a little after seven had had adrenaline pumping through her veins.

"Stephan," she said, not wasting time with pleasantries.

"Diana, where are you?".

"I'm getting ready," she lied and glanced at the clock. "It's only seven. What's up?" Because as surely as he was calling before their regular time, something was definitely up. Silently, she cursed Marco.

"How well *exactly* do you know Logan Parrish?"

Bingo! Give him a prize!

Stephan had asked in his Stephan way. When he had information he wanted you to figure out, he played dumb, letting you fill in the blanks or hang yourself with the rope he handed you. One of his favorite expressions was, "Maybe I'm confused..." Confused? Not likely.

As for his question, if she hadn't been more awake, she might have replied, "Intimately." But he was her boss, who tended not to find fault with her. It would be best not to give him any reason to start.

She had told him on Monday that she went to school with Logan. She hadn't elaborated, but obviously, the D'Salvos were trying to get her into trouble.

"Better today than I did a week ago. We've already talked about Logan Parrish and his vineyard," she reminded Stephan.

"The D'Salvos are concerned that you are spending a lot of time with Logan Parrish and that your role as their consultant might have been compromised."

"I take issue with what sounds like a very serious accusation," she said, thinking that Marco might come off an eager, sweet kid, but down deep, he was a snake. She'd already explained to Stephan about the balloon ride, and yet he was starting to show a little solidarity to the wrong side.

"Be that as it may—"

"Stephan, damn it, there is a problem here that is a lot larger than Marco or Salvatore's insecurities. Mountain Valley Vineyards wine isn't the best product in the competition. To be honest, it is actually pretty bad wine. I think it is the worst among the wineries. They are trying to undermine my credibility with you so that if for some reason, we don't win the competition, they will claim that I had compromised loyalties. That could cost Wave a lot of money. Don't let them get away with this."

"Then you'd better make sure we win this contest. I don't have to remind you what they are paying us."

"And may I remind you, I already told you that I went to school with Logan Parrish.

"I hadn't seen him since college. I think he wishes he'd have hired me instead of the D'Salvos. By the way, the next time you speak to the D'Salvos, make sure to mention that Marco is starting to create a hostile work environment."

"I'll do nothing of the kind. You eat men like Marco for breakfast. Keep him in line."

"I'm trying, but having to keep Marco, especially on a leash, isn't what I signed up for. He's a creepy, little snaggle-toothed bastard. I'm getting a little tired of taking crap from him."

At this, her boss just laughed, and disaster was averted for the moment. She wondered if they had noticed Logan's nocturnal visits to her cabin. She didn't want to think about it too much and decided she wouldn't need any morning coffee to wake up after all.

"Stephan, if you don't have faith that I can pull this off for Wave, and you want to replace me, then you should. It's business, do what you need to do," she offered, putting a little steel in her voice and then bit her lip waiting for his response.

"No, no, of course not! I need you on this, Di. You're the best strategic consultant I have. If D'Salvo calls me again, I'll offer to join you for a few days, but I'm not going to replace you. Just watch yourself with Marco. He sounds like he doesn't quite know his place in his family business. And if you can dig up any dirt on Logan Parrish, it could go a long way toward the loyalty angle."

"I don't like getting dirty," she said, and he laughed again.

If Stephan came down to Yamhill County, her nights with Logan would have to end.

"Keep your chin up. You can do it."

"Thank you, Stephan. I'll try my best," she said, thinking she had a few reasons to keep him in Seattle, where he belonged.

They ended the call on a good note, which should have pleased Diana, but the fact she was keeping secrets made her feel like she was lying for all the wrong reasons. Her loyalty had never been brought into question, and she wasn't sure the accusation wasn't without merit. Neither she nor Logan had shared one tidbit of information. Something was happening between them seemed a lot larger than some competition.

⋅⟨⊙⟩⋅

Logan was extremely pleased with the new rules set into place by the Stark Hotel committee. He bet it was causing Diana a lot of strife, but it wasn't like he was going to ask her.

When he arrived at her cottage each night, business was the

168

furthest thing from his mind. She was his oasis, his salvation. She was also his obsession, and he missed her when they weren't together. He couldn't think about her while he was talking to his staff or trying to do simple math because his focus would go all to hell. He dreamed of taking her out to a romantic, candlelit dinner in town, watching a trashy movie under a blanket, and hitting the pause button to kiss. He wanted to play Monopoly with her only to watch her cheat. He wanted to drink coffee with her in the morning, not scurry away like a thief in the night. He missed her. When he was with her, he was already sad knowing that he'd have to say goodbye before the light of day.

He remembered this from long ago, this pull that she had on him. No one had ever gotten under his skin, not the way she had.

When she'd gone to Wharton, he'd returned to the vineyard and worked himself to death that summer. His aunt and uncle had worried about him so much that when they finally confronted him with what was wrong, even he couldn't deny the truth. Diana had taken a part of him with her.

They'd wanted him to fly to the East Coast and tell her how he felt that he'd been wrong and lied to her so that she would take the fellowship.

He'd come so close, even booked an airline ticket for early November. He was going to see if she'd honor him by going ice skating at Rockefeller Center. It was risky. There was a strong chance Diana would tell him to go to hell, but he had to try to make amends, to make things right between them. He'd been a fool, and it was time to admit it to her.

But life rarely turns out as planned.

Several life-altering events happened in a short period of time. Logan's Aunt Mini, who worried about him day and night, for he was the child she'd never had, died of suddenly of a heart attack that September. His Uncle Jack was overcome with incapacitating grief, a condition Logan came to understand with the passing of time.

When Diana asked him, he hadn't been completely honest with her about the timeline of his aunt's passing. She might not have put it together, but the Diana he knew was wicked smart. She'd know that his aunt's dying that September had changed the course of his life.

He was immediately thrown into a new role as the second in command at Forget-Me-Not.

Ill prepared for such a heavy responsibility, he was terrified he wouldn't make his uncle proud, but for a large part of that fall and winter, his uncle wasn't there. Physically, he was present, but in many ways, Uncle Jack died with his wife.

A little shy of twenty-three, Logan became the man people went to at when they needed answers or to get something done at Forget-Me-Not.

The flight to see Diana had come and gone. He'd never even taken the time to cancel the ticket.

As the months passed, he tried not to think of Diana, believing that she was better off away from the drama happening at Forget-Me-Not. And he honestly didn't have time to think of anything as he tried to run the business and learn the industry at the same time. Even so, Logan didn't forget her. He thought of her daily. Time passed, and days turned to months, months to years, and here they were.

The bottom line and his biggest fear was that after the way he had treated her, she would have found someone else. Now, he knew, he should have called her, surprised her, done anything he could to try and get her back.

Then he'd met Julianna, whose family ran a bakery in town. One day when Logan was taking a rare break, he stopped in to buy something for his uncle, who had a legendary sweet tooth. And he met Julianna, who told him she thought it would be fun to work at a winery. She ended up taking a part-time job at

Forget-Me-Not in the tasting room, and he saw her almost every day.

She didn't have large career ambitions or large dreams, so he thought. She led him to believe that it was her dream to get married and have a family, just like her mother and her two sisters. To a man, who had very little in the way of family, it didn't take long for the wheels to be put in motion. She was easy to love, and he was looking to mend his broken heart. In reality, she hadn't been honest, and neither had he.

Now, his past was circling around back to him.

Diana awakened feelings in him that he thought he'd only imagined. No, that's not it — feelings he'd tamped down and tried hard to forget. Passion vs. love. With Diana, he could have both. Spending time with her made him think more about his marriage. Julianna was safe in that she couldn't break his heart because he never loved her like he did Diana, and sadly, his wife pretty much knew that. Not the details, of course, but she knew there were more than two people in their marriage. She'd had an affair and threatened to be with Marco to get his attention. Only he wasn't sure there hadn't been a bit of relief in his punishment.

He needed to get a grip. Not for the first time in his life, he felt at the mercy of fate.

"Boss, what are we taking today?" Peter, his summer intern, asked, pulling Logan out of his old memories where he seemed to drift for hours on end.

"Ben has it handled," he answered. Not for the first time, wondering why his intern was so interested in what he was serving.

"So, you already decided what you're serving?" Peter repeated.

"I'm serving the good stuff," Logan replied dryly. Despite his sex-muddled mind, he was starting to suspect that Peter was a teller of tales to his neighbors. He had no reason to suspect

Peter of anything but too much curiosity, but lately, the pointed curiosity had begun to nag at him.

"Who all is going?"

"We can only have four people, so I'm taking Ben, Tess, and you." It was the first time he'd invited Peter, but he wanted to watch him around the competitors. Scrutinize him a bit. And it was time to make sure that what he suspected wasn't true.

"Cool," Peter said and walked away, looking very pleased with himself.

Ben met him by his truck. "There is something off about that kid."

"I know," Logan agreed. "You know what they say. You aren't paranoid if they really are out to get you. Listen, watch him today. See how he interacts around the competition."

"What? You think he is talking to the D'Salvos?"

"Stranger things have happened."

"Why don't you ask the blonde? You seem to know her pretty well. She still speaks to you, even after the sprinkler."

"You know about that?" Logan asked.

"Everyone knows about that. We heard her yelling at you."

"We went to OSU at the same time. She's an old friend, but she never talks business. She's too damn professional and competitive. I just wish I'd hired her first," Logan said, not liking the direction this conversation was taking.

"Interesting."

Picking up on the too cute tone, he asked harshly, "Is there something you'd like to ask?"

"I just find it curious that your uncle once told me you had your heart broken by a girl named Diana in college. How many Dianas do you know in a lifetime?" Ben asked.

"Just one, if you get lucky," Logan said. He wasn't a man used to discussing his feelings or his reasons for doing anything. If Ben wanted to know about Diana, he'd tell him. But despite how he felt about the competition between the wineries, he didn't want her to get fired over him. However, if she did, he'd hire her in a New York minute.

"So, she's the one? *The* Diana?" Ben asked.

"She's currently the enemy, and who knows what will happen today, tomorrow, next week, or a month from now."

"Are you going to let that stop you?"

"Stop me from what?" Logan asked.

"A chance at happiness."

"What choice do I have at the moment?"

"You know Tess and me. We loved Julianna like family. But damn it, she isn't coming back, Logan. We all worried we were going to lose you too. But lately, you're more like your old self. This competitive side, that fighter, he's back. I don't know when I've seen you this motivated. That Diana woman, she brings it out in you, and just like that, Forget-Me-Not has a dog in this fight."

"I hope you're right."

"I hope you can find a way to win this thing and get the girl. That's what we want for you."

Logan started to speak, but Ben held up his hand. "I know, it is none of my business, and I've said what I want to say."

And then he just waved as he walked away.

An hour later, they were in two cars, headed to nearby Lake Oswego. Ben and Tess were following, and Logan didn't want to think about the conversation they were no doubt having in their truck.

"So, how much wine do you go through at events like this?" Peter asked. "What is the favorite vintage of the crowd?"

"It all depends. The main thing is to have enough. If we run out, it will cost us votes. We need to keep the Chardonnay good and chilled. We are lucky it isn't a really hot day." As he said the words, he looked up at the sky. It was a muggy, overcast day that looked a bit ominous.

Black clouds were gathering, and he wondered if they'd get

rain. They had an awning, so a little rain would be fine, but a downpour of hail could be disastrous, not just for this event but also to his vines at Forget-Me-Not.

They arrived and parked in the VIP parking lot at the edge of the Luxury Home Tour with a special pass given to the contestants. The venue was a recently paved street in the new neighborhood that had been built over the last year. Logan noticed their staging area was mid-way down the street, right in the middle of the action. All five booths were next to each other. Logan didn't like the arrangement. He preferred to have them facing each other. It was a better way to keep tabs on the competition. The first booth in the line was The Honey Bee Winery, who would naturally have an advantage. He didn't think they were leaders in the competition, but today, with their new position, it could change the tides. He didn't want to take an advantage for granted.

He was between Honey Bee and Mountain Valley. He was strongly considering re-arranging the placards before the other contenders arrived but knew even as the thought entered his mind that the committee had chosen the placement specifically. Maybe Diana would have a similar idea. Let her move the placards, and then he could turn her in. She'd be furious, but that was okay. She could take it out on him later. He smiled lustfully at the thought.

She was a woman whose emotions flowed through her body in waves of colorful passion. When she was happy, sad, excited, or mad, he knew it just by the way she responded when they made love. It was a unique characteristic to her. He knew that she was cautious around him, holding back a little, not that he could blame her. Trust was an issue for her. There wasn't much he could do to change her feelings. He didn't trust himself to be able to maintain what they had.

As if thinking of her could somehow conjure her to appear, she arrived next, with her trilogy of Italians. Logan didn't mind being close to Diana, but the thought of being in close proximity to Marco all day was another matter altogether. She looked gorgeous in a simple black silk sheath dress and a big, black straw hat to shade herself from the sun. She wore big sunglasses; her lips painted a perfect cherry red. She was glamorous. A ruby among rocks.

Logan couldn't stop himself from wondering what color panties she was wearing under this particular outfit. His bet was red. Red was, by far, his favorite lingerie color on her.

The blonds he liked to think of as "the Pirates short of a boat" had their hair all pulled back in matching ponytails, with wide black silk ribbons tied in sloppy bows. They were in black silk blouses and tight black jeans. It was a good day for the pirate supplier when these guys came to town. No doubt they had each other on speed dial. Logan was glad they'd left their swords and parrots at home.

He touched his hair, which he had ignored for the better part of six months. It needed a cut. This semi-hippy look was starting to bother him. It had never been longer, and at this moment, he realized how much it bothered him. He could easily pull it back in a ponytail, or, God forbid, a man bun.

Nope. This had to change as soon as possible.

The decision was made. As soon as he could arrange it, he was scheduling an appointment to reclaim the short, uptown haircut he'd had for most of his life. He didn't want to resemble those Italian pirate freaks in any way. The thought of a man bun had pushed him over the edge.

"Hello, Logan," Diana said, sounding very professional, but under that thin layer of control, he saw a flicker of a smile.

"Still working for the inferior vintner, I see," he said to give her a little jab as Tess, Ben, and Peter started arranging the glasses and wine bottles.

Ignoring him, she addressed the fake pirates. "I like our placement. The façade will be perfect."

"Diana, we'll be right back," one of them said, with a strong Italian accent and a bright smile that Logan didn't like. Then he started walking. Logan wondered if he could walk and talk at the same time.

Tess and Ben laughed. Logan turned to them and said, "What?"

"Where did she find them?" Ben asked. "They can barely speak."

Diana turned toward them, having overheard their discussion, and said, "I didn't find them. They came with the vineyard. They are cousins from Italy."

"They're something," Ben quipped.

"At least they like to work," Diana said. Then she went back to fussing with her booth as the other wineries arrived and started setting up.

The two pirates came back lugging a large wooden frame that resembled the outline of a house, complete with a red roof, a little copper cupola at the very top of it, and white picket fence.

"Oh, hell no," Logan muttered as Diana scurried out to the front of her booth and helped them to position the frame dead center among the booths.

Diana smiled at her ingenuity and met Logan's eyes. The look was easy to interpret. *"I won this."*

"I see someone's playing fast and loose with the rules again," he muttered to Ben and Tess.

"Can she do that?" Ben asked.

"Unfortunately, she can," he answered.

"We got to step it up, boss," Tess said.

She'd bested him again. If only he'd read that Oregon Stater magazine three weeks earlier when it originally arrived at his house, this could be his display. Diana would have been working for him. He wanted to break apart that cute little house façade with his bare hands.

# CHAPTER SEVENTEEN

L ogan didn't look happy. Too bad there was nothing she could do about that. If she had a little pillow talk about her plans to build the façade, he'd have made one too. How she had wanted to tell him her plans. Each night she'd used turpentine to remove the paint from her skin. Then she had used scented soap to hide the scent of the turpentine.

She especially loved the little copper cupola with a weathervane on top of it, which had not been easy to find but could be seen from the entrance to the entrance to the event.

It had been so hard for her to hide her idea from him. But, at the same time, she'd proved to herself that she could keep her business and her personal life separate. They'd once been best friends. After the contest, could they be that again? It was her most secret wish and desire. Suddenly she thought about family, kids, a home, friends, and living in a community that she could be part of in some way. And she wanted it with Logan.

*She was falling in love all over again.*

Looking at her booth, the darling house she'd designed and decorated, she felt a huge sense of accomplishment, but there was also a little regret that she hadn't made it for Logan. When she'd put flower boxes on the house, she'd added geraniums as the cousins added the red roof with the copula and weathervane. For a brief moment, she'd pictured forget-me-nots and a dark periwinkle roof. Working with him as his wife his partner would be a dream come true. *Stop that.*

By the time the Luxury Home Tour officially opened, there were four plain booths with minimal décor, and then there was an adorable mini house. Her house was so damn cute; she could barely stand it.

Logan walked in front of the booths, scrutinized her little house and the rest of the competition. Then he walked up to her booth and said, "Hey Diana, keep this up, and the judges won't even let us use logos. By the next event, it will be a completely blind tasting."

"I would look forward to that challenge, Logan. No problem," she replied, trying to show her bravado.

"Me too," he said, "That would separate my wheat from your chaff."

"Confident are you?" she asked, thinking that he'd win hands down if they went to a blind tasting.

The others around them started chiming in, but they ignored them.

"Well, you have to admit that it is a very interesting idea. Replace all the labels with numbers. I might suggest it to the judges," Logan said, trying to call her bluff. "My wines would stand up."

Diana knew hers wouldn't.

"Sounds like a plan. Let me know when you want to present that idea. I'll back you up."

Logan just nodded with a satisfied grin and started greeting attendees in front of his booth.

Marco returned from wherever he'd disappeared to and said, "Our booth kicks ass."

It was such a compliment for the snaggle-toothed adversary she didn't know what to say except what she held in, which would be a sarcastic, "Don't act so surprised, snaggle." Instead, she took a cue from Logan and just nodded with a satisfied smile.

The realtors, who were in a good mood at getting free admittance to this annual coveted event and free alcohol, loved the "House Booth." She knew it didn't matter what the wine tasted like. They were going to win the realtor vote for sure.

About half an hour into the festivities, the gray sky turned dark and ominous. The first strike of lightning blossomed white in the sky at the same time an ear-splitting crack of thunder penetrated the air. It was close to them.

Diana looked up at the gray sky. Dry lightning. Lightning without the rain to drown out a fire was very dangerous. Before she could open her mouth to shut out a warning, a second lightning bolt hit not a block from where they were standing. People started screaming and running to get to cover.

Diana turned to Davide and Antonio to discover they were already running with Marco to the house behind their booth. Antonio looked back at her and yelled, "Diana!"

She yelled back, "I'm coming!"

She was at the front of the booth, so she ran in a straight line across the street to the nearest house instead of running around the booth where Marco and the cousins had gone. She looked for Logan but couldn't find him in the stampede of bodies. Mothers were shrieking, grabbing their children, and abandoning their metal strollers in the street. Women were pulling off their high heels and running barefoot. Men were shouting, kids, were crying, and then a third bolt of lightning struck, and Diana didn't look back. She just ran.

Once inside the McMansion, she walked through the crowds of people chattering like geese. Their voices were unusually high-pitched and afraid. Despite the fact they had all just experienced the same thing, they retold their version of the story as if adding new drama would somehow make their particular tale of perceived near death more spectacular.

Diana looked for Logan. A couple of the other competitors had escaped to the same house but weren't looking her way. They were mad about her facade and were now snubbing her.

Add it to the growing list of proof, the D'Salvos; they were not well-liked in their industry. No wonder they'd needed to hire her.

She stood next to a bookcase in the library room, trying to get as far away from the windows as she could. Another crash of lightning made the fine blonde hairs on her arms stand on end. There was definitely electricity in the air. When she'd been a small child, thunder and lightning had her hiding under her bed. It was a fear she had never quite gotten over. It wasn't as bad as her fear of heights, but it had some bones.

A little gasp escaped her lips as a hand touched her arm from inside the bookshelf.

More curious than scared, she turned to see Logan standing in a well-concealed opening. He held a finger to his lips and motioned her to follow him. She stepped inside, and he pulled what she now realized was a fake door shut behind her.

"What are you doing?" she asked.

He pulled her to him and kissed her.

"Hi there," he said, his lips still touching hers. "Took you long enough to walk over to the bookshelf."

"If I'd known what was behind it, I'd have made a beeline to it," she said.

She didn't care that he knew just how much she wanted him at that moment.

His hands roamed over her body as she rubbed up against his.

"You look beautiful today," he said and kissed her again.

She reached between them, felt the erection pushing against his zipper. She wasn't the only one who was suffering. She no longer cared where she was, how she had gotten there. She just wanted to melt into Logan.

When he broke the kiss, one hand was holding her up while the other stroked her breast through the silk of her sheath dress.

"What if someone comes in here?"

"I locked us in. This is the house's safe room." Electronic equipment with television monitors and gadgets lined the walls of the windowless room. Above them, dark clouds shadowed the skylight above.

"How much time do you think we have?" she asked, her mind thinking very naughty, very reckless thoughts.

"Enough," he said as he pushed up the hem of her dress, his hand running along her thigh.

"Still, we'd better be quick," she whispered, her voice sounding husky in the shadowy light of the safe room.

"You want me to take you quickly?" he asked, his eyes bright and sparkling.

"I don't care how you do it. I just want you to take me."

He kissed her deeply, his tongue taking possession of her as he pushed her up against a cool, metal wall.

"Oh nice," he murmured, his tongue teasing her lips as his fingers closed over the red lace panties she wore under the silk.

Easing them down over her thighs, he smiled and let them drop to the carpeted floor in a pool of red lace.

She didn't waste any time unfastening his belt. When she unzipped his shorts and pushed them down along with his familiar white cotton boxers, she bent down and kissed the tip of his erection. She heard him moan as she took him in her mouth and sucked.

"Diana, please...."

She released him only to be lifted into his arms, leaned against that smooth, cool metal wall, and speared with his hot, pulsing erection. She had to cover her mouth to keep from crying out when he entered her. She was ready for him, but he was too gentle. She didn't want him to be this way with her, not today.

"Harder," she murmured. He obeyed, his hands cupping her butt as he drove into her.

Her senses rose and shattered, bringing her to a climax that she was barely able to muffle by screaming against his shoulder, her lips smearing red lipstick on the white Forget-Me-Not logo of his polo shirt.

Logan soon followed suit. He groaned through his climax, which was scarcely contained as his face contorted in sweet release.

She heard a strange sound and realized it was rain pummeling to the Earth. It was raining so loudly they could hear it even in the insulated safe room.

"Damn," Logan muttered as he slowly lowered Diana to the floor and steadied her until she could once again support her weight.

"With you, I lose myself," he said.

"Good," she replied as she cleaned herself with a few tissues from her purse.

The last thing she needed was a sex stain on her dress.

It was like they were a couple of wild animals. It had always been like this with them. That afternoon they'd gone hiking to Mary's Peak had been no different. After her panic attack, they'd found a secluded spot and made love. At the time, Logan had explained that he was getting her mind off what had happened. She knew he was getting his mind off of what happened. He'd been just as terrified as she that day on the mountain. Sex was how they grounded themselves.

"Do I look okay?" she asked after she'd reapplied her lipstick and brushed her hair.

"You look more gorgeous than you did twenty minutes ago," he said. "Hot sex and strong orgasms have always agreed with you."

She stepped up to him, and he finger brushed her hair.

"Same question for you," he said. "How do I look?"

"You look damn handsome," she said and considered ruining her makeup all over again.

"I don't want to go back out there," he said as he bent and gave her a delicate kiss.

"Me neither. How are we going to do it?"

Logan glanced at the monitors and said, "As soon as they start flocking out, we can join the flow of bodies."

"How did you know about this room?" she asked.

"I came here yesterday, toured all the houses."

"So, you planned this?"

"Planned the weather? Hmm, I'm gifted, but no, I don't know if I've ever been so happy to see lightning."

"Where is the rest of your team?"

"Ben and The Intern were back at the car to get another load of bottles. Tess ran to a different house."

They heard another rumble of thunder and felt the ground tremble. Diana didn't hesitate; with ears ringing and the vibration of the thunder still pulsing in every nerve of her body, she stepped into Logan's outstretched arms.

"That was much closer," Logan said, his voice concerned.

"Yeah," she whimpered.

"You don't like thunder and lightning?" he asked, his mouth close to her ear as he held her.

"No. Never."

"We never experienced this when we were dating before," he said, his voice taking on a sentimental edge she found interesting.

"Just lucky, I guess," she said, pulling back to meet his eyes.

"No, not lucky. This would have been fun back then. Making love during a thunder and lightning storm. Holding you and giving you comfort as Mother Nature has her way with the Earth," he said, then paused and playfully asked, "What else makes you want to be held? Besides heights, flying, and weather?"

"The night. I want to be held every night by a man who loves me," she said and felt him tense. That hit a chord. Good. Let him feel it. He should know the truth of it all.

But Logan didn't respond because something just over her shoulder held his attention.

Diana looked to see he was looking at one of the monitors.

"What is it?" she asked, turning more she couldn't make out what was happening.

"That last bolt of lightning hit the booths," he said, his voice concerned.

Diana now saw that her little house no longer stood upright. It was perched at an odd angle. There was so much smoke and steam that she couldn't see the area too clearly, but what she could see was bad.

"Oh damn, the weathervane," she murmured. It would have acted as a lightning rod, drawing the lightning to it like a moth to a flame. Unfortunately, it hadn't stopped there. The bolt had taken out all the booths. The tables looked like they'd been tossed by a giant. Bottles of wine, some broken, some intact, lay on the ground. The asphalt had jagged cuts running in the otherwise smooth surface where the lightning had fanned out from its strike, ten feet in all directions.

"Damn," Logan murmured. "Look at that. That's power."

"I don't want to go out there and face that," she said, and he pulled her closer.

It was another five minutes before the storm dissipated as fast as it had arrived, and people started moving back into the street. Logan left the safe room first, but Diana took her time. She didn't want to face the other wineries. They'd be angry and blame it on her. They were right to say that her house façade had attracted the lightning, but could they blame her for an act of nature? Yes, they could.

Marco stood in the middle of the street with his hands on his hips. He was arguing with someone from Blanc et Noir, one of the other vineyards in the competition. When she approached, they both stopped and turned to her.

Marco asked, "Where were you?"

The man from Blanc et Noir scowled at her, pointed toward the booths, and said, "Hey lady, thanks a lot for ruining this event."

Logan helped the other vintners right what was left of their tables, but at the other man's words, he stopped and turned toward the noise.

Diana knew that moments like this were what made her the sought-after consultant she was. It was time to sing for her supper and defend herself and her client.

"Really?" she said, approaching Marco and the other man. "You want to blame me for an act of nature?"

"You caused this!" the man yelled, his red face going a shade darker. Marco merely watched.

Diana smiled and shook her head as if she were in the company of idiots. She was standing before Marco and this angry guy, so it wasn't much of a stretch. "I'm sorry you don't understand the unpredictability of the weather. If I'd set out to ruin this event, I wouldn't have chosen lightning."

"You—," he began, but she held up a hand in front of her to stop him.

"Let me bottom line it for you. If your wine is any good, you'll stand in front of what once was your booth, and you'll hand it out to people. If they like it, they will vote for you. If they don't, well, then you are shit outta luck. You're mad because we came up with an ingenious marketing idea to draw people in? Tough. This is a competition. We are supposed to bring it at these events. But it looks like Mother Nature just evened the score. So, stop complaining, and let's get back to it. We've got wine to serve and votes to earn."

To Diana's great surprise, Davide and Antonio applauded and

gave her catcall whistles from the curb. Several other vintners joined in. She could hear Logan's laughter among several others who'd enjoyed the performance she'd just given. It felt good.

Within five minutes, all the vintners were standing in front of what used to be their booths and handing out samples. Visitors to the Street were eager to get to free alcohol after the freak storm scared them.

She didn't dare look at Logan. She knew he'd heard every word she'd said. Whether he'd approved or not, she didn't care. She did care on a personal note. But this wasn't personal. It was business.

Standing in front of the smoking wood and surveying the damage that used to be the little house she had so painstakingly designed, Diana wanted to cry. But as the event goers started coming back to their area, attracted by both the carnage and the element of free alcohol, something very heartwarming started to happen. People didn't just come for the wine; they wanted to talk. Diana spent the better part of the rest of the day chatting with people and sharing stories about their other events and Mountain Valley Vineyards.

She was hyper aware of Logan, but she could not look his direction. Every time she thought of what they'd just done in the safe room of the model home, her cheeks heated. A fine sheen of sweat broke out all over her skin, made worse by the humid, damp air. Her dress clung to her like a second skin. All that heat they'd generated was still coursing through her, begging for another kiss, another touch, anything that was Logan.

By the end of the day, she wasn't sure who was victorious. Before the storm, she'd have said she was a clear winner, but in light of the disaster, she wasn't sure.

When she got back to the Merlot Cottage, she had a shower and relived the time she spent with Logan in the safe room. No one appeared to have missed them or even realized they were together, which was good.

She drank a glass of wine from one of the competitive vineyards and shook her head. It was good, better than Mountain Valley Vineyards' and on par with Forget-Me-Not. How the hell they were going to win this, she didn't know. They lost every time on taste, and she wasn't a miracle worker.

When Logan arrived later that night, he brought along a friend. Diana opened the door, ushered them in, and tried to quiet her excitement. Once the door was shut, she said, "Ginger!" The dog attacked her with tongue and wiggle butt.

"I hope you don't mind, but she has been acting sad. I think she felt left out."

"You can bring her over anytime you want," she said. "I love her."

He also brought a bottle of wine. "I thought you could use this after today."

"You know me well," she said and took the bottle from him so that she could open it.

"Are you alright?" Logan asked as they sat on the sofa with Ginger between them, drank the wine as Logan's fingers played in her hair.

"Sure," she replied, "Why wouldn't I be?"

"Some of the other vineyards were mean to you today."

"Nothing new there. Did you want to defend my honor?"

"Possibly," he answered.

"Why didn't you chime in?" she asked.

"I didn't completely disagree."

"You agreed with them?"

"Mountain Valley Vineyards has a magician who distracts people from what is really going on. Lots of color and lights, pretty pictures, really strange men with manes of hair, strippers wearing lingerie or dressed like lion tamers. You're their ringleader, the master illusionist. But their wine, well, it sucks."

"Oh please, the strippers were Marco's idea," she said but wasn't sure if she should feel flattered or angry. But she did see his point. Hell, hadn't she thought the same thing earlier?

"I just wish none of the smoke and mirrors were allowed. I think you can figure out that we are about to go to blind tasting. Everyone was serious today. They don't like what's been going on, and they are going to talk to the committee at the Stark Hotels. Because no amount of smoke and mirrors will hide the flavor when a customer orders a bottle of wine at a restaurant in a Stark Hotel and gets a load of the real flavor of whoever wins this contest."

"Are you going to talk to Daisy Stark?"

"No."

"But you don't like what is happening," she said.

"I respect your business acumen, but I'm a little tired of all the games."

She wondered if he meant between them personally or in business. "What? You don't want to play?"

"If I decided to play on that level, you'd never see it coming."

Before she could say another word, he took the glass out of her hand, placed it on the coffee table, leaned over Ginger, and kissed Diana. She knew he was doing it on purpose to get her to shut up, and she didn't mind. Not one bit.

# CHAPTER EIGHTEEN

L ogan took Ben on a long walk to the far edge of his
vineyard. It was the only place he felt they could find
the privacy he needed.

"Find out any info yesterday from your friend next door?"
Ben asked as soon as they had stopped.

"We don't have that kind of relationship," Logan replied.

"Really?" Ben asked, a little too interested. Logan didn't
want to share any of the details of his time with Diana. Ben was
one of his best friends; he had been incredibly supportive. Heck,
he might even know that Logan made nightly walks to Diana's
cabin, but Logan wouldn't tolerate gossip at his vineyard that
might reflect badly on Diana. He didn't want anything to
intrude or taint what he had with her. It was special for reasons
he hadn't quite made peace with yet.

"No," Logan said, ending the subject. "We have some things
to discuss, starting with The Intern. Do you know where he
went during the storm?"

"No, but I don't know where you went either," Ben said with
laughter in his eyes.

"Tess and I were in the truck."

Logan ignored the part of the comment that addressed his
whereabouts and let the silence answer for him.

"I saw Peter walk back to our booth, after the storm, from
the same direction as Marco. I don't have enough to confront

him, but I have a feeling he is either related to the D'Salvos or is getting paid by them."

"Aw, crap," Ben said.

"Exactly my thought. He wanted to know what we were serving way before anyone needed to know. I thought he was asking so that he could check in with his friends next door. I don't know, but I don't like it. He asks a lot of very leading, very detailed questions."

"I've noticed that as well. Do you think he reports to your friend?"

"No, that kind of thing isn't her style. How much time has he spent in The Vault?" The Vault was where Logan kept the wine he had yet to bottle. It was the largest building on the vineyard.

"I've had him in the tasting room and working in production. He spent a day putting labels on bottles."

"Good. I have plans for the PN 13, and I don't want him anywhere near it. I don't want too many people knowing how good it is proving to be." With that, he pulled the cork out of an unlabeled bottle of wine and poured them each a taste.

"Try this," he said, handing a large, red wine balloon glass to Ben. "This is the three-year-old Pinot. I think it's ready to bottle."

Ben sniffed it, swirled it, and did all things good winemakers do, then he tried it and smiled. "This is fantastic."

"I know. I'm going to bottle it and see what we can do with it. I'm going to take it to the next event out in Seaside. If we make it to the finals, we are building the menu around it. But until I'm ready to bottle it, we need to be very careful with who knows where it is kept and just how good it is."

"You know what, Logan?"

Logan just shook his head.

"You've got it back. You're better now than you ever were."

Logan was humbled by his friend's words but managed to say, "Thank you, Ben.

I'm sorry I let everyone down."

"It wasn't that. It was just that you were good, but now you're just better."

"Thank you. I hate to say it, but this might be the finest wine this vineyard has ever produced."

"I might have to agree," Ben said.

Logan knew just what this wine could mean to him. It was a game-changer. It had the potential to solve a lot of his problems. He didn't know if it would be enough, but it just might be what he needed to keep his land. The problem was, if the D'Salvos knew about it, the price for the water rights, everything, might get priced well beyond even what this wine could bring to him. He knew he was paranoid, but the wine industry was notorious for shady business dealings.

As he walked back to his house after the meeting with Ben, Ginger running figure eights around him, he started to envision a crazy idea. It was such an insane notion that, for a moment, he wondered what was wrong with him. The idea that he could save his land with the three-year-old Pinot Noir alone would mean that he didn't need to win the contest. Diana could win. She could get her promotion.

His obsession with her was making his thoughts reckless. It was ridiculous. He was compromising himself for her. She'd only been back in his life for a few weeks, and he was already thinking of ways to help her? What was wrong with him?

*He was falling for her once again...*

He pictured Marco with his evil smile. And the way he'd looked when the police had questioned him after the accident. He'd broken his arm in the crash. It hadn't been quite enough for Logan. He'd wanted Marco to feel his pain. And still, to this day, Logan, even though Julianna wasn't living with him any longer, he still cared. He wondered just how much Marco had to drink that night. It was the only explanation and one that he had adamantly discussed with the police. But, by the time the police investigated his theory, it was too late. And, of course, Marco wasn't going to admit to anything of the kind. They had been in Yamhill County so long that their influence bled through it, like wine spilled onto a white tablecloth.

No, he needed to win the contest. It wasn't enough to have an alternate solution. He needed to win. Diana couldn't factor into his decision. She had already blurred the lines. She would be gone in four weeks, two if Mountain Valley Vineyards wasn't a finalist.

Then what? Would he run up to Seattle to try and salvage what they were rebuilding? Would he hire her to help him at Forget-Me-Not? He didn't want to think about it. He just wanted to enjoy the moment.

He needed a Plan B. Something more on the scale of Diana's kind of marketing. Smoke and mirrors. Something bordering on devious.

Logan drove the two hours to the town of Seaside. Depending on how things went at this fourth event, the Seaside Wine and Seafood Festival, there would be plans to set into motion. He hadn't wanted to stoop to this level. Hadn't wanted to add cunning to his marketing plan, and the things he contemplated were barely legal. Over the last few days, the ideas had grown on him, and he no longer argued the merits of right and wrong, legal, or just bordering on legal. He wanted to win.

As he set up his booth at the Seaside Wine and Seafood Festival in the Performing Arts Center next to Mountain Valley Vineyards' booth, it occurred to him that once they'd finished this task, there would be only one last competition. The finals would come next and determine the winner of the contest. And as per the rules and the secrecy around the voting, he wouldn't know how they had done until the very end.

Then what?

It would be time to speak again with the bank, which was holding off on his loan request to see how he did in the contest. He didn't quite trust them because Mountain Valley Vineyards also banked with his bank.

He did have his one little ace in the hole. He was going to bottle the three-year-old Pinot Noir next week. He hadn't told the bank about this wine, and at the moment, he was glad he hadn't. He wasn't sure he trusted the local bank. They had a long, love and hate relationship that went back as long as Parrishes had lived in Yamhill County.

Every ten years, the water rights were negotiated. Two things Logan knew for sure, the price would always go up, and the bank seemed to be on the side of Mountain Valley Vineyards. He wondered if the years since his aunt died would have been as bad on them if they'd had better financial backing from the bank. 1998 and then 2005 had been very challenging for everyone but Mountain Valley. When all the neighbors were struggling with poor fruit yields in the feast or famine industry, Mountain Valley was thriving. Maybe it was time to find a new bank, or just even the score.

Best case scenario, he thought he could yield ten thousand cases of his new Pinot. If he sold them for four dollars a bottle or forty-eight dollars a case, it might be enough. He wouldn't know until he met with his distributor, Rob Miller, next week. And the wine would need to be vetted by the usual critics, but he knew, just *knew*; this wine was special.

He glanced over at Diana. If she were his consultant, he'd be talking to her about the Pinot and what to do with it. She was smiling as she set up her booth, chatting with new Mountain Valley Vineyards staff of older ladies from the Sommelier Society. Mixed in with the pirates, they made for an interesting team. Occasionally, Diana would look his way, but by mutual agreement, they didn't speak, but they did catch each other's eye.

For the first time in two years, she gave him a reason to smile, to feel happy. She gave him hope that life wasn't the frozen, lifeless place he'd thought. There was joy, and it came from being with her, talking to her, holding her, making love to her. He was starting to need more. These last weeks, they'd rekindled their relationship, making him think a future could be had. He wanted to share his world with her and find out about her life and the lost years since she'd been at Wharton.

He wanted to keep seeing her when this was over. If he didn't win the contest, his life would change dramatically. He'd have to figure out what to do with his wine, the upcoming crop, and the Pinot Noir that had such potential. If all else failed, he'd have to seriously consider selling the vineyard. And what would happen then? He'd tried not to think about that because not winning wasn't an option. He had to keep Forget-Me-Not alive and thriving. No matter what, he'd make room for Diana. He just didn't know what that looked like yet.

After the doors had opened for that first day of the two-day festival, Logan glanced at Diana, who stood in front of her booth greeting people. Mountain Valley Vineyards were serving fresh oysters with their wine tastings.

He smiled. What an interestingly bad choice...

This particular event involved a small food and wine pairing. He was required to serve food. Despite the complaints of the other wineries, this was not to be a blind tasting. They could have their logos but could only drape their booths in black and white. They could have signage, but it had to involve the seafood or the wine, no ice cream, no gelato. He knew he had a good chance of winning. His servers were currently giving away mini crab cakes paired with their wine tastings, which had proved to be a big hit.

Logan had gone to the extraordinary measure of hiring two off-duty Pacific Coast Restaurant chefs to assemble and cook the crab cakes, and other seafood appetizers in front of the people gathered at his booth.

Every twenty minutes, the chefs traded off giving a class on how to make a different seafood appetizer accompanied by a white wine from Forget-Me-Not. Festival goers even received a recipe with the wine recommendation included. He'd had several patrons standing in front of his booth for over an hour, watching and learning from the chefs.

Tomorrow, the second and final day of the event, a dessert chef would be creating decadent chocolate desserts and pairing them with red wines. It would be the first outing for his three-year-old Pinot Noir, and he couldn't wait. He didn't know for sure, but he thought it was a pretty safe bet to guess that Mountain Valley would be shucking oysters tomorrow as well.

Thankfully, more people liked impromptu cooking classes than raw oysters.

If this had been Diana's idea, it had been a misstep. He'd have to ask her later, hopefully when she was in his bed. He hadn't figured out how to get close enough to her yet to let her know where he was staying, but he was already craving her sweet, hot little body. Heck, he was craving all of her; her mind, warmth, and heart.

Logan lost track of how many people he met and talked to. He smiled so much his face hurt. And toward the early afternoon, he noticed Diana slip away from her booth. He made his excuses and followed suit. He caught up with her just outside the vendor entrance.

"Diana," he said, nodding to her as they stepped into the cloudy afternoon.

She stopped, looked each way, then said, "Logan, how are you today? How is the attendance at your booth?"

"I'm fine, and we are doing well," he said, looking around to make sure he was alone. "Congratulations, by the way."

"It seems early to be congratulating me on the contest, but I appreciate your acknowledgement of what is happening. Thank you."

"I know you won the realtor vote at the Street of Luxury Homes."

"Yes, we did," she said and smiled. "Better to have won it than not."

"So, what did you get for that?" he asked, already knowing but having too much fun with Diana.

"A $500 gift certificate to Home Depot."

"You must be thrilled."

She narrowed her eye at him and gave him a playful punch in the arm. He tried to look hurt, but he wanted to laugh.

"I'm not," she said, "but taking it out on you is highly satisfying."

He smiled at her. "Were you going somewhere when I stopped you?"

"Yes, I have a few minutes of break."

"Where are you staying?" he asked, lowering his voice.

"At the Starfish Inn. My room is between Salvatore and Marco's," she said. Then, after she looked around to make sure they were alone, she whispered, "And tomorrow, my boss is coming down from Seattle to see how I'm doing."

"Aren't you lucky? Sounds like fun. I'm staying south of town at the Driftwood, room sixteen."

"Really?" she said with a small smile.

"You know, in case you find yourself in the neighborhood. I'm usually in by nine o'clock," he said and watched as she nodded and walked quickly away from him.

Mission accomplished. There was something about this cloak and dagger stuff that he kind of liked.

He had cut his beautiful hair.

When she'd noticed, she'd almost dropped the bottle of wine in her hand.

Logan cut his hair after he'd left her yesterday morning and appeared at the festival today. It took his already Keanu Reeves-like dark, brooding features to a whole other level of handsome. It was how he used to look when they were dating in college. Somewhere in her heart, there was a little tug of remembrance that was both sweet and bitter.

She didn't notice if Davide and Antonio had followed her instructions on the décor of the booth or if they had the wine she'd requested. She was easily able to ignore the cutting comments Marco was whispering behind her about the sizes and shapes of patrons attending the event.

She was only interested in Logan's hair. Why had he cut it?

Despite the noise of people around her, Diana could make out one voice through the din.

"Wine is a living, breathing thing. It has personality and moods," Logan said to a group of women who were hanging on his every word.

"It will taste different fifteen minutes from now, one hour from now, three hours from now. It will be subtle. Maybe the almond notes will deepen to cherry, maybe the aroma of fruit will become more pronounced. The key thing is to know when the wine is at its peak for what you are serving. Maybe you aren't serving anything but the wine. It will taste much different than if you take a little cheese or a bite of fruit..."

The expressions on their faces displayed one uniform characteristic: *longing*.

She was not immune to the feeling. She understood it too well.

There was something else she noticed about Logan; he

looked more self-assured, more confident than she'd seen him. Part of her wanted to take credit for his new attitude, but she knew it wasn't about her. It was about his competitive nature. He'd gotten into the fight. She saw it in the way he was moving around his booth. There was more confidence to his swagger, and she wondered how much it had to do with their evening rendezvous. She'd been very careful never to discuss business in front of him. Also, she locked up all her paperwork each night so he wouldn't have the opportunity to see anything he shouldn't when he was passing through her cabin to get to the bedroom.

Glancing around at her other competitors, she began to worry. Her booth wasn't drawing the traffic it usually did. As she pondered why they weren't getting the level of interest they were used to, Marco pushed the local newspaper into her hands.

"Great idea, raw seafood," he said with a scowl. "What the hell are we going to do now?"

She gave him a look that she hoped conveyed her anger and then glanced down at the headline, which told her everything she needed to know. *Shellfish Bacteria Makes A Bad Name for Oysters as Dozens Fall Ill.*

Glancing at her display, she shook her head. Crushed ice poured onto a special table that had been designed just for this event and housed a variety of raw oysters on the half shell. Raw oysters were an idea that Marco and Salvatore had told her was not a negotiation. This wasn't their first wine and seafood festival, and they knew what drew the crowds.

She couldn't help it. She glanced up from the article and said, "Told you I didn't like this idea."

"Can you fix it?" Marco asked, looking like a scared kid.

As she quickly scanned the article about a new strain of bacteria which had been detected two hundred miles away was affecting shellfish, especially uncooked shellfish like oysters and clams, she groaned. Ingesting the raw seafood could wreak havoc with your digestive system.

If you were lucky, you were sick for a few days. If not, you ended up in the hospital on an IV.

Once they had filled the trays with ice, the professional oyster shuckers had done an excellent job of setting up an impressive display. Diana could smell the salty, fresh ocean scent of oysters. Because their oysters had been purchased locally and probably harvested within ten miles of their current location, it was highly unlikely they had bacteria.

"Let me make some calls," she replied and stepped away with her cell phone and called the supplier. He confirmed what she believed to be true. The oysters were local, and they had been grown a few miles away. He reassured her that the product was safe. As she spoke to the supplier, an idea came to her. After explaining her plan, he agreed to help. A half-hour later, several of his staff arrived carrying signs from their warehouse.

"Dancing oysters, it has come to this," she said as she positioned one of the large dancing oyster signs proclaiming locally harvested 'safe' oysters at the end furthest away from Logan's booth. He had a real chef in a tall white hat making something that smelled wonderful, something that was cooked and didn't scare people.

Despite what she'd said to Logan, she was tired of all the gimmicks to get people to vote for wine. She didn't even like the food element. But if she had a fair venue, no gelato, no charities, no food, no sexily clad waitresses, no puppies, no balloon interviews, just one glass of wine against another, she would lose this competition.

She was edgy besides just the seafood controversy. Diana hated working next to Logan's booth and not being able to talk to him. All day long, she watched women swoon as he offered them Pinot Gris, Riesling, and his sparkling Chardonnay. If he had any idea how appealing he was, had paid any of them one drop more attention than he had, he'd have to beat them off with a stick. He was easily the best-looking man in the room.

Around two o'clock, after her chat with Logan in the parking lot, which had her already thinking of ways to get out of her hotel unseen that evening, Salvatore D'Salvo appeared at her side. He asked her how many tokens they had in their little lockbox. This part of the competition was about tokens. Each party that entered the event and showed their tickets got two tokens per person to drop at the winery booth as 'votes' for their favorite winery.

Marco had already been reprimanded for trying to buy tokens from patrons in the parking lot. He had merely shrugged it off like an errant child caught with his finger in the cake frosting.

"We are up over a hundred and fifty. But if you look at some of the other wineries, we are neck-and-neck," she said, glancing at the four other competitors and finally landing on Logan.

"Why aren't we beating them?" Salvatore asked, indicating Logan's team.

Diana handed him the newspaper and waited for him to connect all the dots.

She'd have a better answer for her boss, Stephan, when he arrived tomorrow. Between Salvatore and Marco, she was getting challenged in every direction. The article in the paper that morning had only added insult to injury.

When Salvatore didn't say anything, she pointed to their display.

"The oysters," she finally said. "That article this morning was very bad timing. I'd hoped it wouldn't affect us, but I fear that it has."

"What are you going to do about it?" he asked, and she could hear the underlying challenge in his tone. When it came to short memories, father like son.

"The signs have helped, but not enough. I've got another idea," she said. When she noticed no change in her traffic, the idea had formulated over the last hour. "It won't cost much, and I think it might really work."

"Talk," he said.

She explained her plan to Salvatore, and he nodded, agreeing that it was an interesting idea.

"Best part of all," she said, "It takes no time. I just need the equipment."

An hour later, she was lugging that equipment to her car, having cleaned out the local hardware store. She had two large crock pots, a large cooler, ladles, etc. Her next stop was the grocery store, where the bought cream, half and half, butter, salt, pepper, Tabasco, oyster crackers, bowls, and spoons. One thing she'd learned from old friend and mentor Bonnie Elder was about how to preserve holiday traditions. She'd been the extra daughter at their house for Christmas for the last twenty years. And every Christmas Eve, Bonnie served her famous oyster stew.

Diana hadn't been exposed to a lot as a kid. She didn't get out of the state until she was eighteen. She hadn't traveled on an airplane until she went to Wharton. The one saving grace was that she always was looking for opportunities to improve herself. She didn't want to be thought of as someone who was lacking in etiquette or didn't have a good education.

When Bonnie had set a bowl of oyster stew in front of her that first Christmas Eve she spent with Bonnie's family, Diana feared the worst. She could see the black and gray oysters floating in the milk. She couldn't eat them. Bonnie, sensing her distress, told her to add the crackers and just try a spoonful. Diana did as Bonnie instructed, summoned her courage, and then tried the stew. It was rich, the cream and butter transporting the oyster from a slimy little clump to a delicacy like no other she had ever tried. And for the first time in her life, she felt a little sophisticated for having tried something so foreign to her.

She liked the oyster stew and felt the distance widen from the poor little trailer park kid she had been. Little did she know that someday being able to make the rich stew would come in handy. She couldn't wait to tell Bonnie and thank her again for taking a chance on her.

By three o'clock, the ice tray table had been replaced with a flat table. She had two large crock pots of the cream, milk, and butter mixture going. She made the oyster stew to order, dropping three small oysters in the scalding broth at a time. The oysters cooked in less than thirty seconds, and while people waited, they got to try a glass of wine. Then, she would serve up the stew and sprinkle the surface with oyster crackers and a pat of butter.

Out of the corner of her eye, she noticed Logan watching her from his booth. She did her best not to smile at his scrutiny but felt her cheeks grow warm.

The stew increased the traffic to their booth by double. By eight o'clock that evening, they had to shut down for the night. Diana lost track of how many times she'd explained the recipe for her oyster stew, but the feedback had been extremely positive.

The official judges stopped by, unlocked the token box, counted out tokens, and made note of their numbers.

"You have four hundred and sixty-two," Daisy Stark remarked.

"Is that good?" Diana asked.

"We will see what tomorrow brings, but I'd be happy if I were you," she responded and walked over to where a smiling Logan waited.

Back in her hotel room, Diana was exhausted. She hung her head under the stream of the warm shower water and wondered when the last time she had stood on a cement floor for twelve hours. People did it every day, but she was thankful she wasn't one of them. It was a good reminder to her why she had worked so hard to stay in college.

When she got back to the Merlot Cottage on Monday, she was going to send Bonnie Elder flowers. If she hadn't taught Diana how to make stew all those years ago, they would have been SOL today. As it was, she didn't think she'd caught up with Forget-Me-Not, but at least they'd increased their traffic in the late afternoon and early evening. And there was always tomorrow.

Diana dried and styled her hair, put on a scant bit of makeup, added her favorite Jo Malone Orange Blossom perfume, and then glanced out the peephole of her door. When she was sure the hallway was empty, she left her room and headed to her car.

Ten minutes later, she knocked on Logan's door. When he opened it, wearing a robe fresh from his shower, she got the full intensity of his smile, and felt a part of her stomach turn warm and molten. Without saying a word, she stepped inside and fell into his arms, their lips seeking each other as their hands sought to free themselves from layers of annoying fabric.

Diana couldn't stop running her fingers through Logan's short hair. It made him look younger, reminded her of the man he'd once been. Her jeans and blouse were tossed into a chair, followed by his robe, and then they were on the bed, the firm mattress hard against her back, the crisp sheets a little too starched and scratchy. Logan's skin was warm and soft as satin, where it wrapped over hard muscle. He smelled of honeysuckle shampoo and minty toothpaste, pure intoxication to her senses. When he kissed her like this, ran his hands over her body, she couldn't think, didn't want to have any thoughts that didn't involve him.

"You smell good," he said.

"I was thinking the same of you."

"What is that? It is familiar."

"Orange blossom."

"I didn't smell it on you earlier today."

"I only wear it for you," she said.

"Nice."

"I like your haircut," she said.

"I was hoping you'd notice."

He unhooked her bra, murmured something sweet and naughty as he kissed a trail to her breasts. She lifted her hips, pushed against his erection, and felt it bump insistently against her lace-clad thighs. He pulled her lace panties away, cool air teasing her skin and bringing goosebumps to her flesh. Where Logan touched her, she smoldered.

He moved her to the edge of the mattress, and she knew instantly what he wanted. It had been a long time since they'd done this particular position. She liked it. She'd always liked it.

"Come here," he said as he sat up and pulled her onto his lap. Face to face. They kissed with long, deep ferocity. Their tongues danced in sensual play as his hands helped guide her onto his straining penis. Inch by inch, she slid down him, his body going deeper and deeper into her. She should be directing this scene, her body in control. But as he pushed up into her with short upward thrusts, she could no more control his body than her own. She was overcome with the feeling of complete surrender with each spike of pleasure.

Unable to breathe, she broke the contact with his lips and leaned heavily against him. Her breath came out in short, uneven gasps.

"I'll never forgot this," he murmured as he grabbed her hips and drove into her body with piston-like motion—smooth, quick, hot strokes.

"Logan, I've missed you—"

Her voice wasn't clear. It didn't sound like her. It sounded like the lovesick woman she was. And that was her last conscious thought before the orgasm wracked her body, making her feel warm and molten in his arms.

As her breathing slowly returned to normal, every inch of her felt heavy with relaxation. Logan lay on top of her. Their bodies still joined as his lips kissed slow trails along her jawline. She whimpered as she came down. He could be relentless with her. It was something she'd never found in another lover.

He once took it as a challenge to see how many orgasms he could give her in a weekend. They'd made it well into double digits on the first night. No one had ever been as affectionate, as free, as generous a lover as Logan.

When at last, he slipped away from her, she could barely raise her head to watch him slip into his robe and cross the room to the fireplace. Dropping before it, he lit a pre-laid fire, which quickly sparked to life. He opened a bottle of wine and poured two glasses that he set on the coffee table by the couch.

"Come sit with me by the fire. We can watch the ocean. They have floodlights on the breakers."

Leaning up on her elbows, she touched the curve of her breast, letting her hand run along the length of her body. Logan's eyes followed the path of her fingers as she replied, "But I don't have a robe."

Reaching for the belt of his robe, he pulled the fabric open. "There is room enough for you in here."

Much later, Diana sat on Logan's lap, the erection she'd once straddled now nestled warmly between her legs. They watched the effervescent waves crash on the beach just beyond the hotel room. Occasionally, they'd look away from hypnotic waves to kiss and explore each other. Sometimes, Diana would simply lean against him, shut her eyes, and pretend that he was hers forever.

At some point, she must have fallen asleep because the ringing phone had her opening her eyes to an unfamiliar, sunlit room. Logan snuggled against her, his breath warm on her ear. As he moved away to answer the phone, she groaned and reached for him.

"My wake-up call," he murmured, gently kissing her shoulder and back.

"What time is it?" she asked.

"Seven," he said.

"No!" she yelled, scrambling from the bed. "I needed to get up at six!"

"Wear what you had on last night. You can shower here. You can shower with me," he said, smiling mischievously.

She didn't have time to think. She ran for the shower only to be joined by Logan a half a minute later. When he started kissing her, she felt her body weaken. It was all she could do to push him out of the way so she could lather up and get rinsed.

"You're no fun," he said with a chuckle as she brushed her teeth with a finger and his toothpaste.

"I have a contest to win," she said as she borrowed his deodorant and reapplied the mascara and lipstick she always kept in her purse. As she shimmied into her jeans and top, Logan emerged from the bathroom and blocked her path.

Relenting, she went into his arms and kissed him. She didn't want to leave. Heck, in another minute, she'd be pulling him down onto the bed and asking him to do all sorts of things to her.

"I don't want you to go," he said.

"That makes two of us," she murmured.

"Tonight, back at the vineyard."

"I want to. My boss is in town to see how we are doing at the festival, but I hope to drive back tonight."

More than anything, she wanted to be with this man tonight and have him make love to her. She was already counting the minutes.

"The vineyard."

"Tonight," She said, with one last kiss.

As Logan shut the door behind her as she left, she could've have sworn she'd heard a faint, *Love you.*

# CHAPTER NINETEEN

With Diana still on his mind, Logan got dressed for the second and last day of the festival. He felt good. Better than he'd felt in months. Maybe it was the competition, and maybe it was his Pinot Noir, or maybe it was all the sex he was having with Diana. He didn't want to think too much about any of those things as he grabbed his keys and headed for the door. As he got inside the company's black Ford Explorer, his cell phone rang, and he recognized the number as coming from Forget-Me-Not.

"This is Logan."

"Logan, it's William." William was his factory manager. Logan knew him well enough to know from the tone of his voice something was very wrong.

"William, what's up? Is Ginger okay?" he said by way of greeting. Ginger was staying with William while Logan, Ben, and Tess were at the festival. It was irrational, but he worried about his little red fur girl.

"Where are you?" There was hesitation in the other man's voice, and it immediately put Logan on edge.

"I'm on my way to the festival. What's wrong?"

"Pull over."

"I'm not driving yet."

"I don't know how to tell you this...

"What, what is it?" Logan asked, feeling the panic seize his chest. He hadn't answered Logan about Ginger. Not Ginger. Not his sweet fur baby. "Seriously, is Ginger okay?"

"Yes, Ginger is fine. But something's happened to a lot of the three-year-old Pinot Noir. It's gone."

"I don't understand. What do you mean it's gone?" Logan asked, his heart in his throat.

"Someone broke into The Vault last night and dumped a bunch of the barrels.

They got through the first row and into the second."

"PN 13?" he confirmed.

"Yes," William said. "I guess we can be happy they didn't get all of it. Of the four hundred barrels, they got between seventy and a hundred."

Logan breathed a sigh of relief. He'd lost something, but not as much as he could have.

He leaned his head against the steering wheel and let the gravity of the loss sink in. He'd wanted to get a security system put in that area of his storage facility, but when money got tight, he hadn't implemented the plan. It certainly wouldn't have been as expensive as what he'd just lost.

"Have you called the police?"

"Right before I called you. They are on their way. Whoever it was busted the lock on the door and must have used a battering ram to break in. The wood is split."

The doors to The Vault were big barn-style doors, solid and robust. How someone couldn't have heard it on a quiet summer night, he didn't know. Banging on that door would have sounded like a shotgun blast.

"What else did they get?"

"Just the PN 13. Something must have spooked them because they didn't finish the job."

Logan could hear Ginger growling menacingly in the background.

"Are you sure they're gone?"

"Pretty sure, but to be on the safe side, I'm back in my car with Ginger, and the doors are locked. I've got my pistol with me. Ginger, stop it. It is okay. Sorry Logan, she just saw Peter. He's walking up the road right now. I don't know what to tell you, Logan. All that wine, well, it looks like a murder scene. I saw it the moment I drove up. The ground is soaked with it. Looks like blood. I knew we'd had some sort of accident. Then I saw the busted door. Ginger started barking before I even stopped the damn car. It spooked the hell out of me, and she hasn't stopped growling."

"Stay out of the storage area until the police get there. Did Peter hear anything?" Logan asked. He couldn't help the suspicion leak into his mind.

"When I called him a few minutes ago, I woke him up. He sounded hungover but told me that he'd help with clean up."

"I'm on my way back from the beach. Don't let him near The Vault. Have him stay in the tasting room. Tell him to do an inventory of the shelves. That will keep him away from this until I talk to the police. And be prepared. I want to get the remaining PN 13 bottled as soon as possible. Let's start on it tomorrow morning."

"I understand, boss. Will do."

"And William?"

"Yeah, Logan?"

"Two things, hire round the clock security. I don't want any more surprises. And tell everyone that we lost all of it. I want them to think we are decimated."

"Are you sure?"

Thinking of how deep the D'Salvos connections ran, he said, "Very."

Logan's next call was to his tasting room managers, Ben, and Tess, who were just arriving at the festival. He quickly filled them in and told them he was counting on them to handle the today's events. He checked out of his room and started driving the hour and a half back to Yamhill County.

As he drove, anger pulsed through every nerve with each mile. He thought of the shortlist of suspects. Marco D'Salvo was at the top of the list for more than one reason. Did Marco know about his special Pinot? Was Peter a spy for Marco? He hated to question the kid but to be honest with himself. He'd been suspicious of his intentions soon after he hired him.

Had he mentioned it to Diana? She'd asked a lot about his wines. And then he remembered. He'd told her he had a special vintage of Pinot Noir. It was what had distracted him from his sparkling wine. The real question was: Who had she told?

Diana was wicked smart, which was why he hadn't given her a tour of his facility, especially The Vault. She would have no idea how much wine he had or where it was stored. Did he really think of accusing Diana? She'd been with him the night before. He'd held her in his arms and made love to her as if they were back in his warm attic room. It had been one of the best nights he'd had in years. He was falling in love with her again. Hell, maybe he'd never stopped. He couldn't think her capable of this.

It all came down to trust…Did he trust her?

If she'd told the D'Salvos about the Pinot, even mentioned it in passing, that would have been all it would've taken. He knew they were capable of anything. If she did anything, he was sure it was unintentional, but even then, she was smarter than that. No, if he were a betting man, his money would be on Peter.

As Logan drove back to his vineyard, he felt sure it had to be someone who knew that he and most of his key staff would be away for the weekend. He'd have to talk to Salvatore D'Salvo, or at the very least, the police would have to have a chat with him. He'd have to do the same with Peter. For all Logan knew, the vandals could have hit several vineyards, but he doubted it. He was pretty sure he was the only one who'd been targeted, and he knew why. The only question he had now was, just what was Diana's role in this? She had a promotion on the line, but just what would she do to get it? Deep down, he couldn't believe it.

He did the ninety-minute drive in a little over an hour. When he arrived at Forget-Me-Not, Ginger was the first to see him, sticking her head out of William's black company Explorer and making her familiar "rooing" sound. He walked over to her and gave her a pet through the window, then opened the door and greeted her wildly shaking butt. When she had greeted him enough to calm down, he attached the leash to her collar and walked her over to where Sheriff Baker, a man he'd known his whole life, waited with William.

"Sheriff," he said and extended his hand to the man and nodded to William. He clearly remembered each time he'd ever encountered the lawman. Sheriff Baker was tall and thin with kind brown eyes, which worked in his favor when he delivered sad news. He'd been the one who told Logan that Julianna had died in the auto accident, showing up at their house, his hat in his hand, his expression unreadable. Logan had still technically been her husband at the time, and the sheriff didn't know the complicated situation that existed in the love triangle of Logan, Julianna, and Marco.

He remembered how the sheriff told him that Marco would live, although he didn't know how Julianna had come to be in Marco's car at the time. Marco had been taken to hospital. Logan thought it was common knowledge that his wife had left him for Marco, but since the sheriff didn't know, Logan had to share the less savory details of his life with the kindly man who spent much of his time shaking his head.

Logan remembered his humiliation and embarrassment. Not only had Julianna started seeing Marco, but she'd also moved out of Logan's house a couple of weeks earlier to live with Marco. Logan told the sheriff that he'd hoped she'd get over it, let go of the strange infatuation with horrible Marco, but then she'd had Logan served with divorce papers two days before the accident.

And the last time Logan and the sheriff had spoken was a year and a half earlier when Logan was in the worst moments of his grief and contemplating suing Marco D'Salvo for wrongful death. Logan was sure that Marco had been impaired when they'd had the accident. Julianna might have been in the process of divorcing Logan, but they'd been married for almost eight years. He owed her the justice he thought she deserved. Her life had mattered to him. Was he just mad about the affair and wanted to get even? Yes, and no. He wanted Marco to feel the impact of Julianna's death. Once Marco had gotten out of the hospital, it was as if Julianna hadn't existed. Marco's life returned to normal. He even had her clothing and personal effects returned to Logan in cardboard boxes. The boxes had been given to her family, but her touch and the occasional item still remained. Logan had taken care of the rest of it after he started seeing Diana, which had helped.

The sheriff had listened to all Logan's reasons, talked to him about it for the better part of an afternoon. In the end, he persuaded Logan not to pursue the case against Marco. It had been the right, rational decision, but it still hurt.

Now, Logan had an automatic reaction to the sheriff. The mere sight of him made Logan's stomach lurch and flip. If there were bad news coming, the sheriff would always be the one to deliver it.

"Hi Logan. It's a hell of a thing. They sure made a mess of your storage area. When I first heard your name, I wondered if there was a fire somewhere based on you being a fireman. Sorry, I know you'll think this is much worse," Sheriff Baker said and offered his hand. They shook heartily and walked toward The Vault.

Logan looked down at the ground and saw the deep stains in the soil, puddles of dark crimson that had flooded the lawn, turning it the color of an eggplant. Ginger sniffed at it and dared to touch her tongue to one of the puddles, and then quickly pulled back. William was right; it looked like a murder scene.

"I don't suppose there have been any other sorts of vandalism at any other vineyards around here?" Logan asked.

"No, Logan, you're the only one we've found so far. I'm sorry. Do you have any idea who might have done this?"

"You can't be serious," Logan said, and the sheriff couldn't quite meet his eyes.

"Now, Logan, the past is done. You of all people know we can't go back in time. I've been proud of how well you've been doing. We love how you are such a part of the community. Why, we know if we need help, you're one of the first people we call. Don't backpedal on me now."

"The D'Salvos want me out of here. They want my land and will do anything to get it," Logan said, ignoring the sheriff's concern and compliments.

"Do you have any evidence of that?" the sheriff asked.

Logan ignored the sheriff and walked slowly around the crime scene, remembering how just a few days earlier it had been pristine. As he stepped on the soiled ground, an idea so dark and so devious formed in his mind that it pushed away all the other negative thoughts.

He returned to the sheriff and William.

"What is it, Logan?" William asked.

"Let's not bullshit each other. We've been through too much in this lifetime. We all know who did this. Just because I don't have a note from Marco confessing to it doesn't mean that he didn't do it."

"Now, Logan, this is the kind of talk that leads to vigilante justice, which I just can't have here in Yamhill County," the sheriff said.

Logan laughed after all he'd gone through, and the sheriff thought he was stupid enough to do something that would endanger his safety or freedom. He was plotting something, but it wasn't something that would land him in jail for the rest of his life.

"You don't need to worry, Sheriff. I don't want to see Marco dead, not anymore."

"Logan," William warned.

"There was a time when that was all I thought of, but time healed that particular wound. Have you heard about the Stark Hotel's contract and the stupid contest that five of us local wineries are participating in to win it?"

The sheriff nodded but didn't say a word, obviously deciding it was better to let Logan talk and possibly get him to admit to something.

"And did you know my water rights are up for renewal?"

The sheriff just shook his head again.

"Why don't you come up the house? Let me tell you about the contest, and then you can see what's at stake...And if you're officially off duty, I've got some wine for you to try."

# CHAPTER TWENTY

Diana felt better about their chances of success at the Wine and Seafood Festival on Sunday. They were switching to red wine, which meant her days of cooking oyster stew were over. She'd had a lovely evening with Logan, and as far as she could tell, the D'Salvos hadn't even realized she had snuck away to be with him. She was not looking forward to Stephan's visit but she wanted him to see the D'Salvos in action.

Luckily for Mountain Valley Vineyards, red wine was something they did well. And by well, she meant it wasn't vinegar, which was all she could say. Diana spent the first fifteen minutes opening and defusing red wine as two of the sommeliers arrived and started arranging trays of sinful chocolate desserts.

Now and then, she would glance over at Logan's booth. He had not arrived by the time they were set to open. Where could he be?

And maybe it was her imagination, but his staff seemed to be watching her. It was a paranoid notion, but one she couldn't rationalize away. They'd had a semi-friendly attitude with each other yesterday, but today she was feeling the chill.

Marco arrived right as the crowds were starting to flow in from the entrance at ten o'clock. Heaven forbid that he should arrive early and help set up the booth.

"Slacker," Diana muttered under her breath.

By noon, Diana was more than a little worried about Logan. It wasn't like him not to be where they were having a competition. He'd never missed an event. But then he hadn't brought her into his circle of trust and let her in on his game plan, and she was fine with that. The competition was kept separate from their relationship, and they both had come to that understanding. But she thought he would surely tell her if he'd decided to go back to Yamhill early.

Ben, one of Logan's people who had been guarded but friendly to Diana on several occasions, walked over to their booth during a lull in the afternoon.

"Hi Ben. How is it going?" Diana asked as the unusually solemn man stopped in front of her.

"Did you hear about what happened?" he asked, regarding her suspiciously.

"What do you mean? Is Logan okay?" she asked, sensing the tension in the other man. Something was wrong, very wrong. She could feel it deep in her gut. Had he been in an accident? Was he alright?

"Would it bother you if something happened to Logan?" Ben asked, shrugging his shoulders as if he didn't believe her sincerity.

"Damn it, yes! Is he okay? Is he hurt?"

Ben shrugged and asked, "What, you mean you haven't heard?"

Diana came out from behind the booth and stepped away from the crowd assembled. "Damn it, Ben! Is Logan hurt? What happened to him?" Tears were challenging the corner of her eyes. Fuck yes, she was worried.

"Physically, Logan is fine," he said, watching her closely.

She took a breath, the first breath she'd taken since he'd come close to her table.

"Okay, then what is wrong?" she asked, shaking her head, then asking, "What about Ginger? Is she okay?"

"The dog is fine. But last night, someone broke into our vault and dumped a fantastic vintage of pinot noir he's been aging for the last three years."

"Who—?" She asked but quickly stopped and motioned for Ben to step to the side out of earshot from anyone at Mountain Valley Vineyards.

"Do you know who did it?" she asked once she'd felt that her composure was back in place. Her thoughts immediately ran to Marco. He had been acting strangely all weekend. And she bet she wasn't the first to suspect the other men. She hadn't been around the hotel last night, so she couldn't even be sure they'd been there.

"No. Do you?" he said, his face angry.

"Could we stop with this? I have no knowledge of what happened. I feel bad for Logan. I care about him, okay?" she said, a little louder than she intended and almost spilling her true feelings.

"Well, we have an idea who did it," he said, his eyes narrowing.

"Do you want to tell me?" Diana asked, trying to distance herself from the accusation she could feel creeping in on her. But when Ben said nothing, she added, "If someone is out vandalizing vineyards, we all need to be careful."

"Oh, something tells me that you don't need to be worried," he said, turning on his heel and walking away from her.

Diana bit her lip. There was a lot she could think to say but knew she shouldn't. It was one of those times she had to remind herself who was currently signing her paycheck. It also told her that Ben was a little more aware of her relationship with Logan than she had earlier suspected.

Logan had told her about the Pinot Noir. It was the vintage that made him abandon sparkling wine. He hadn't elaborated at the time, but she just knew it was something special. She'd not told anyone about the Pinot. As far as she was concerned, it was none of her business.

Glancing over her shoulder, she saw that Marco was carefully studying her. She stared right back at him. If he'd done something criminal to Logan, she wasn't going to be a part of it.

"What did he want?" Marco asked as she made her way to the tasting table.

"It seems that someone broke into Forget-Me-Not last night."

"Really?" he asked, interested, his misaligned tooth catching on his bottom lip as he smiled.

"You mean you haven't heard about it yet?" she asked, watching him as she did. There was the briefest scowl on his face. A little hitch, but then he shook his head as if not hearing her.

"I don't know what you're talking about, Diana. What happened?" he asked, finally turning serious.

"Someone broke in and dumped an entire vintage of Pinot Noir. From the sound of it, they knew what they were looking for. You wouldn't know anything about that, would you? Because if you did, I'd call the police myself."

Marco looked sullen and folded his arms. "You know, when you first started with us, I liked you. I thought I could learn from you. But as time has gone on, I realize you're nothing special."

Ignoring the nasty remark, she said, "You've expressed a lot of hostility toward Logan Parrish. I know your car was involved in the accident that killed his wife. It only makes sense for me to discuss this with you. If you are uncomfortable, that is an unfortunate side effect, but it is necessary."

"Where do you get off questioning me?"

"The contract both of our mutual parties signed on our behalf. It gives me the right."

"Well, I didn't sign it," he said.

God, he could be a little asshole. These last few weeks dealing with his attitude was more than she could bear.

"You're still a part of it."

"There is a word for women like you in Italian. *Cagna*. You should look it up some time," he said.

Diana didn't know a lot of Italian but did know the meaning of that word. *Cagna* meant bitch in Italian.

"Your father is paying me a lot of money to help you, so call me whatever the hell you want. I simply don't care. I'm going to do my job, and if you happen to get upset...tough. That's just how it goes. But hear this, I didn't sign up to participate in illegal activity. If you had anything to do with the vandalism and burglary at Forget-Me-Not, our contract is void."

"*Cagna*," Marco repeated, pointing his finger at her.

Diana knew her confidence always bothered Marco. But today, she was trembling on the inside. The lines between what was right and wrong, where professionalism crossed the line to doing what it took to win, had suddenly appeared very ominous. She might be facing down someone capable of violence. It certainly didn't feel like the smartest thing she'd ever done, kicking at the angry lion's door. But the fact he'd called her a bitch twice made her want to clock him with a wine bottle.

Any snide retort she might have added was cut short by the perfectly timed arrival of her boss, Stephan. She hadn't seen him approach, but he'd heard enough of their conversation to come to his own conclusions.

"Ms. Hunter is there a problem?" he asked, his pale Scandinavian skin bright red with anger as he walked them a little further away from the patrons.

"I was just explaining to Mr. D'Salvo that the property owner next door to him was vandalized last night. I was trying to determine if Mr. De Salvo had any knowledge of the burglary due to the fact the property owner is one of his neighbors."

Stephan Victor was exactly the man to put Marco in his

place. At well over six feet, Stephan was tall, blonde, and handsome. He wore round tortoiseshell glasses that he used to intimidate. He didn't wear his hair in a mane like Marco or his cousins, but his ego could kick Marco's in a fight. The fact he was the most masculine gay man Diana had ever met was just what the current situation needed. With one knowing glance, Stephan regarded Marco with a look of instant disdain.

Stephan had been quick to criticize her after the story of her ill-fated balloon ride made it back to him, but now he'd seen Marco in true form.

"In response to my question, Mr. D'Salvo referred to me as a bitch, in Italian," she said, her eyes never wavering from Marco's angry, twisted face.

"Mr. D'Salvo, I'm Stephan Victor, President of Wave. If you ever speak to my associate in this fashion again, we will execute section two, paragraph twenty-six of your contract. To refresh your memory—derogatory, inflammatory communication with any associates at Wave will result in the termination of the contract. The unpaid balance of the agreed upon amount is due within seventy-two hours of termination. Have I made myself clear?"

Marco scowled at Stephan, turned away from them, and knocked into one of the booths, taking with him three full bottles of red wine, which spilled onto the carpeted floor of the convention center. Two of the bottles broke when they hit the floor, splattering several people. The rest did significant damage to the carpet.

With barely a backward glance, Marco looked at Diana and said, "Clean that up," then, he headed toward the exit. Unfortunately, the bottles that had fallen to the floor belonged to Forget-Me-Not. Ben was already charging after Marco.

Stephan muttered a curse and charged after both men. Diana wished she could be a fly on the wall when he finally caught up the other men, but at the moment, she had her hands full.

She started by apologizing to Tess, who was already fuming. "Look what that little asshole did to my booth!"

"My sentiments exactly," Diana said as she started taking the names and addresses of all the people splattered with wine. Once that was finished, she said to Tess, "Write up a bill, and I'll make sure it gets paid. Do you have enough red wine? I could send someone to the store to buy several bottles of your vintages. Are you carried here locally in any of the stores?"

"We have enough," Tess said angrily. "Besides, this wine is irreplaceable. It is probably the last of the Pinot we lost last night."

Diana felt sick to her stomach, not to mention the scene they'd created. Wasn't it enough she was trying to win the competition? Did Marco have to sabotage her at every move? Maybe Stephan would get them fired, and then she could go help Logan. That would be the best news she could get.

Knowing she couldn't say anything to make this better, she said the only thing she could think of. "I'm sorry. He's a jerk."

"I'm sorry you work for an asshole. You seem pretty cool. I could like you if you didn't work for them," Tess said. Aside from Ben, who regarded her suspiciously, Logan's staff had always seemed like nice people.

"Thank you," Diana said and gave Tess a tentative smile, which fell away as Ben came back to the booth. He gave her a dirty look and then whispered something to Tess.

Diana didn't know if she should apologize or just stay where she was. She chose the latter.

An hour later, Stephan arrived back at the festival.

He stepped to a quiet corner and looked at her. Diana didn't need to be told that he wanted to speak to her. She could see it in his eyes. Like an obedient dog, she lowered her head and met him in the corner.

"Please, please tell me I'm fired," she said, thinking it might not be so bad.

"Sorry, no. I talked to him, chewed on him a little, and then we got some beers at the Rip Tide. He's not too bad. He's a dick with hair, frustrated with his dad and taking it out on everyone in range. I told him to be more respectful of you."

"How did he take that?" she asked. Sometimes, he blamed her for bad client behavior.

"He needs us. He likes you. He just needed to lash out, and you were there. You know the story, Diana. They are a family business with growing pains. As soon as they take over the Vineyard next door, the place will be big enough for all the D'Salvo egos."

"What about Forget-Me-Not? Did he do something to them? You have to understand he and Logan Parrish hate each other."

"So, you've told me. Yeah, they really hate each other," Stephan said. "I don't know if you know this. Logan Parrish's wife was in the car that Marco was driving when they had the accident that killed her. She was divorcing Logan to marry Marco."

"I know. It is the worst kept secret in Yamhill County. Rumor is that he was probably drunk and got away with murder," Diana said.

"Yeah, I thought that as well. Regardless, he denies having any knowledge of what happened last night. We have to give him the benefit of the doubt. It is our circus, but he isn't our monkey."

"How did you keep Ben from killing him?"

"I offered to write Forget-Me-Not a check for a $1,000 for their trouble if he walked away."

Diana couldn't help it. She smiled. "That worked?"

"Apparently, but it cost me $2,000. Glad I had my checkbook in the car. I'm pretty sure they are going to turn you in for unsportsmanlike behavior."

"Turn me in?" she asked.

"Mountain Valley," he corrected her.

"And who is to say they will acquire Forget-Me-Not's land?"

"It is a foregone conclusion. As a matter of fact, I all but convinced Marco that we might need to extend the contract another three to six months to help them get through the transition with the additional land."

Diana started to shake her head in response but caught herself. "Tell me that he asked for another consultant. Please."

"No," he answered. "He didn't. On some level, he likes you. But for some reasons, you push his buttons. Try not to do that."

"Like it is as easy as that," she said. "He's a punk asshole."

"Well, do your best. Your ability to get along with a wide variety of personalities is a key component to being a partner at Wave."

As he said the words, she felt a little ill. She wanted to be a partner at Wave, right? At that moment, she was no longer sure. And it had little to do with her job but more to do with falling in love with Logan. He made her want things that she hadn't before, and even if things didn't work out between them, Diana now knew family and the white picket fence were a necessary part of her future.

"Okay, kid, I'm going to sample all the wines in the competition. Then I'm going to sober up and drive back to the Vineyard to have dinner with Sophia and Salvatore. Let's circle back around tomorrow morning. Nice job on cleaning up after the temper tantrum. Looks like you are one of the most popular booths. Definitely the most entertaining..."

She watched him stride away without a care in the world. If she made partner, would she be able just to buzz in and out without really doing anything? Somehow, she didn't think so.

When it was six o'clock and time to wind up their booth, Diana was exhausted. She dared a glance at Forget-Me-Not only to receive a scowl back from Ben. The tentative détente she'd reached with Tess did not extend to her husband. Did they really believe she had something to do with vandalism? She was sure they suspected Marco but to think she had any hand in it was ridiculous. All she wanted to do was to finish cleaning up their workspace and get her car loaded. When she could slip away, she needed to call Logan and make sure he was okay.

As Diana drove back to the Vineyard, she kept waiting for her cell phone to have service. When at last she had enough bars for her Bluetooth to connect, she called information and asked for Forget-Me-Not. She was connected to someone who wasn't Logan and asked to be connected to him.

"Mr. Parrish isn't taking calls this evening," the man on the other end of the line informed her and then asked, "Who may I tell him called?"

"Just a friend. I'll call him another time," Diana said and quickly hung up.

When she'd made it back to her cottage at Mountain Valley Vineyards, unloading her gear in the twilight, she wondered if Logan would visit her tonight. He would have to know that she had nothing to do with this, but he might correctly assume that she was close to the people responsible. She had no proof, just her gut, but it had never lied to her.

She took a long shower, letting the hot water roll over her body, remembering how just a night earlier it had been Logan's hands gently running over the contours of her skin. Wrapping a towel around her middle, she stepped from the shower and opened the door. She came face to face with a very angry Logan, who had somehow found a way into her cabin and done it without her knowledge.

"Damn it, Logan, you scared the hell out of me!"

"Hello, Diana," he said, his expression grim, hostility oozing from him in dark waves as he filled the doorway to her bedroom.

"I don't mind that you're here, but just how did you get in?"

"The lock is crap. I used a credit card. We need to talk."

"I tried to call you as soon as I had cell service, but 'Mr.

Parrish wasn't taking any calls.' I was really worried about you. I think it is time for us to exchange cell numbers, don't you?"

Diana didn't let the angry look she got in response bother her. She was more than a little relieved to see him and decided to act on her feelings. She pushed against his body, past his initial resistance, wrapped her arms around him and let the towel drop to the floor.

"When I heard something happened, I thought you'd been hurt, then I was worried about Ginger," she said pressing her warm cheek to his slightly cool one.

His hands rose to push her away as he whispered, "Diana—"

"Shh…just let me hold you for a minute," she said, not allowing his rejection to affect her. His body relaxed by degrees. "I'll ask about getting the lock fixed. Just indulge me. I've been worried about you all day. I didn't have your cell number, and they wouldn't put me through, and then I couldn't talk to you. It was a bad day."

He sighed in resignation, and then his arms were around her. Cool fingers, tempered by the cool evening air, slid along her back and down to cup her buttocks.

A moment later, he lifted her in his arms, and their lips met. He walked her into the bedroom, his body covering hers in a mix of textures. Cool denim wicked away the moisture from her legs while the buttons on his cotton shirt tickled her breasts until she pushed it away to expose his chest. Hands worked feverishly to free bare skin from the restrictive fabric. Before long, he was as naked as she, and their bodies were fit tightly together, moving as one.

Diana clung to Logan, recalling how she'd felt when she'd heard something had happened and thought the worst. She bit back a small cry, felt a tear form at the corner of her eye, and roll down her cheek. None of this was lost on Logan. He wiped away the cheek and held her tighter.

"What is wrong with you tonight?" he whispered in her ear.

"I told you. I heard that there had been an accident. I was worried that you or Ginger were hurt. I had to call directory assistance...And then when I called the Vineyard, they wouldn't let me talk to you. It bothered me."

Logan leaned away from Diana, looking down at her face.

"So, I take it you didn't mastermind the destruction of my Pinot Noir? Those tears aren't guilt or crocodile?" he asked, his face serious and more than a little distrustful.

Seeing the questioning in his eyes hurt.

"Of course not! I would never do that to you."

"The stakes are incredibly high."

"In case you've forgotten, I was with you last night," she said, as his fingertip brushed away one of her tears.

"Be that as it may, Marco wasn't in my bed last night."

"Well, that is probably a good thing," she said, trying to make the accusation light-hearted.

"Where was he?" Logan asked.

"I don't know where he was, nor do I care," she said, wondering just where Marco had been. She didn't like the direction this conversation was taking. "He's a troll. Today he called me a bitch in Italian."

"He's an ass. Did you tell him about my Pinot?" he asked, his eyes blazing into hers.

"Was there something to tell?"

"I told you about it. How I was saving it. How I'd abandoned my sparkling wine because I had a very promising Pinot."

She just shook her head and said, "I didn't put that together. For all I knew, it was already bottled. I certainly didn't know where you kept it. How could you think I'd do something like this?"

Logan sat up, the cool air hitting her bare skin, making Diana feel exposed. She reached for a blanket as Logan wiped a hand over his face. "I have no doubt that Marco is somehow behind this. I just can't prove it yet."

"I see why you'd come to that conclusion," she said and pulled the blanket more tightly to her. "Logan, contest or not, if I knew he'd done something like this, I'd be the first to call the police."

It was only then that Logan looked down at her, shaking his head. Did he not believe her? She'd never lied to him. Ever. He couldn't say that about himself.

"You're really on the wrong side of this."

"I'm actually in the middle. Either way, I lose."

"What do you mean?" he asked, stretching out next to her.

"If Mountain Valley loses, I lose a promotion I've worked years for. If you lose, you potentially lose Forget-Me-Not. There will be no clear winners here," she said as his fingertips lightly traced the skin along her thigh.

"If I lose, I bet your contract gets extended to cover the new acquisition of my land. That would be a mighty pretty feather in your cap, or is it a notch on your lipstick case?"

"How did you know about that?" she asked, thinking that Stephan had only mentioned that possibility to her that afternoon.

"I guessed, and it appears I'm right," he said as a look of sadness flashed in his soft blue eyes.

"I won't do it," she said, clutching the blanket to her body like a lifesaver. "I told my boss today. I'm not sure I can handle an extension of the contract. I won't watch them dismantle your winery if it comes to that. I don't look at the end of other people's dreams as a notch. Despite your opinion of me, I'm not that fierce and cold."

"Are you sure?" he asked, leaning closer to her. "What happened to all that confidence? That bloodlust that I've come to expect from you?"

"Is that what you think of me?" Bloodlust? Was he teasing? Suddenly, she didn't think so. She didn't know how to answer or what to say to keep from escalating the situation. Then he filled in some of the blanks for her, and escalation was achieved.

"You need to do your job, Diana. Don't hold back on my account. Heck, I know that you are at a disadvantage because you are competing against me. I don't envy you."

"Thanks for understanding that this isn't personal," she said and rolled away from him.

"With you, it never is," he said and sat up to pull on his boxers.

"Just what is that supposed to mean?" she said, sitting up.

Logan slipped into his jeans. His back turned to her. "I'm under no illusions that you would ever put a personal relationship ahead of business."

"I would have twelve years ago. I'd have given it all up for you, Logan. I was so in love with you. And you broke my heart," she said as Logan's hand paused on one of his shirt's buttons.

"I get it. You think I broke your heart?" he asked, not waiting for an answer. "Why do you think I did that?"

"I've tried to figure it out for twelve years. I think you finally filled me in at your house after you turned the sprinklers on me."

"As I've said, Wharton was a phenomenal opportunity. Nothing should have stood in your way."

"Nothing, including you?" she asked, her voice cracking, "Including my feelings?"

"It was the right thing to do. I don't regret it for a moment, and it isn't like you ever looked back," he said, his blue eyes ice cold in the dim light of her bedroom.

"You hurt me," she said. "You made it clear you didn't want me, so what was I supposed to think?"

"Diana, be reasonable. Look at the big picture. This situation is just like Wharton twelve years ago. When are you ever going to get this kind of opportunity again?"

What was he trying to do, be the sacrificial lamb? This was ridiculous.

"Right, because I'm still the low rent trailer trash who has so far surpassed my station in life. If I'd followed my destiny, I'd be a cocktail waitress somewhere. Wait a minute, that is what I did today! I served wine like a waitress. I just did it on behalf of a bunch of egomaniac assholes. I should have felt lucky that someone like me should have such an opportunity."

"That isn't what I said."

"You didn't have to, Logan. I've always known that down deep, you never thought I was good enough for you." There, she finally said her mind. Logan always made himself the martyr, but in truth, he probably never felt like she was worthy of the Parrish dynasty. She wasn't exactly the sweet little girl his family wanted him to bring home to his aunt and uncle twelve years ago. She could tell by the way they looked at her, the way they had reacted to her. They knew she was close to her trailer park roots. They didn't think Logan was serious about her, and they were right.

"Diana, that has nothing to do with this. If our relationship had been that strong, we'd have survived Wharton. We didn't."

Diana sat up, wrapping the blanket around her. "You didn't give us a chance to survive, Wharton. You ended it. What did you expect me to do, beg you?"

"I expected you to fight. Fight for us, but you didn't. You just believed me, didn't even question why I was doing it." Diana thought about that — that wasn't true, was it? She asked him why the change of heart. She was sure of it. He was so cold and decisive that evening. That evening, she tried so hard to forget.

"So, this is my fault? You walked away, and I didn't chase you down, so it was my fault?"

"I thought I would at least hear from you. I thought you might call and tell me that you missed me. Anything. But I got nothing."

He had to be kidding. She said, "You broke up with me!"

"Anyone could have seen through that, Diana. I made it easy for you to break it off. I did you a favor. I was devastated when you left. It almost broke me."

Holding up her hand, she said, "Don't do me any more favors. I seriously can't believe you. I'm still not over what you did, and you have the gall to tell me it was my fault and you were hurt? And now, history is repeating itself. I can't do the right thing because there is no right thing in your mind, you fucking martyr. Get over yourself."

With a quick glance at the ceiling, he said, "I knew that starting something between us again was a bad idea."

"Really? Well, fuck you—it seems I just can't get it right when it comes to you, Logan. But then, maybe you don't want it to work. Poor Logan, always unlucky in love. If you give this a chance and it works, I've robbed you of an excuse for self-pity."

"Come on, Diana, we are both adults. We both got what we wanted."

"Quite frankly, you need to leave before you impart any more of your wisdom on me tonight, Mr. Parrish."

"Fine," he said and strode toward her front door. Once he opened it, he called back, "Get the lock fixed."

"Well, fuck you very much, you coward! I'm not going to chase after you and beg you to stay with me. Go be a fucking martyr, you tool."

Diana picked up the nearest thing she could reach, a hairbrush sitting on her nightstand. She tossed it after Logan, knowing that even as it left her fingers, it would fall way short of its target.

# CHAPTER TWENTY-ONE

Three days after the disastrous scene with Diana, Logan walked around his house, moving from room to room with Ginger following silently behind him. His aunt and uncle's house, this house, the land, the vineyard meant so much to him. How was he going to leave it if it came to that? He'd have to move to the east coast to a state where they didn't have vineyards or beverage specialists. Could he leave? Leaving his family land was one thing, but leaving Diana, he wasn't sure he could bear it. His life, in every area, was a disaster. He heard Diana's words again and again. He couldn't say she was too far from the truth. But he'd wanted the best for her, always the best. That is why he sacrificed his feeling so that she would excel. She didn't look at his sacrifice as selfless. She looked at it as the ultimate act of selfishness. Diana was crazy to think that he ever thought she wasn't good enough for him. She knew him better than that. Why would she even think that?

This wasn't the end of them. He couldn't let that happen. Never again. But he needed to wait until after the contest. Enough of these confused loyalties and subterfuge. He needed his head in the game until this was over. Then he could make it right with Diana.

Would she tell the D'Salvos that he was thinking of moving to the east coast? Would she use it to her advantage? She wouldn't. He knew that.

The ringing phone snapped Logan out of his silent musings. He answered with a gruff, "Logan Parrish."

"Hello, Mr. Parrish. This is Daisy Stark from the Stark Hotels. How are you today?"

A knot inside Logan's stomach tightened. Daisy Stark told all five wineries that she would be calling them after the votes were tabulated. The thought he might not be a finalist kept him from even thinking about the call. His palms were damp with unpleasant anticipation.

"Good morning, Mrs. Stark. How are you?" He didn't care how she was, but he needed to get on with the torture. If he wasn't a finalist, he might as well start packing his bags. He didn't know how he could keep Forget-Me-Not. It was unlikely that what was left of PN 13 would save him.

It would be over, the death of his dreams, the death of his family's dreams, his future. The winery had seen five generations of Parrishes, but Logan Parrish had been the one who couldn't cut it. He'd been the one to disappoint all the relatives before him.

"It would appear that I'm the bearer of some good news this morning," Daisy chirped happily into the phone.

Had the chair not been underneath him, Logan would have fallen to the floor.

"I can't wait," he managed. And he couldn't. He'd been holding his breath.

"I'm very pleased to tell you that Forget-Me-Not is one of two finalists in the Stark Hotel contest!"

Logan released a breath and felt the room spin a little out of focus. He'd done it, taken this extremely large step. Now, he just needed to win.

"Thank you. This is the best, most fantastic news. Can you tell me who the other finalist is?"

"Unfortunately, I can't tell you because they haven't been notified yet. I called the high scorer first. Yes, that is you, but by only a few final votes. Now, an announcement will be in the Yamhill Times tomorrow. I'm also going to do a press release and splash it all over our website at Stark. Allow me just to say, you probably know the other winery fairly well," she answered.

That told him all he needed to know, not that it was any surprise.

He had the high score. Maybe it wasn't as bleak as he thought.

Over the next few minutes, Mrs. Stark went over the list of rules for the final competition. It would be a head-to-head blind tasting at a dinner service of four courses, appetizer, salad, main course, and dessert. The competition would be a week from Saturday. He had only a week and a half to consult with his assigned Stark Hotel chef and develop a menu that would highlight the strength of each of his wines and, therefore, his vineyard.

At the end of the dinner service, the six-person Stark Hotel panel would reveal their votes. Majority vote got the coveted three-year contract.

When Logan got off the phone, he had to sit at his desk for several moments and collected his thoughts. He'd done it; he'd really done it! He was a big step closer to getting the deal of a lifetime. Now, he just had to figure out how to ensure his win.

And if he could win, he would keep his vineyard.

It was time to implement Plan B.

+—————— •◦❁◦• ——————+

Diana walked along the rows of vineyards on autopilot, trying to clear her head. It had been three days since she'd seen Logan. How could he walk away from her? If he wanted her to fight for them, she would. She wasn't a twenty-two-year-old anymore. She was a grown woman who went for it. And in this case, she wanted Logan more than anything else in the world.

She grabbed a leaf on one of the plants and felt the velvet smooth texture tickle her skin. This was all wrong. There should have been a way for them to work it out. She loved him. And after all that she'd been through in this life, didn't she deserve a chance at happiness?

When he'd broken up with her before Wharton, she didn't have the self-esteem nor the trust in her feelings to ever think they had a chance. He'd made it pretty clear.

*"I don't see myself spending my life with you…"*

How would he have spoken to her if he really wanted her to go away forever? Maybe her interpretation was wrong, not what he intended, but when you grew up how she did, you think no one wants you…even your parents. Regardless, Diana was too young and too timid to fight for what she wanted. Well, that wasn't the case now.

Sometime last night, while she was looking at the beams that made up the ceiling of her bedroom, she decided on a plan of attack.

Despite Logan's bend to the martyr within him, she wasn't going to let him go. He didn't get to decide this time. She did, and he better get on board. Once they figured out who the winners were of this competition, Diana was going to get Logan back. Screw the driving back to Seattle. She was staying, even if that meant packing her car, driving it next door, and sitting on Logan's front porch. He wanted her to fight for it? Well, watch out, buddy, it was on.

Diana's cell phone whistled at her. She had a text message, and the only thing that made her look at the screen was the thought that it might be Logan calling to tell her that he wanted to apologize. But it wasn't a message from Logan. It was from Salvatore.

RESULTS ARE IN. GET TO MY OFFICE ASAP!

That was just great, another order from another D'Salvo. And the use of capital letters, she could almost hear them shouting at her. Marco was starting to rub off on Salvatore, and their mutual treatment of Diana was slowly disintegrating. Wait until she moved in next door. They would scream their little heads off. No amount of capital letters were going to save them then.

She took a deep breath. Time to *focus on the good.*

Today was the day they were announcing finalists for the Stark Hotel contract. Note to self, the next contract she negotiated that was tied to a big competition, if there was another contract, would have different phases. They should have negotiated to have the contract end on the day the finalists were announced with the caveat to another contract that took them through the finalist stage. She knew they were finalists. How could they not be? She knew they'd won the first and possibly the third task outright. And if she were guessing, Forget-Me-Not had to be a close second.

As she entered the tasting room ten minutes later, she could hear a champagne cork popping. Ah, yes, they were obviously finalists.

Salvatore was the first to greet her, engulfing her in a bear hug that made her feel like she'd been accosted by a creepy old man with lots of cologne and body hair. She did her best to act happy...thrilled even, but the truth of the matter was her heartbeat with happiness for Logan, who Salvatore had already discovered was the other finalist.

She put a smile on her face as she lifted her glass in a toast, "It is on. Now, all we have to do is win the damn thing!"

# CHAPTER TWENTY-TWO

T
he next few days crawled by, causing Logan endless sleepless nights.

How many times had he considered going to Diana's cabin?

Every night he had contemplated it. What would it take for Diana to come to him? Was she as invested? Did she feel things was different this time? This time he needed to know that she loved him. He needed someone to fight for him.

It had taken every ounce of his self-discipline not to knock on her door and tell her that he had made a mistake. That he was being an ass. But soon, the contest would be over, and he'd have a chance.

Diana hadn't shared any secrets, but if the D'Salvos discovered their affair, she could lose her job. And Logan wasn't about to cost her everything she had worked so hard to achieve. However, he wasn't purposefully going to lose the contest so that she'd win. As far as he was concerned, the contest was between the two of them. This was the last time they'd be on opposite sides.

Logan smiled sadly as he looked down at the grape leaves in his palm. The once healthy leaves were now laced with large, dried brownish-red patches known as lesions. Each lesion was littered with tiny black spots. To a vintner, such a vision was terrifying. It was a disease Logan had studied well. Black rot. It was a fungus not widely seen in less tropically humid areas. But the rains that spring had been very humid, and it had been a slightly wetter spring than they had liked, which had opened the door to such an evil invader.

Logan hoped for an Indian summer to compensate for the wet spring, but black rot was a game-changer. If he'd found it on his plants, the crop for this year and potentially for years to come would be lost. And it didn't stop there, for the disease could go dormant and reappear years later. There was no way to compensate with chemical and cultural methods to eradicate such a predator so late in the season. The chemicals would ruin the fruit, and he didn't want to be known as the vintner who bottled wine with the aftertaste of toxic chemical residue. Besides, he was an organic farmer.

And if his plants had black rot, untreated, they would all be dead within a year.

He smiled at the idea of Salvatore D'Salvo hearing the news of black rot so close to his land, let alone land that he intended on buying. It would scare the living hell out of him. Or so Logan hoped.

He looked at the specimens in his hand. They were very convincing examples of black rot. Textbook. He sniffed it. It smelled like a dried grape leaf, which is exactly what it was.

He knew with certainty that some of the "infected" leaves had blown their way very close to the D'Salvo property line. He had been careful. None of the leaves were actually on D'Salvo land. He smiled again as he glanced at his watch. By now, his neighbors should be doing their daily walk through, looking at the crop. It wouldn't take long for them to start seeing a few well-placed lesions covered leaves on their land. And if they didn't, he had taken steps to ensure they knew about it. At the thought of their reactive panic, Logan smiled again.

He and Ginger walked down to the tasting room and called to Peter, who had been rearranging stock and learning how to run a tasting room since the day after the robbery. He couldn't shake the feeling he'd had about the boy since he had hired him on.

"Yeah, Logan?"

"I need you in a meeting. They can spare you for a few minutes," he said, nodding to the two part-time women who worked in his tasting room.

Ginger growled at Peter as he approached.

"Ginger, it's just Peter," Logan said. But she would not be discouraged. The closer he got, the deeper her growl. Good girl.

Logan looked at her and the way she was looking at Peter. "You'd better make sure to stay on the other side of me," he said as Ginger tensed. He placed his body between his dog and the intern. "She can be vicious if she thinks you mean me harm."

He patted her head and said, "Easy there, girl. It's okay."

"Why doesn't she like me?" Peter asked.

"She is fickle," he said. "Takes her a while to warm up to people."

But as they walked up to Logan's house—where William, Ben, and Tess were waiting—Ginger muttered a low, menacing growl. She kept at it even when Logan locked her in the kitchen. She lay down on the other side of the door and sniffed at the crack in the floor. Occasionally, she would paw at the door or utter a single bark of frustration.

"Thanks for coming. Let's go sit down."

They all settled in the living room, and Logan opened one of his new bottles of the rare PN 13. They all had a glass, and at last, he spoke.

"We have a problem. I need to discuss it with you all, and I need you to promise that what I tell you will not leave this room."

They all nodded and muttered their pledge that they wouldn't share whatever he was about to tell them.

Setting his glass down carefully, he reached into a large grocery bag and slowly removed what was inside.

He then held up several of the lesion covered grape leaves, which were in small plastic bags. Logan instructed, "Have a look, but keep them in the bags."

"Does anyone know what this is?" he asked.

"Holy shit," Ben murmured, staring at the little baggie in his large hands. "Is that black rot?"

"Yes," Logan said. "I had it tested this morning to be sure at a very discreet lab out of the area. It is textbook black rot, and I've never been more frightened in my life. It is on three plants right on the edge of the property line next door to Mountain Valley. And if we have it, it has to be next door as well, maybe even began there."

"I wouldn't put it past the D'Salvo's to bring it in," Tess muttered.

"I doubt he knows he has it," Logan said.

"Can you kill it?" Tess asked.

"Not exactly," Logan said vaguely.

"You don't understand, Tess," William said, looking into his wine glass. "No one wants this disease. By the time you find it, your vineyard is infected. It is like acid to these plants. The grapes will shrivel up and die. It might look like the plants have healed, but next year at about this time, it will wake back up. It can be dormant for years. Most vintners remove the plants, sterilize the land, which doesn't do much for the flavor of the grapes, and they start over. Or they removed deep pockets of earth and replace it with fresh sod—also a big, costly mess."

"Others go out of business, forever," Logan said with a pointed look at Peter, and then he downed his glass of wine.

"What are you going to do, Logan?" Peter asked, with a note of excitement in his voice.

Good, he was engaged.

"I'll show you the three plants. I want them covered with plastic and removed. Remove every leaf you find on the ground. Then I want us to remove any plant that is touching them. We'll dig out the root, spray the ground with a mixture of vinegar, salt, and organic dish soap. Then we wait and see."

"Dish soap?" Peter asked.

"It is organic RoundUp. Safe and effective," Ben interjected.

"I just hope it will stop the progress of this stuff, or we are completely screwed," Logan said, placing the effect of defeat in his voice on just the right words.

⊷──── ⋅๑⋅ ────⊶

Diana didn't have the time to answer a summons. She had all but memorized the Stark Hotel's extensive restaurant and room service menu and was trying to decide what they should serve at the finalist dinner. She had consulted not only with their designated Stark Hotel chef but also some of her friends in the culinary world to see which herbs and spices brought out the best aspect of any wine. Certain flavors could take a mediocre wine to higher levels. She liked to think of an old Southern term she knew. "No matter how thin you slice it, it's still baloney." Bad wine was bad wine.

She had a headache, her eyes burned, and she wasn't sleeping. She knew she looked awful, as if she'd aged ten years in less than a week.

Whatever new and different little wrench Salvatore or Marco wanted to throw at her would not be appreciated today.

Her fuse had been getting shorter each day. She hoped they'd fire her. Then she could leave this place, leave the cabin that only reminded her of Logan and nights in his arms. The feeling of Logan's body holding her own, the sound of his heart beating in her ear, the memory was enough to make the sanest of people go crazy. It was sweet torture. Unlike anything, she'd ever experienced. At least in twelve years.... Who was she kidding? If they fired her, she'd drive to Logan's and refuse to leave. Damn, she hoped she was fired.

241

As she marched to the tasting room, she tried to distract her murderous thoughts with those of dessert.

She pictured the selection Stark Hotel Restaurants had to offer. There were a few holes and gaps. Maybe a nice bread pudding with dried cherries or a molten lava cake would make a lovely dessert option. Red wine went well with chocolate, but she'd intended to serve a dessert wine, not a heady red. Logan would probably serve chocolate. He loved chocolate, *dark* chocolate.

He'd go with dark chocolate. And he'd serve a red. The problem was that head-to-head; any of his reds would outshine any of the reds at Mountain Valley Vineyards. If they both did a chocolate dessert, the judges would get a head-to-head challenge. She was pretty sure she couldn't win that.

After greeting Antonio and Davide in the tasting room with a smile that was more of a half grimace, Diana made her way to Salvatore's office. Marco and Salvatore gave her a dirty look the moment she arrived.

What had she done now? Did they know about Logan? She hadn't seen or talked to Logan for over a week.

"Close the door behind you," Salvatore said gruffly.

She hated closed door. Crap. It was always bad when doors were closed. By way of greeting, she asked, "Okay, I'm here. What's up?" It was better than: *Why the hell did you summon me like a damned servant?*

"How familiar are you with the horticulture surrounding a healthy vineyard?" Salvatore asked.

"I know what fertilizers work, things like that. I know that you are an organic vineyard, so you don't use pesticides, which is good because they can affect the taste of the wine. Why?" she asked, thinking that of all she had expected to hear, it wasn't this.

Salvatore held up a grape leaf that had seen better days and asked, "What do you see?"

Sighing, she held out her hand for the leaf.

It was a dead leaf. So what? But, since they were all upset, it must be something important.

The normally vibrant, uniform green surface was interrupted with several yellowish-brown spots. On closer inspection, she could see little black spots on the leaves.

"I see that something is very wrong. What is it? Mold?" she asked, staring intently at the leaf.

"Hardly. It's only the worst of the worst. It is black rot," Salvatore said.

Black rot? She'd never heard of it before, but it wasn't like she knew much about the plants that grew the grapes. Her expertise was more in line with what to do with the wine after it bottled. She knew how to keep mold off a cork, but not off a leaf.

"Have you ever had it before?" she asked.

"No, and I don't have it now, but I have it on good authority that it is showing up on the vines next door," he said, studying her a little more intently. Was he looking for a reaction? He would be denied. What did it mean for Logan?

"What does it mean for Mountain Valley? Is it contagious?" she asked as dread crawled over her skin. From the looks the men across from her were giving her, she knew this was much more serious than some mold.

Marco said, "We probably have been exposed already. This late in the season, we are finished. It will kill us! It starts with the leaves, moves to the fruit, and consumes the vines. Eventually, it kills the plants, and then we are done."

She wanted to…. Do what? Call Logan? Talk to him, help him? Get fired and sued for breach of contract?

She asked, "Can you stop it from coming over here?"

"I'm not sure we can," Salvatore said. "When the first signs appear, it is usually too late. This season is potentially an entire loss. I have all the hands out searching the vineyard, looking for signs."

"Does Forget-Me-Not know they have it?" she asked.

"My source tells me that Logan Parrish knows, but he wants to keep it quiet. I doubt he knows how serious it is. He thinks he can remove the plants, and the issue will be solved. He is naïve," Salvatore warned.

"I work for you. I'll do what you say," she said, feeling a little burn in the pit of her stomach. "But wouldn't knowledge of this swing the contest in your favor?"

"Our properties are too close. This is potentially the worst news we could have received," he replied. "If this gets out, it hurts us!"

"You have a spy at Forget-Me-Not?" Diana asked, knowing that had to be the case since Salvatore mentioned his 'source' and now wondering just which of Logan's employees wasn't to be trusted.

Marco just looked at her, the secret knowledge burning a hole in his small brain. It wasn't much, but it was enough. She had her answer.

"It doesn't matter how we heard," Salvatore said, ignoring her question. "If we were to be proactive and treat this disease, it would ruin the fruit for this year. We are going to have to prune the plants severely when the full rot shows itself, which will happen in about six weeks, right before we would be normally harvesting."

"By that time, the grapes will be shriveled up and look like peppercorns," Marco added.

The silence stretched between the two men until Diana asked, "What do you need me to do?"

"You can start thinking of ways to get us out of this contest," Salvatore said, shaking his head.

"You can't be serious," she replied, slightly dumbfounded.

"Damn serious. I already have commitments with different

vendors that I have no idea if I'll be able to fill. This year isn't the problem. It is the next two to three years when this harvest would have been perfect. There is no way we can fill the Stark Hotels' order if we lose this harvest. The action we take now will sacrifice this season to save the future seasons of Mountain Valley."

"Don't you think you might be over-reacting just a little bit? We don't even know if it is conclusively black rot," she said. "Or if you have it on your plants."

"The infected plants are only thirty feet away from my land. I had no doubt."

"If we win the contest, we'll examine the contract. We can add an addendum about exceptions, like black rot, that would get you out of it."

"I know it when I see it. I don't want to take any chances. Get me out of the contest," Salvatore said. His decision was made, and he was in no mood to discuss it.

"What will you do about Forget-Me-Not? Are you still on track to buy it?" she asked.

"I can't think about buying his land now! Think of it. He has much more trouble than we have. Let some other sap buy him out. I need to close the water rights deal sooner if I can. I want to get the money out of him while he is still solvent. I'll use it to buy grapes from other vineyards to fulfill my orders if the worse happens."

"Isn't he almost bankrupt?" she asked as her brain tried to digest everything they were telling her. She had been so focused on winning the contest that she couldn't think of just walking away from it. She was competitive, but even as she thought of the win, she thought of Logan. He could lose everything. What could she do?

"Not yet," Salvatore said.

"Wasn't he burglarized a couple of weeks ago?" she asked, feeling like she was treading on a fine edge.

"He didn't lose all of it. And from what I hear, what he has will sell for a very good price if he realizes the value," Salvatore said.

"He is probably too stupid to figure that out," Marco added.

Of all the things she knew Logan to be, stupid wasn't one of them. He knew exactly what he was doing. He knew about the virus; she was sure of it. But he'd not taken one proactive step forward to do anything about it. That in itself was strange.

Salvatore added, "Depending on how fast this appears on the vines. I'll need capital. We need to rent some land far away from this virus or start buying grapes from other vineyards. I need the money from Parrish's water rights to buy inventory."

"Papa, we don't need his money!" Marco protested.

"If this virus progresses as it is known to do, we will need all the capital we can find," Salvatore said, giving Marco a harsh look.

"I've called my attorney and told him to offer Parrish a price he can't refuse for the water rights. I need to get that settled as soon as possible. I just hope he doesn't question my motives."

"Papa, please don't give in to him," Marco complained, sounding like a bratty child.

"When you've been in business as long as I've been, Marco, you learn to strike while the iron is hot. Now is one of those times. I will gladly take Mr. Parrish's money while he has it."

He turned his attention back to Diana and pointed a stern finger at her. "Make it look like we tried to win, but by God, make sure we don't get that contract. Once Parrish has it and cannot fulfill it, we will be in a better position to take his land if we still want it."

"So, you want me to lose it for you?" she said.

"Yes, make sure you give them no other choice."

"I need to speak to Wave. This goes against everything you hired me to do. We might need to redraft or add a clause or addendum. We'll keep it private, but I can't purposefully lose something for you without your request in writing."

"Fine," he answered flatly. "What else will it take?"

"I'm going to need four of your worst performing wines. Two white and two red. I have an idea which ones they are, but I'll want to get your opinion as well," she said, already making the list of bad wine in her head.

"Have Davide help you to find what you need," he said.

"I'll speak with Stephan today," she said and added, "What do you think about getting some of those leaves tested to confirm they are infected with black rot?"

"They've already been tested," Salvatore answered. "We heard from a very reliable source that the leaves tested positive. I don't want word of this to spread. With each person that knows, there is a potential for a leak to occur."

"You know that you have my word. You have a proprietary relationship with Wave," she said as she stepped to the door, quietly opened it to escape the tense silence of Salvatore's office.

He nodded and waved her away.

Diana stopped in the tasting room, and with Davide's help, they found the four bottles she was looking for. He put them in a dark green wine bag that was sectioned to carry four wine bottles at a time, and then she went back to her cabin.

Finding her contract, she called her boss and quickly explained the situation to him.

"You can't be serious? They want you to pull out of the competition?" Stephan asked.

"No, they want me to purposefully lose it."

"This is completely unheard of."

"I agree."

"Damn it! This is the kind of thing that could invalidate the contract. They might tell you to throw the contest, but we need it in writing. If we lose the contest without written authorization, it could come back on us like a herd of ambulance-chasing attorneys. I suppose we could sue them after this is over if it hurts our reputation, and we can prove it. Hell, I don't want our name anywhere near this. We will have a PR nightmare on our hands."

"For starters, email me the document you want him to sign, and I'll get it done," Diana said.

"Now listen, we need to get a disease specialist in there to fix this thing," said Stephan.

"No," Diana said, "I already tried that. They don't want anyone to know. He's invoking confidentiality. We can't say a word to anyone. Salvatore said that word of this could be fatal to any vineyard. Forget-Me-Not is just in too close physical proximity for comfort. They want this buttoned up, but they need me to lose the competition."

"That will damage our reputation! It is totally unacceptable."

"Which is why I'm calling you, because if we throw the competition, it damages us, right?" she asked, hitting her hand against her forehead after stating the obvious. "If we win, we potentially ruin a client. What am I supposed to do? I've only got six days to do something. You got any solutions?"

"Yes, I know just what you need," he said. "I don't want to trust this to some addendum I might write. I need them to have a face-to-face with one of our lawyers."

Oh no.

Don't say it.

Oh, please don't say it...

"I'll get on the horn with Brad and send him down there."

"Stephan—"

"You've done a great job with this family of egos, but I need them to know you've got a little more muscle behind you. Marco and I have an understanding, but Salvatore needs the lawyer speak, nailing it all down for him. Don't want him weaseling on the compensation. Heck, we might need a bit more compensation to deal with the fallout."

"But I—"

"We contracted for the food and lodging of two of our people if we deem it necessary. Well, heck, you and Brad are old friends. You could share—"

"Stephan!" she yelled in the phone.

"Yes, Diana?" he asked, his voice calm but irritated at the interruption.

"I cannot share a living space with Brad. I hate Brad. He is my ex-fiancé. I caught him having sex with another woman, my neighbor, in our bed. I threw his clothing out the third-floor window of my condo a few months ago. Our relationship isn't tenuous. It is adversarial."

"Whoa, that's probably more information than I needed to know. Explains a few things. Listen, Di. This is business. Make nice, finish the contract, and make the money, 'kay?"

"He can't stay with me. This isn't a negotiation."

"Alright, alright, I'll spring for a hotel for him. He probably wouldn't stay in a cabin anyway. Lawyers are so pretentious," he said, laughing at his own joke.

Then, as she wasn't even in the conversation with him, he went on, "I'm going to make sure that old Sal can't blame this on Wave. Have Brad add a little well-written penalty with a monetary consequence. And damn, if they refuse to sign it, we'll threaten to move forward with the objective of winning the damn contest."

"You know what, Stephan?" she asked and then answered without waiting for him to reply. "This is the ultimate worst moment of my career. This is a humiliating ending to this project."

"Di, don't worry about it. We're still getting paid. Hell, it might even give you and Brad a chance to extend the olive branch."

The only thing she wanted to do with an olive branch was shove it up Brad's ass.

# CHAPTER TWENTY-THREE

L ogan smiled with disdain as he watched the game camera footage from the day before. He had secretly installed several of the camouflage cameras near his property line with the D'Salvo's land. Last evening, a little before midnight, Marco appeared in a black Ninja wannabe outfit. The camera caught him slowly looking just beyond the property line into the Forget-Me-Not vineyard. He didn't have to wait long. Another familiar figure captured in the glow of the night vision camera appeared on the screen. Only this person was on the Forget-Me-Not side of the property and bore a striking resemblance to his overly eager, suspicious intern, Peter.

The two figures began talking, and Peter passed a clear food storage bag to Marco. Logan knew instantly that it contained some of the tainted leaves from the plants.

It hadn't been easy to ensure that plants on the edge of the property line showed evidence of the disease. Worse yet, everything he had planned to use on the plants smelled like chemicals. It was Tess, who'd gotten a little creative with some of the more toxic organic products. If he was still in business a month from now, he was going to give Tess, Ben, and William surprise bonuses. He had no idea that their loyalty to him ran so deep. They were willing participants in Plan B. They embellished it for the intern, especially demure Tess.

Logan watched the camera as Peter gestured behind him to the leaves on the vines in the close proximity.

Good.

"Hope you got a good look, Marco," Logan muttered.

That ought to put things in motion. Diana must be going nuts next door.

At the very thought of her, he sighed and tried to ignore the longing in his heart. He loved her. He'd always loved her. The question now was, did she love him like he loved her? Was it enough for her to abandon her career to share a life with him? He couldn't ask her to make the choice, but he hoped she would choose. He hoped he was her choice.

He could see her there, helping with the harvest, learning to be a winemaker, working alongside him. When they were in college, she would've done it, but Logan was sure she would have resented him for missing out on Wharton. It had been a crazy notion whenever his mind had touched on it, fantasized about the possibilities.

He heard what she said about being a cocktail waitress. She was still aspiring for something he wasn't sure of, though he knew this wasn't the life for her.

Even when she'd been in school, she'd been quite clear about what she'd wanted. If he'd asked her not to go to Wharton, not only would their relationship not endured, but they probably would also have ended up hating each other. Some things just weren't meant to be. It was just hard to keep that perspective when he thought of those moments when they were in each other's arms. When they made love, the emotions were so overwhelming; it felt like they were the only two people in the world. Meant to be together. He hoped they'd get that second chance.

Sensing his sadness, Ginger placed her head on his knee and demanded attention. He rubbed his palm over her velvety fur, giving her ears a rub as she sighed contently.

"At least I have you, girl," he said as he scratched his dog on the head.

His phone rang, disturbing the moment with Ginger. He picked it up and wondered what fresh hell awaited him now.

"Mr. Parrish, this is Jack Alton of Alton, Dean, and Jacoby."

He recognized the name. The guy was the lawyer represented the water rights on the side of the D'Salvos. Logan grunted in acknowledgment. He had yet to hire his own attorney.

"I've been asked by Mr. Salvatore D'Salvo to set the price in the renewal of your water rights..."

Usually, when it came to the water rights, Logan had to initiate the negotiations and any of the phone calls to even open the discussion.

Something was wrong about this. He just wasn't sure what he was getting into.

A moment later, the lawyer said, "In the spirit of neighborly friendship, Mr. D'Salvo would like to offer you the following price..."

Logan listened and then had a hard time speaking. He asked the lawyer to repeat the price, which he did.

It didn't change, but it was significantly less than Logan had expected. He didn't think this surprisingly good news was a coincidence. The D'Salvos knew about the diseased plants and were concerned. Nonetheless, he did not trust how easily the other man had opened up the dialogue. He thanked the lawyer for his call and vaguely offered that he would think about it and get back to him.

The phone rang a second time in as many minutes, and he didn't want to answer for fear that it was the lawyer calling back to say, "Just kidding!"

But it wasn't the lawyer; it was his wholesale distributor, Rob Miller. The day they'd bottled PN 13, he'd had Rob come by to taste the wine. Rob had taken six sample cases with him when he'd left. The last few days, Logan had worried what he'd hear from the man when he called. He usually took his time between picking up a new product and calling him with news of how people were responding to it. Logan knew Rob was a busy man, and despite his desire to ask him to drop everything for this special wine, he knew a call so soon was unusual.

"Logan, it's Rob. Got some news for you."

Logan didn't think his heart could take much more of this. He needed to hear good news. Everyone at Forget-Me-Not loved the wine, but that meant nothing. Rob was a business partner but also a friend. He would tell it to him straight.

"Tell me."

"That Pinot is kicking ass everywhere I take it. I dropped a bottle off with the editor of Yamhill Wine Review late in the afternoon after I'd stopped by to see you. I told him that it was good and that I'd appreciate it if he could taste it and give me his opinion. He opened it right there. We drank it out of paper cups, and it was still fabulous. He's going to be calling you for an article. I've spent the better part of two days talking it up because I know it is important timing. Well, I've got commitments from everyone I've talked to. I sent two cases of it out for the critics. The reviews are going to be spectacular. This is the best wine to come out of Forget-Me-Not in the entire time we've worked together," he said, the excitement clear in his voice.

"Rob, I don't know what to say. Thank you for this," Logan said as he took a deep breath for the first time in months. Maybe all the dead ancestors would be proud of young Logan after all.

"Wait, it gets better. I bumped the price. Thirteen a bottle for you, four for me, retail is twenty-six. Heck, we might be able to push it to thirty-five or forty a bottle after the critics chime in."

Logan was speechless. When he could find his words, he thanked his friend again and said, "Take five-fifty and give me eleven-fifty. You've earned that and so much more."

"I can't do that, Logan. There is an old saying, be a pig and get fat, or be a hog and get slaughtered. I'd rather take less and let you get your water rights so we can keep doing business together. This is going to fully establish you as a premier wine-maker. Don't be surprised if you start getting hit up for consultations. Hell, I'm already feeling that I priced it too cheap. If Wine Spectator gives it a 90 or greater, I'm doubling the price."

The current price would more than pay for his water rights. He'd have a very nice profit. Rob's men had picked up the last of several shipments of PN 13 the day before. It was now securely being held at his distribution facility.

"There is something I need to tell you," Logan said, treading carefully. Rob didn't distribute Mountain Valley Vineyards. It was part of the contract between them. He didn't service the winery next door. "You might hear rumors of a disease called black rot invading my vineyard. We don't have it. We never did. It was a rumor."

"Started by Marco or Sal?" his savvy distributor asked.

"A very conniving, desperate man named Logan Parrish," he answered honestly.

Rob chuckled, "I don't think I want to know. But, if I could guess, that is one way to make your land look unattractive to neighboring predators."

"Exactly."

"Tell you what I'm going to do. If you win this Stark Hotel Restaurant contest, I'm going to have a little A-frame brochure produced. Full-color, spotlighting all of your wines, pure class. We'll make enough of them for every table in every restaurant in every hotel Stark has. Hell, maybe we can put them in every room. And then I'm going to make some kick-ass cutouts for the stores you're in for the end of aisle displays."

"I feel like Christmas has come early."

"Kick some D'Salvo ass."

"I'm trying."

"Good to hear. Expect your first check-in a week or so."

"Now, that is really good to hear."

Logan didn't wait. He called his bank and talked to his loan officer. When he mentioned the new loan amount for the water rights and how he expected the loan to be fully paid in six months, the loan officer replied, "I can work with that, Mr. Parrish. I'll get started on the loan. Would you like to sign papers later this week?"

He could, and with a quick call back to the lawyer, he accepted the presented amount for the water rights. They would sign the papers as soon as they were ready, within two business days.

"Yes," he said, and they set an appointment.

The deals coming his way were so good he was more than a little suspicious. He wasn't used to having things go his way. He'd gotten used to disappointment. He couldn't believe D'Salvo had taken Peter's word for black rot and hadn't had the leaves tested. He supposed it was like lice. If you've got it, take care of it, but don't talk about it.

"Paranoia is the first step in the process to insanity," he said, looking down at Ginger, observing the intensity in her amber eyes. "The second step, I suppose, is talking to a dog."

---

Diana was exhausted when she made her way into the tasting room. She'd spent the entire day with her designated Stark Hotels chef discussing meals. His name was Frank, and he wanted to sample the wines she was thinking of pairing with the food. Explaining to him that they were still deciding what to serve had not gone over well.

"I'm sure the other competitor is building a menu around the wine, not the other way around."

What could she possibly say to that? "Well, we want to lose, so forget about it...."

She was angry. She was mad at Logan, mad at the D'Salvos, mad at her boss, mad at the situation, and mad at the world. And when Brad arrived, she'd have another item to add to the list of mad. Possibly she'd let her anger over her feelings for Logan get the better of her. She had certainly put the chef in his place with a few choice words about who was running this show. He probably hated her. Fine. Join the club. Heck, ask The Snaggletooth how to call her bitch in more than one language.

She was exhausted and just wanted to go back to her cabin and take a shower. Instead, she was going to meet with Sal at the tasting room to discuss her wine selections. Hopefully, he would agree that they would be bad enough for the finale.

Davide was pouring at the bar but paused when she stepped inside the tasting room. He looked at her intently, and she wondered what she'd done now.

Stopping mid-stride to the back hallway offices, she said, "Do you need me for something?"

But he didn't answer. He merely nodded to one of the café tables behind some large display barrels that created a private enclave.

Intrigued for all the wrong reasons, Diana stepped toward the enclosure and peeked around the corner.

There, in all his handsome, perfectly tailored glory, sat her ex-fiancé, Brad.

"Oh crap," she said by way of greeting. She'd only talked to her boss late the night before. Brad must have dropped everything, packed his Louis Vuitton, jumped in his white Porsche Panamera, and driven like a freaking maniac. She only hoped he'd gotten a speeding ticket, the jerk.

His dark blond hair was perfectly combed, set off by the white button-down, starched shirt, and crisp khaki trousers. A country club tee time was missing their fourth for golf.

"Diana," he said as he stood and took in the disarray of her stressed, emotionally wrought expression. "My goodness, this hasn't been easy for you, has it?"

Stepping close so that she wouldn't be heard by any other sensitive ears in the tasting room, she whispered, "The fact that fate has chosen to throw us together is just some strange coincidence, like a freak meteor killing you in the street. So, I'm going to be nice, professional, and defer to you for all things legal. But know this, nothing you can say or do will make up for what I walked in on in my own bedroom, in my own bed. You are a pig."

By now, the tasting room had grown eerily silent. Davide and Antonio were obviously trying to take in every little nuance of her conversation with the human Ken doll.

Had she loved him? She thought of Logan's smile. Just his smile. No way had she loved this pretentious jerk.

She and Brad had picked out a china pattern and registered at Williams Sonoma and Nordstrom because that is what people of a certain level of affluence did. Certainly, he'd been faking it just as much as she had. Hell, he'd cheated on her with her next-door neighbor. There was a phrase that came to mind: *Don't shit where you eat.* He had.

Plastering the smile on her face, she turned and said to Davide and Antonio, "Did you both meet Brad? He's our lawyer from Wave. He keeps it all legal. Brad, have you met the guys?"

After the introductions had been made and the blonds had sized one another up, Brad asked, "Diana, is there someplace we can go and have a chat?"

She laughed so loud that it echoed against all the wood and vaults, making her sound malevolent, like the evil queen in a fairy tale.

"Excuse me, gentleman. Would you let Sal know that I'll be back in a few minutes? Brad and I need to catch up."

They told her they would. She led Brad out of the tasting

room through the parking lot to a picnic table that was very popular with customers who wanted to enjoy a bottle of wine on-site.

"Is this about business? Because that's all I'm going to talk to you about. We are in a big mess here."

Brad sighed and carefully arranged himself on the bench of the picnic table as if he worried he would get dirty. Ignoring her last comment, he said, "It has been four and a half months, Diana. I've given you an adequate amount of time to put everything into perspective."

"Did the ring hit you in the head harder than I thought?" she asked. "I mean, I wanted it to hurt, maybe cut you and leave a scar, but did it hurt you a little more than intended? Because you're not making any sense."

"Diana, please. I've come a long way."

Same dense Brad as always.

"You came here because Stephan ordered you to come here," she replied. "I've said all I need to say."

"I only did it to get your attention."

"Excuse me? You thought sleeping with another woman was a good way to do that?" she said. "You could have just vacuumed or mopped the floor. Maybe brought me flowers occasionally."

"I got tired of competing with your job, so I decided to compete on a playing field you might notice," he said with an edge of anger she remembered all too well.

"A bed isn't a playing field," she said, her anger starting to well up within her. "And it sure isn't a place to fight a war against someone you love."

"I wanted to get a reaction. I wanted to see if you'd get mad," he said, as a little blush crept into his cheeks.

"You got your answer. I hope you and neighbor Janice will be very happy. Now look, we have a mess here."

"It was just a fling. Once the sex wore out, I missed you."

Diana squeezed her eyes shut and felt the urge to scream. Scream until she didn't know where she was, didn't even know her own name.

She gritted her teeth and said, "I hate you so much. I have no words. Now, I want to talk about business. If you don't, I'll just call Stephan."

"I'll be staying here until the final day of the competition. I hope that in that time, you'll be more open to a civil conversation."

"You can't be serious," she said. "I thought you'd only be here one night to get the addendum signed."

"Stephan wants me here until the end. That way, I can handle any surprises that might arise. The D'Salvos offered me the Chardonnay Cottage."

Damn it to hell. Chardonnay was right next door to Merlot. She had been fortunate in her stay at Mountain Valley Vineyards in that she'd avoided all the paying guests quite successfully.

"Why are they so nice to you?" she asked.

"The original contract is quite clear. It has an escalation clause if they damage our reputation. When I shared it with them, they got a little more accommodating."

"Great. Really great," she said and stood.

Over the next several days, she did her best to avoid him. He would stop by her cabin and knock on the door, but she refused to let him inside. How he occupied his time, she didn't know or care.

When she was on her way to the final wine tasting to pick the worst of the worst, he found her just outside the tasting room.

"Where are you going?" he asked, like a lonely puppy.

"I'm going to a special wine tasting. A dress rehearsal for the final competition. In the spirit of extending an olive branch, why don't you come with me?" she offered secretly, hoping he'd trip and fall on an olive branch that might impale him, someplace in a soft, warm area that would hurt. If that didn't work, she had something else in mind.

They met with Marco and Salvatore in the tasting room. Davide had laid out glasses next to each bottle of wine. She could almost enjoy the angry looks between Brad and Marco, natural born enemies. They were in competition as to whom was the best-looking man in the room. Diana thought it was a draw. She thought they were both ugly.

She picked up the first bottle for consideration and poured tastes for everyone. It was an especially dark and tart Pinot Noir that Mountain Valley had bottled five years earlier under the name "Dark Night."

"Okay, this is candidate number one for the main course."

She took a sip and almost gagged. Everyone, including Brad, had a grimace on their faces. The wine was swill. The fact Salvatore had even thought to bottle it convinced her that they didn't deserve to win the contest.

"That's rather unpleasant," she said, and Salvatore agreed.

"Not our shining star, which makes it perfect," he said, with a sad cadence to his voice. Maybe he was rethinking the contest. She no longer knew how she felt about that.

"You don't have to do this," she said. "Let's go back to the original plan. It is not too late."

"I assure you. I have not made this decision lightly. We must not get legally bound to a contract we cannot fulfill."

Brad added, "Well, now you know how Wave feels about the contract."

Salvatore had signed the special addendum Brad drafted that afternoon. For him to be continuing with this conversation was too much.

"I understand, Salvatore," she said and gave Brad a look she hoped he would interpret as an order to shut up.

She didn't understand purposeful losing. Her pride did not allow such defeatist attitude. If the situation were reversed, she'd have sent the sample leaves to three different labs and gotten results before doing anything as rash as what Salvatore was planning to do. The D'Salvos wouldn't do anything of the kind because they didn't want anyone to know. Secrets. Like what happened on the night Julianna Parrish died. Had Marco been drinking? Was the accident his fault? More secrets.

Diana was tired all the way to the core of her bones. She felt like the rest of her life was in the balance over this stupid contest. She wanted to win for selfish reasons, but her heart wanted Logan to blow them away. Diana pictured the bliss of simply setting down her glass, packing her bags, and driving next door. It was far enough away from all the mess that surrounded her as if she'd bought a one-way ticket to Kenya.

When she'd won that marketing presentation in school, scoring three points higher than Logan, it felt so good, so amazing. She was so proud of herself, of her accomplishments. She hadn't thought beyond that moment, that hour. Then he'd caught up with her and asked her to grab a burger. And that was the first day of the love affair that would define the rest of her life. It was so much larger than the damn marketing presentation. She'd barely noticed when Dr. Bekker approached her about putting her name in for the Wharton Fellowship. He'd made Logan the same offer, but Logan had turned him down. At the time, he explained it away.

"Why do I need to do something like that? My future is right here. I know what I'm going to do with the rest of my life."

He'd known he wanted to be a vintner. It was his dream and his passion. He'd known since the day he'd been born a Parrish on Forget-Me-Not soil.

How did all those little, tiny events in the scope of her long life, in reality, shape the entire course of her future existence?

If Logan had won that day instead of her, would he have still passed on the idea of the Wharton Scholarship? Dr. Bekker always wrote a personal recommendation for the top student,

CRUSH

just as he had done for Diana. It might have been just the one thing that pushed the decision in her favor.

If Logan won that day, would he have still taken her out for that sophomore bacon cheeseburger at the MU? She thought so. More accurately, she hoped so. Would they have had their spring term affair?

If it had been Logan who won the Wharton Fellowship, would he have promised to write and call? Or would he have broken up with her just as he had? Maybe he would have made her false promises and then met another girl at Wharton. She hadn't met anyone that year away. She was still so in love with Logan, so devastated by his cold detachment, that she couldn't think of another man. The fellowship had only lasted ten months. Would their love have endured if he had been the one to go away? She knew this: She would have waited for him. And she wasn't giving up now. He didn't think she'd fought for it then? Well, she'd show him.

This contest. The stakes, the lives, the twist of fate...

Was this fate offering her a do-over? Fuck it. She was making sure that she and Logan had another chance.

She silently asked the question again: "Who, in your heart, do you want to win this contest?"

She picked up another glass of red wine the color of blueberry juice and took a sip. It was the kind of wine that kept dentists in the money for whitening products. It was as if someone had switched wine with non-diluted vinegar.

The answer to her question made her heart beat a little faster, and tears threatened to overwhelm her in front of the least sympathetic group she could ever think to assemble. She smiled a blue-toothed grin and announced, "Winner, winner, chicken dinner! This has to be one the worst wine I've ever had in my life." She wanted to add, "Shame on you for even bottling this crap. Serve it, and I guarantee you will lose."

Brad followed her out of the tasting room later that night.

Unfortunately, he was going to try to have another conversation with her. She wished he'd just keep hanging out with Davide and Antonio; they were so much more his people in intellect and self-absorption. Heck, Marco was even warming up to him. Rumor was, they'd all gone bar hopping the night before.

"Diana, wait up!" he said as she quickened her pace.

Whirling around, she almost ran into him. Brad put his arms up to stop her.

"What do you want?"

"Could we please talk?"

It was inevitable.

They ended up standing between the two cottages, talking in the dark. She wasn't about to invite him inside.

"I just wanted to let you know that I forgive you for what you did," he said.

It was hard to keep from laughing at such a ludicrous statement.

"What exactly did I do?" she asked.

"Throwing all my clothes out of the condo."

"You should be happy I didn't throw you out of that condo window, Brad."

"What is wrong with you? Why do you say things like that?"

"When do you think you will own up to your bad acts? You cheated on me in my bed with a woman who was my friend. That creates a lot of rage."

"Well, at least it got your attention."

"It is old news, Brad. Be thankful we didn't do something really stupid like getting married."

"We can pick up—"

"No, we can't."

"You love me. I still love you," he said, "Don't throw that away."

"I don't love you anymore."

"Don't say that—"

It was then that they heard it, the screech of something rather inhuman.

Brad asked, "What the hell was that?"

Diana didn't want to wait around to find out. She pulled out her pepper spray.

And then she saw a large shadow moving through the vines about a hundred feet away.

"Holy shit!" Brad yelled. "Do you see that? What is it?"

Brad sounded scared. She would have taken satisfaction in that if it hadn't been for the fact that she was terrified of the large shadow slowly meandering toward them.

"It might be a cougar," she said calmly.

"A what? You can't be serious."

She was very serious. Logan had been right, damn it!

"They have cougars here. Get behind me. I've got pepper spray," she said as she armed the spray.

"Are you fucking kidding me? Pepper spray isn't going to take down a cougar," he said as he stepped toward her and tripped.

He tripped on one of the little boxwoods that outlined each cottage. His ensuing scream as he went down caused several things to happen at once. First, he bumped into Diana, who had her finger on the trigger of the pepper spray. When he hit her, she tensed, and the released streams of the potent bear spray. As it happened, Brad's body was dropping, but his face was at a perfect angle to intercept the potent chemical. His ensuing screams awakened the dead and scared away the cougar.

The shape simply vanished as Brad fell to the ground screaming like the graceless wonder that he was. Unfortunately, Diana got caught up in his legs and landed on top of him.

Marco and Davide arrived first with flashlights. Diana ended up on the grass, spread eagle from where Brad had tossed her off of him. Brad lay next to her, crying, rubbing his eyes, and screaming obscenities.

The other men looked down at them with confused expressions. They had no idea what to make of the scene before them.

"We saw a cougar. He tripped and fell on me. The pepper spray went off in my hand. It hit him in the face."

She spoke in short sentences, which they appeared to understand. In the end, they were laughing as they helped both her and Brad to their feet.

It took over an hour for the pepper spray to stop reacting with Brad's mucous membranes. Brad complained like a little kid as his eyes swelled shut and liquid poured from his nose. Diana couldn't help it; she thought, on some level, he deserved it as she opened a second box of tissues and placed them before him.

"I can't believe you did this to me," he cried.

"I didn't do it to you on purpose. It was an accident."

"It was assault," he countered.

"Let's just say that it makes us even."

"Wait until I tell Stephan."

"Let's get him on speakerphone and tell him together."

"Does anything rattle you, Diana?" he asked.

She thought on that for a moment and replied, "Not doing my best for a client. I still think the next-door neighbor shouldn't be underestimated. He is smart and cunning."

"Would you give it a rest?" Brad said, his voice sounding so husky, she had to smile.

"I could have the leaves tested."

"No, the client has told you what he wants. Let it go."

Good, she thought. At least she offered. Her conscience was clear.

# CHAPTER TWENTY-FOUR

L ogan watched the footage from his game cameras as he drank a glass of his special Pinot. This was becoming his daily entertainment. And it had already been a good day, and he felt like celebrating. His water rights had been renewed. He had another loan, but soon he would have the funds to pay it down. If only he could go back in time and negotiate the riparian rights at the beginning of the land purchase 150 years ago that had created Forget-Me-Not winery and had stipulated renewal of water rights every ten years, he would. His relatives had been naïve. If he had enough money in a year or two, he was going to hire a hydrologist and get his own damn well. He never wanted to be in this position again.

Whatever happened tomorrow night at the final competition, he still had a fighting chance. If he lost, he'd have to work harder than he'd ever worked. But if he won, all the problems that seemed so large would simply dissolve. And then he'd have new challenges, challenges he wouldn't mind having, like expanding his operation to include sparkling wine. And proving to the love of his life that she needed to give them another chance.

Did he feel bad outsmarting the D'Salvos? No, the last few months had triggered a very basic need to fight within him. He was in the middle of a Hatfields and McCoys battle, and it was happening when he stepped out of the front door of his house. They had seriously underestimated him. They needed to be taught a lesson, and he couldn't wait to school them. From what Logan could piece together, there had been bad blood for years. His uncle had noticed a closeness between Logan's mother and Salvatore D'Salvo when they were teenagers. He'd put a stop to the budding relationship, and it hadn't ended well. Salvatore married Sophia, but Logan's mother hadn't had the happily ever after. She'd been denied her true love and died giving birth to Logan. His uncle had told Logan that his father was a seasonal winery worker, the result of a rebound love relationship for his mother, but Logan was always suspicious.

Then history repeated with the next generation. Logan remembered the day he'd finally figured it out. Julianna was distant even before the affair, but then she started acting giddy. There were new purchases of lingerie appearing on his credit card. Lingerie he wasn't seeing. And her reading to children one day a week at the local grade school became four days a week. Then he started watching the game cameras on his land, and they caught something they shouldn't.

He still remembered the day he saw Julianna and Marco kissing where their properties met on Game Camera Seven. The same place where, two years later, he had staged the tainted black rot. He still couldn't believe Marco was so stupid as to not put it together.

He pulled up Game Camera Seven to watch for any more clandestine meetings with Peter and his neighbors.

His thoughts had drifted once again to Diana, who, like some sort of magician, appeared on the screen of his computer. He set the wine glass down hard, almost knocking it over. His heart gave a little quiver. Damn it! He missed her.

What was the hell was she doing?

He knew she liked to walk along the property line, but she hadn't done it since they had that final, stupid blowout.

He checked the time on the camera. She'd walked out early that morning before it got hot in a pink t-shirt and a pair of navy shorts, which completely distracted him. He hadn't seen her in shorts in years, but she looked good. Hell, she looked great. Her long legs were tan and shapely, as he remembered. He hoped she had remembered the pepper spray. He had seen fresh cougar sign just that morning and was considering a warning phone to her.

Now, as he watched, she climbed the short fence between the properties and walked over to where six of his grapevines had been removed. He'd purposefully left a few leaves behind to further put fear in the hearts of his neighbors. That possibly hadn't been a good idea in retrospect.

Pulling a little plastic bag from a pocket in her shorts, she placed a couple of leaves in the bag and then took a large sniff of the contents.

She wouldn't be able to smell anything on those leaves. He'd made sure of that.

"Clever girl," he muttered and felt that little chill of discomfort grab hold of him. What was she planning to do?

Run to the nearest lab and get them tested?

Had he expected less of her?

No, in fact, he'd have been surprised if she hadn't wanted to take a look. He was just a little surprised she wasn't taking the D'Salvos at their word. They'd taken enough samples a week earlier that he thought if anything was going to come of it, he'd know by now. Obviously not.

He wasn't out of the woods yet, but the delay had given him the time he needed to negotiate the water rights and strategize. It had been so worth it. And knowing that the game with Diana was still on, the thought of what was yet to come made him quite happy. This would tell Logan the truth of their relationship. Would she out him to the D'Salvos? Or side with him? That was yet to be seen. She liked to win. She was the most competitive woman he'd ever met. He turned to his computer and browsed the Wave website to see her photo again.

Logan glanced down at Diana's photo. He had it bad. Contest be damned, this thing between them wasn't over.

He didn't know how this could possibly work, but Lady Luck seemed to be looking favorably upon him.

He'd gambled so much. Why not truly raise the stakes and go all in?

Before he picked up the phone to implement what he now considered to be his "Plan C," he called down to the tasting room and asked to have Peter sent up to the house.

While he waited for the intern to arrive, he gave Ginger a peanut butter-filled Kong toy that he'd placed in the freezer. It was one of her favorite treats and might make her a little more amenable to Peter. Secretly, he loved his dog's ability to judge character.

But when Peter appeared, she started growling. Logan banished her to one of the large leather chairs, deciding he wanted her in the room when he talked to the now scared intern. Ginger would lick at the frozen peanut butter in the Kong eight or nine times, then would raise her head, narrow her eyes, look at Peter, growl a bit, lower her head, and go back to the Kong. It felt right.

"Sit down, Peter. Would you like glass?" he asked as he grabbed one of the bottles of his prized Pinot Noir.

The kid didn't know what to say, so Logan poured him a glass and handed it to him. They sat across from each other, Logan's desk between them.

"We need to talk," he said and hit the PLAY button on his computer and turned the screen to face the boy. It was the footage from a week earlier. The screen clearly showed Peter handing Marco a baggie of leaves.

Peter set the glass down on Logan's desk and put his face in his hands.

"Would you like to explain?"

"Logan, I'm sorry—"

"Why did you do it?" Logan asked.

"I didn't want to. I wanted to learn from you and help you this summer. I never meant to hurt anybody."

"What changed?"

"I met Marco. He talked to me one day over the fence. And then he just like wouldn't leave me alone. He, like, knew about my mom and dad, even knew their names and where they lived."

Peter had never mentioned his family. Logan knew they lived in Portland, but other than that, they were a mystery to him. Perhaps he should have asked more. Peter was over twenty-one, so he hadn't needed any parental consent to have their son work in his winery.

"What about them? What do they have to do with anything?" Logan asked.

Peter looked away, but when his eyes returned to Logan, he started talking and didn't stop until he spilled his entire story in a rush of confession.

"My dad lost his job last year. And then my mom was like diagnosed with breast cancer, and they don't have health insurance. Mom's going to be okay, but they're about to lose the house. Mom's medical bills are like $10,000 a month. Marco offered to pay for Mom's treatment. I didn't know what to do. They're my Mom and Dad, you know?"

Logan has suspected there were issues, but he didn't know they were this bad. His heart went out to the kid.

"How did it start?"

"He approached me when I was working on the irrigation. He already knew me, knew about my parents and stuff. He said he wanted to help, and it wouldn't hurt you. That it wouldn't like make a difference in the end."

"Which was probably the moment you should have come to me?"

"Yeah."

"What did you tell him, and what did you get for your trouble?"

Marco had given him envelopes filled with money for information, but he was disappointed with the lack of information Peter was able to provide.

"Then he asked me to break into The Vault and, like, dump all of PN 13."

"How did he know about it?" Logan asked, hoping he wouldn't hear Diana's name.

"I gave him samples of all the wines in The Vault. I know, I know, I shouldn't have done that. The Pinot was the one he thought was the best. But I couldn't do it, Logan! Not after I got to know everybody like you are really cool, and you've been really nice to me."

"But you still broke into The Vault and poured out the wine."

"I couldn't go through with it. I felt too awful. I got through about seventy-five barrels, and I just couldn't do another. All that wine. It looked like blood. When Marco found out, he was pissed. He threatened to go to the police and turn me in."

"How ironic."

"I'll make it up to you, Logan, whatever you want me to do. Please don't call the cops. I could work for you for free and make it up to you."

"You dumped almost a quarter-million dollars worth of wine. And that is the very low-ball estimate. I don't think that working off that balance is a viable solution."

Peter looked like he was about to be sick. But despite what he had done, this stupid kid was giving Logan a lot to think about.

Logan hadn't known his biological parents. It had taken a long time for him to come to peace with it. From his birth, his aunt and uncle had been there. They hadn't been able to have children of their own. He had been everything to them, and they had been the most wonderful parents in the world. He respected them for keeping his mother's memory alive. He just wished he could have met her. As for his father, the possibilities that kept circling back to him weren't all that positive.

"Tell me about Marco's reaction to the black rot."

# CHAPTER TWENTY-FIVE

The day of the competition had Diana out the door before eight a.m. She made the early, last-minute appointment the day before, and there was no way she was going to miss it.

The kid who opened the classroom door at the local community college hardly looked old enough to be out of high school. But he was the Head of the Plant Biology Department and had a doctorate in Botany. It had taken a few phone calls, but he had agreed to see Diana. She thought it was probably her use of the words confidential and top-secret that swayed his decision in her favor. Deep down, everyone enjoyed a little cloak and dagger.

As "Dr. Greg" looked at the grape leaf through a microscope, she paced, knowing that she looked as nervous as she felt.

He jerked his head up and asked, "You think this is black rot?"

"No, actually, I don't. It is something that is made to look like black rot."

After the man-boy said his next words, Diana quickly thanked him and felt vindicated.

There was still time. She had twelve hours until the competition. Mountain Valley Vineyards would win or lose, but it would be a fair fight. She would see to that. Damn Logan, he'd almost bested her, but in time, if everything went the way she thought it would go, he'd thank her for her integrity.

Once in the car, Diana paused. Should she tell Marco and Salvatore?

No.

She loved Logan, but she had a contract with Mountain Valley Vineyards. But she loved Logan. Marco and Salvatore didn't want her to get the leaf tested, so she wouldn't tell them the result.

For her own peace of mind, she had to find out. She had a feeling Logan was being a strategic businessman as much as he was testing her. Seeing what she might do, judging her reaction, personally and professionally.

On the way to her cabin, Brad opened the door of Chardonnay and stuck his head out.

"Diana?"

"Brad."

He was still brooding and angry about the pepper spray. They'd done a good job of being civil to each other in front of the client, but when they were alone, the gloves were off.

She wondered for the hundredth time how she could have ever gotten so close to someone who was so wrong for her.

"Good morning, Diana," Brad said as he buttoned one his starched oxford shirts. His eyes still looked a little bloodshot.

Turning, she regarded him with narrowed eyes. What now?

"Good morning, Brad. What can I do for you?" she asked, trying her best to be cordial.

"We need to talk."

"No, we don't."

"I know about you and Logan Parrish."

"What exactly do you think you know?" she asked.

"He's the guy who ruined you for everyone, including me. Isn't he? That's why this is so personal for you."

"He's our competitor. Anything else you have to say isn't relevant," she replied as her heart beat faster and face flushed.

Brad was right, it may have started out that way, but now things were different.

"When Salvatore called Wave, I told Stephan about your past relationship with Logan Parrish. How much you hated him. It was why Stephan chose you for this. You're ruthless any day of the week, but when someone displeases you, you go for the jugular. I should know. I mean, just look at me," he said, indicating his face.

"I told Stephan about knowing Logan Parrish. I didn't hide anything," she replied, discomfort creeping into every cell in her body. She had told Brad about Logan when they were dating, but she hadn't mentioned his name, never quite went into all the details. How he had guessed as much, she didn't know. Now he was playing the victim. She didn't want to step into this, needed to keep her head straight for the night ahead.

"Stephan dangled the partner carrot in front of you, just in case you had any second thoughts."

"Thanks for cheating on me. Made me see your true character," she said as she slowly burned.

"What's it going to take for us to go back to the way it was, Diana?"

"What do you mean?"

"You need to lose this for the client, but I know you want to win. Because if you win this thing, you will finally have your revenge. Will you finally be able to give yourself to someone, to be vulnerable, to love? Can we finally forget the past and move on with our future?"

"I know how to love, and because I know what love is, I know we don't have a future. And the client wants us to lose, so we will lose."

"I was serious when I told you that I only had the affair to get your attention."

"And I was serious when I threw your clothing out the

277

window of my condo. We're finished. I don't forgive that kind of betrayal."

"Give it a little time, Diana. You'll forgive me."

"No, Brad, get it through your thick skull—we are over."

Now it was time to fight for the man she'd always wanted. *Logan.*

Diana stood before the mirror in her cottage, feeling nervous. She had done something and hoped it wasn't the worst mistake of her life. She'd found the best wine that Mountain Valley had to offer, and it would be on display tonight. She'd discretely switched the bottles less than an hour ago.

The man she loved would win tonight based on the merits of his wine, not because of any gimmicks. He'd never have to wonder if he was good enough to beat Mountain Valley. When this was all over, he'd know he had done it on his own merits as a winemaker. She'd tell him.

She had done something scary and rash and out of love.

And if he didn't win? Well, she'd go anywhere he wanted to go. Fuck the partnership, not that she'd have a job to worry about anyway.

Tonight, she was the designated representative of the Mountain Valley Vineyards for the final event. Logan was representing himself. They alone would work with the chefs in the kitchen at the Stark Hotel in downtown Portland. The rest of the competition was anonymous. The wine would be poured into lettered decanters, and no one would know which wine belonged to whom. The panel of six judges would vote, ranking the dishes with a "1" or a "2." At the end of the night, the votes would be tallied, and the competitor with the most "1's" would be a winner. There were four courses with six judges made a total of twenty-four votes to be cast. In the event of a tie, the six judges would have a final, head-to-head tasting of Pinot Noirs. The Majority vote wins.

The press, the guests, and the competitors that didn't make it to the final round got to sit in the same room as gallery observers. They would dine on wine and appetizers, courtesy of the Stark Hotels, as they watched the competition and heard the comments of the judges. They could not speak or comment.

Diana reached into her closet and grabbed the black cocktail gown she had planned to wear for this final competition. It was a tasteful black silk crepe sheath with clear sequins. It was from some Italian designer and had cost a small fortune, but it was insipid, and it looked boring to her now as she stared at it. It was conservative and professional, just right for the occasion. Just safe enough to make Diana look perfect. She was glad in that moment that she had planned so well as to know what she was wearing for the final competition, but the very sight of the dress now made her angry. Her mind was very much on other things as she struggled into her silk stockings and conservative heels.

She had to hand it to Logan; he was very clever. The fighter she always knew he was, and not only did that lite a fire in her belly, it made her proud of his protectiveness of the family business. Once again, he confirmed by his actions why her love for him has never dwindled. If only they could have the happily ever after she longed for. Tonight was the ultimate leap of faith.

He was too clever for Marco and Salvatore. They'd never seen him coming. But she had. She suspected him, and then she'd been proven right.

"Damn it!" she yelled as she stuck a fingertip through the fine knit of her expensive silk stocking. As she pulled off the ruined stocking, she dropped onto the soft mattress in the Merlot Cottage. She was taking a personal gamble tonight. Everything was on the line, the contract, her job, and Logan. She only cared about Logan.

She grabbed her pillow and buried her face in it. What if it didn't work out? What if it blew up in her face? What if she'd made a mistake? Why was it never easy?

She marched back to the closet and started pulling at the clothes until she found the dress she hadn't had the nerve to wear. It was a low-cut, backless halter-style silk dress that hugged every curve of her body. The skirt was short, and the heels were high. Thanks to her ruined stockings, her bare, tanned legs would get a lot of exposure.

She didn't feel like being "safe" or "perfect." She felt like kicking some damn ass!

⸰⊛⸰⊛⸰

Logan wore a navy suit with a patterned dark red silk tie the color of Pinot Noir. He wasn't used to dressing up, but this occasion called for a certain image. He hoped once he had secured this contract that, he could revert to his comfortable jeans.

As he tied his tie in the master bathroom mirror, he thought of Diana. He wanted to see her tonight. He wanted to make this right. And he could, once the damn competition was finally over.

He'd played with her. He could admit that. He had tried to mess with her confidence, and based on all the activity he had witnessed, it had worked. But unlike their college days, this time, he hadn't meant to hurt her. He'd played dirty. He only hoped that in time, after he explained it all, she could forgive him. Logan had done what he'd done to take a stab at his real, intended enemy, Marco. Maybe Diana would understand that.

His life was forever changed because of Marco's actions. It was one thing to forgive, quite another to forget. And a lesson too that Marco and the D'Salvos needed to learn and should have been taught generations ago. You do not mess with the Parrish's. And Logan was a Parrish, through and through.

Bending, he petted Ginger, who had been watching him from the corner of her perch on the bed.

"I'll make you proud, and after tonight, it is done. I promise. After this, we move forward," he said as she looked earnestly into his eyes.

She tilted her head as if she understood every word he'd said.

"And if we are lucky, she won't be able to walk away. You'd like having her around, wouldn't you, girl?" He gave Ginger's velvet ears one last rub for luck and kissed the top of her head before he left for the competition.

# CHAPTER TWENTY-SIX

Diana arrived at the flagship Stark Hotel in downtown Portland, the site of the competition, where she had begun this journey over two months ago. She immediately went into the kitchen to make sure her chef was already there. He greeted her coolly.

"I upgraded the wine, but I need it to be our little secret," she whispered.

"Thank God," he said and shook his head, then whispered. "That was some of the worst wine I've ever tasted."

A waiter helped her carry the wine inside so that it could be decanted and labeled. Logan was already there, her heart skipping a beat, when she saw him looking wicked handsome in a navy suit. He was chatting with his chef and didn't seem to notice her, but the moment he did, she felt it, her heart beating double-time.

"Diana," he said in a tone that was infused with intimacy as he took several steps toward her. "Good luck tonight."

She leaned in close and whispered, "I know what you did."

Leaning back from her, his expression quizzical, he said, "I'm not sure I follow you."

"The black rot. You purposefully killed several of your own plants right next to the property line," she said through clenched teeth.

Logan ran his eyes over her body and the black halter dress that hugged her every curve. His gaze lingered a little too long on her cleavage and then finally met her eyes. The dress had been a great decision.

"I don't think anything that happens on Forget-Me-Not land is any of your business," he said as a slow, calculating smile graced his lips.

Diana wanted to punch him. And hug him. After her stint working for the DeSalvo's and knowing some of the past saga between the two families, she was glad he was getting his revenge.

"Maybe I want to make it my business," Diana said.

Logan smiled and asked, "Really?"

"Yes, I hope you have extra room in your closet because I'm moving in tomorrow."

"What?" Logan asked, taken aback and then smiling, confused. "Aren't you going home?"

"Nope. I'm moving in. I'm fighting for us. Think on that for the next few hours," she said and then turned to walk away.

Logan caught up with her ten seconds later. "Hey, we need to talk. Are you serious? Because I hope you are."

Diana said, "I'm serious, but I'm in business mode now. We'll have to talk about us later. You now know my plan, so deal with it. Now, let's talk about your little black rot scheme. You didn't keep it to your land; you tried to intimidate us—"

"You trespassed, stepped over to my property, and took samples," he said, cutting her off. "Not to mention Marco keeping a spy on my staff for the last three months. Don't try to deny it. I've got the camera footage to prove it."

When she didn't respond, his smile grew larger. "Oh gee, you mean Marco didn't tell you they had my intern, Peter, on their payroll?"

Diana didn't know what to say. "I have no idea what you are talking about."

"Come on, Di. Think about it."

"Peter? That little nerd with the bad hair who is scared of his own shadow?" she asked, trying to piece it together. She'd met the awkward boy a couple of times at the different events but never thought he was connected to Mountain Valley Vineyards.

"So Salvatore and Marco didn't tell you? Ah, I see…That way, you could try to deny it if you were ever asked. But just so we're clear, I know all about him. I've let him think he was a valued member of my staff, but all the while, I've fed him exactly the information I wanted him to share."

"I didn't know about Peter," she said. Thinking back on it, she might have seen him talking with Marco but never thought much of it. Marco spoke with many of the winemakers in the county, so him speaking with Peter on rare occasion wasn't unusual.

"Well then, you've been the perfect little pawn, and for that, I'm thankful," he said.

"I know you faked the black rot. I know you wanted us to sabotage the competition for fear we wouldn't be able to fulfill this contract when we win. But guess what? I discovered it in time."

"Good for you. Bet it made you the hero in their eyes."

"Really, Logan—" That's when Diana decided there was no need Logan needed to know that she never told them.

"And there is the whole other matter of you collecting samples two days ago… trespassing on my land."

"Oh, like I've never done it before? Please."

"And since we are being so honest," he said, his tone a little sharper, "Just when did they ask you to get close to me? Or is this little threat to move in something you came up with to throw me off my game tonight?"

<hr />

Logan watched the color drain from Diana's face. Good. He wanted her angry. Mad at him. It was the only way he'd know the truth. Possibly the only way they'd be able to get everything out in the open. Though his gut suspected what they had wasn't part of her contract with the D'Salvos.

He saw her lip tremble a moment before she grabbed a loaf of French bread from a basket that was conveniently next to her and hit him with it. The first blow caught him on the side of his face, the second on his chin. He let her get in three hits before he grabbed her wrist and pinned her to the cool brick wall behind them.

"Enough," he said, gazing into her angry tiger-striped eyes.

"I'm just getting started," she said as her left hand reached for and found a second loaf of the hard bread. "How dare you accuse me of trying to get information out of you? After what we shared? I love you, you asshole. And you deserve to get hit after the sprinkler."

The noise around them ceased as the chefs, and sous chefs stared in open-mouthed horror at their two rival wineries got dirty in the kitchen.

"Do you mean it? You love me?" he asked. Logan did not want to cause her another moment of pain. Nor did he want to be away from her for one more day; not one more moment. That was the second he decided he was going to marry her.

"Yes, you dumbass. Nothing matters but us," she said and as a tear trickled down her cheek.

"I just needed to know—" He'd discuss this all with her later, but right now, Logan was the happiest man on earth.

"Two minutes to the first course!" the maître de from Stark Hotels interrupted as he came through the door. Noticing the silence he was greeted with, he promptly took in the scene before him and crossed to where Logan and Diana were leaning against the wall.

"What is going on here?" he asked. He looked at Logan. "Your chin is bleeding."

"Nothing," they both said in unison as Logan let go of her arm, and the bread fell to the floor.

"I won't have a brawl in my kitchen. Step back, Mr. Parrish. Ms. Hunter, stop abusing him with that French bread."

Logan did as he was asked. Diana looked at him with a tenderness that struck his heart.

"If you two can't get along," the maître de continued, "You will be removed from the kitchen and relegated to the gallery. Is that understood?"

They both nodded, but then Logan said, "We aren't arguing. We were just discussing how we love each other."

"You love me?" Diana asked.

"Yes, Di, I'm in love with you."

Diana smiled and said, "I'm sorry about your chin."

Feeling a little dampness on his chin, he touched it. His finger came back crimson. The crust had sharp edges. He had two minutes to clean himself up before appearing in front of the judges.

She grabbed a damp paper towel and pushed it against his chin. When the bleeding stopped, they parted to their mutual corners of the kitchen.

He looked at the plates that had been assembled by his crew and nodded as Diana did the same across the kitchen.

The dishes were taken out side by side, followed by Diana and himself.

The judges, who were all owners of the Stark Hotel, were introduced. They were Alex and Daisy Stark, Adam and Laura Stark, and Mitch and Rebecca Wilder. Daisy waved warmly, having met them all before.

"Welcome, I know you know all our names, and you might recognize the ladies from the tastings, but let me make it a bit more informal. This is my sweet husband, Alex. That pretty lady at the end of the table is his sister Rebecca with her handsome husband, Mitch. And this gorgeous couple in the middle are our cousins, Adam and the very famous artist, Laura Hokensen Stark, his wife."

Logan was shocked. He'd heard of Laura Hokensen. She was incredibly talented. Maybe with Diana's help, he could get her to paint the view at Forget-Me-Not.

Diana and Logan had each written a brief description that was read to the judges by the supposedly impartial maître de, who still looked pissed off during the blind tasting. Logan had started with his Pinot Gris and a seafood crostino of lightly smoked scallops sliced thin over a puree of Tuscan white beans, flavored with a little shaving of black truffle. Diana had also picked a Pinot Gris with a light appetizer of roasted vegetable pate that looked elegant and colorful but wouldn't be a match for his scallops.

The judges' careful comments were benign. Logan observed that they ate more of his crostini than they did of Diana's pate, but the wine was what mattered. They held the glasses up to the light, sniffed them, tasted, and then made notes on their score sheets.

The plates and glasses were cleared.

Logan had glanced at the gallery of observers before he returned to the kitchen. He saw Ben, Tess, and William, who waved his way and smiled. Peter looked at him sheepishly. They'd been through a lot in the last forty-eight hours, and it wasn't over yet.

He eyes narrowed on Diana's ex-fiancé, Brad. Aware he was being watched, the other man smiled and blew a kiss toward Diana. Diana ignored the kiss, her eyes laser-focused on the judges. Logan fought every urge he had to stop himself from crossing the room and starting something with Brad. He looked like a jerk.

They filed silently back to the kitchen and watched as the finishing touches were made to the salads.

"I'm sorry about your chin," Diana said, looking at the Caesar salads on her side of the kitchen.

"No, you're not. We are now even for the sprinklers," Logan said, with a half-laugh, then he kissed her quickly.

"You're right," she said, "I'm not sorry, but I'll never do it again."

"Two minutes!" the maître de yelled as he gave them each a glaring look.

"What are you serving with the salad?" he asked, his question taking her by surprise.

Turning her eyes on him, she smiled sweetly and said, "A zesty little Sauvignon Blanc."

"Did I tell you that I'm getting back into the sparkling business?" he asked.

"Good, you should," she said. "I love your sparkling."

"Because it reminded me of our first reunion date. I wish I'd handled that a little differently. I shouldn't have stopped kissing you when I did."

Placing a hand on his arm, she warned, "I know we have to be all professional, but I wish we could leave and go home, open a bottle of your sparkling, and you could make it up to me."

"My home, our home," he said, trying on the phrase. When she nodded, his heart fluttered.

"Why did you do it?" she whispered.

"Stop kissing you? I was a little out of practice, I suppose... I couldn't believe you were back in my arms. I can't believe that I have been away from you for the last two weeks."

"It has been a really hard two weeks," she said.

"Never again, Diana."

# CHAPTER TWENTY-SEVEN

Diana had made him bleed. She felt bad. She hadn't meant to hurt him, not like that anyway. Diana had wanted to get his attention and make a point. Instead, she had clubbed him like a little girl punching a bully.

He'd forgiven her. He said he loved her. She told him she loved him. It was going to be okay.

They stood before the judges and listened.

*"This sparkling Chardonnay is such a fun choice,"* Laura Stark *commented.*

*Alex Stark said, "It was a little flashy, but it is good with the beets and the balsamic vinegar…"*

*Rebecca said, "I didn't think sparkling wine has any place in the menu except with dessert…"*

*Mitch said, "Then it probably shouldn't be your drink of choice in the afternoons, honey."*

*Laura scrunched up her face, "Is it my imagination, or is this Sauvignon quite lemony…"*

*Daisy agreed, "It is a bit harsh for the delicate lettuce…"*

The points and counterpoints went on and on. And mostly, the positive comments appeared to be for Logan. Good!

After listening to mediocre reviews of her wine, Diana looked to the gallery, where Salvatore gave her a shrug. Eventually, he'd figure out that she switched the wines. She only hoped he wouldn't figure it out until the competition was over.

Back in the kitchen, the chefs were making the final preparations on their main courses.

"Let me guess," she said to Logan, "You've made chicken."

He smiled and said, "No. Filet with Port reduction and my new, spectacular three-year-old Pinot Noir. You know, what's left of it."

She thought he had lost all the Pinot Noir in the vandalism. Without thinking, she blurted out as much. "I thought you lost that vintage in the burglary."

"Don't you mean the vintage Peter tried unsuccessfully to destroy because Marco was bribing him to dump it?"

"To repeat, I had no knowledge of it then, and I have no knowledge of it now," she said, feeling the blood pump in her temples. "Do you have any proof Marco is involved? And by that, I mean anything that could nail the little snaggle-toothed bastard?"

"Yes, I do. And Peter isn't a bad kid. He just got manipulated into doing something he knew was wrong. You should have seen him the next day. He looked like roadkill."

"How does Marco fit into this?" she asked.

"You'll see. He isn't going to get away with it."

"Good. I hope you nail his ass. How is sweet Ginger?"

"She misses you," he said, his eyes meeting hers. "Why wait until tomorrow? Come home with me tonight. The closet space is available."

She kissed the tip of her finger and touched it to the cut on his chin. "I think that can be arranged."

She didn't want to be here. She wanted to be with him, curled in front of the fire on a stormy night with Ginger lying at their feet.

"I'm glad you didn't lose your valuable wine," she said, but unable to stop herself, she added in a low whisper, "I hope you don't lose your business. I hope you don't lose your vineyard. We can't lose us."

"Two minutes to main!" the maître de yelled and then cut them a look of warning.

"This time is forever. And Diana?" Logan asked softly. "I want you to know, I bought an airline ticket to see you that November."

She didn't understand. "But you didn't come."

"My aunt died at the end of September, and I couldn't leave. She was the only mother I'd ever known. I was hurting. My uncle was destroyed."

"You never told me that." She felt the shock cover her face with this revelation.

"I started running the vineyard in a matter of days. I'd never felt more alone until...well...these last two years."

"I could've helped," she said, her throat painful and tight.

"I should've told you," he said, his eyes so earnest she couldn't look away.

She shook her head. "You shouldn't have ever let me go."

He leaned in until his lips were touching her ear. "I can't let you go again. I can't—"

"I love you," she said.

"Diana!" her chef called, pulling her attention away from Logan. With a quick, apologetic glance to Logan, she turned back to her chef.

"I need you!" he yelled.

She went to him as he held up two spoons. She tried both sauces and made a decision.

"That one," she said, holding up the spoon in her left hand.

The chef looked frustrated as he said, "You just picked the one that doesn't have your wine in the sauce."

"Yeah, no surprise there," she said.

"Yeah, well, what do you want me to do?" he asked.

"Use the one with our wine, of course," she replied.

Stepping back to Logan, she met his eyes and waited. His arm encircled her waist, and he pulled her close, his hand warm and lovingly stroking the bare skin of her back, and then he kissed her. Somewhere in the background, someone dropped a metal ladle on the metal countertop; someone whistled, and finally, there was silence.

When Logan broke the kiss, it took her a moment to remember where she was.

"What the hell is wrong with you two?" the maître de asked.

"Would you prefer I was hitting him with something?" she asked, blinking away a tear, not looking at the little man, her eyes focused on Logan.

Logan kissed her again, so softly that some rough part of her insides melted like warm chocolate.

"For the love of God, stop gawking.... Go, go!" the maître de yelled to the staff.

Feeling like the world had shifted off its axis, Diana let Logan lead her out of the kitchen.

As they prepared to listen to the judge's comments, Logan's hand brushed hers. She fought the urge to grab it and hold on for dear life.

Then the judges began their discussion.

*"I really hate to say this, but I simply don't care for the sauce, it's just, well, harsh,"* Laura complained.

*Her husband agreed with her, "Laura, you are right. I don't like the sharpness of the Pinot, and knowing it is in the sauce is a rather unpleasant experience..."*

*"Yes, I like the other sauce over the filets because it isn't made of a very complementary wine. And wasn't one of our competitors clever? They found a way to incorporate a fifth wine into our experience,"* Daisy said.

*Her husband added, "Darling, that is a port in the sauce, not just wine!"*

The praise for Logan's Pinot Noir and his Port made Diana secretly happy. She didn't even know he had any Port.

*"And this Pinot! I didn't know that either one of your wineries had such a vintage. What a lovely surprise,"* Rebecca added.

*Mitch said, "This is the best thing we tried all evening..."*

She wondered what they'd have said if she used the alternative wines. She didn't think she could have handled what surely would have been a bloodbath.

By unspoken agreement, she and Logan ended up back in their dark corner of the kitchen.

"How fast can you pack up your cottage?" Logan asked, making her head spin for all the wrong reasons.

"Already started. Just give me ten minutes," she said as she leaned against him.

"Two minutes!" the little maître de announced, appearing, holding his fingers annoyingly close to Diana's face.

"What about your job in Seattle?"

"Who cares? I love you more than any damn job," she said. "I can't be away from you."

"One minute!" the maître de yelled, then he walked over to Diana and Logan. "You two," he said, pointing at them, "Get the fuck in the game. What the hell?"

⁜

Sometime the day before, when he'd watched the camera footage and felt his heart warm in a way it hadn't in at least two years, the decision was made. Logan was in love with her, and he wasn't going to screw it up. His heart wouldn't allow it. He wouldn't allow it.

Once he removed all the drama around the contest, realized that Forget-Me-Not was, against the odds, going to survive, he'd seen his future. He'd seen a future with Diana. She was still the same girl who he'd fallen in love with twelve years ago. Fate had given him a second chance, and he wasn't about to mess it up. However, that didn't prevent him from making sure that she would fight for them this time. That she wouldn't let him go.

"Diana!" her chef was calling to her, and they both made

their way to the waiting dessert plates. Flourless chocolate cake with fresh raspberry for him, bread pudding for her.

"Taste this," Diana's chef said, shoving a spoon at Diana as his chef handed him a fork with a sample of the cake. It was decadently rich. It would need the red wine he'd chosen to cut the richness. The port would taste sweet next to the cake. Perfect.

Diana was nodding her head in agreement with her chef.

"That is fantastic," she said and then moved around the table to give him a hug.

Her chef said, "I don't know what is going on between you and your competitor, but I hope it is turning out the way you want it to."

"It's better," Logan interrupted as he pulled Diana close and held her to him.

The dessert plates went out the door to the waiting judges.

Diana walked out ahead of Logan. He smiled. His next move was going to completely surprise her. It had completely surprised her boss.

"Hey," he said before they completely left the kitchen, "Good luck."

"My money is on you," she said.

They stood side by side, close enough that his pant leg brushed against her bare leg. This competition had been nerve racking, and their kitchen entertainment would no doubt be the talk of the industry in a day or two.

They still had one big chunk of unfinished business.

*Mitch started, "Interesting that they chose a brandy for the bread pudding…. It is lovely, really lovely."*

*"This chocolate is death by chocolate, and it brings out the fruit in this chocolaty port," Daisy offered.*

*"But it is so rich. I could never eat a full portion," Rebecca said.*

*"Oh please, you could eat it. When we were kids, I saw you eat an entire chocolate cake," Alex offered.*

*Daisy wrapped it up. "Not only did we try some lovely wines, but we also now have some very wonderful new menu options to consider. Thank you both for a lovely menu. It isn't going to be an easy decision. Give us a few moments to tally the winner, and we will be making our announcement shortly. You both should be very proud of yourselves"*

There was no reason to go back to the kitchen, so Diana and Logan walked to the gallery, where chairs waited for both of them at their respective sides of the battlefield.

Diana gave him one last look that spoke volumes and then sat between Salvatore and Brad, who immediately started talking to her, their heads bent together.

Logan sat with his tasting room managers and Peter. Logan looked at the young man and nodded. It was almost showtime. Peter had spent the better part of the afternoon talking with Sheriff Baker, who now stood next to the doorway with three other officers. The kid was getting off lucky. Logan hadn't wanted to press charges, and the district attorney had allowed Peter to make a plea in exchange for testifying against Marco. That almost made them even for what Marco had done by seducing Logan's wife.

# CHAPTER TWENTY-EIGHT

Diana didn't mince words with Salvatore.

"You had a spy at Forget-Me-Not," she whispered.

"What are you talking about?" Salvatore asked as Marco slid his chair close and joined them.

"Did you pay him to vandalize Logan's storage area and dump the wine?"

Marco merely smiled as if Diana were especially dense.

"He didn't get it all," she replied. "He only got a third."

"Who told you that?" Marco asked.

"Who do you think?" she asked.

Brad finally spoke up. "Diana, stop. Wave cannot be a party to this conversation."

"Maybe I should just go to the police."

"Diana," Brad warned. "You can't. Remember the contract."

"What does it matter now? The contest is finished," Marco whispered, his snaggletooth a little too close. "I want you out of Merlot tonight."

"No problem," Diana said.

"Diana don't say another word," Brad warned again. "Mr. D'Salvo, Wave appreciates your business. If there is anything, we can help you with in the future, feel free to contact us."

Diana wasn't going to let this fly. She had a few choice words to share with the D'Salvos, but she didn't get a chance.

Daisy Stark started tapping a wine glass with a spoon to get everyone's attention. Waiters were lining up with bottles of champagne.

"Thank you, ladies and gentlemen. It is my great honor to announce that after careful consideration and a very close contest, the Stark Hotels has finally declared a winner." She then went on to thank all the wineries, asking for them to stand and get the applause they deserved. Diana looked toward Logan and found that he was looking back at her. Everyone else was looking at Daisy Stark, but not the two of them.

When at last, Daisy said, "Our new beverage partner, the winery to receive a coveted three-year contract with the Stark Hotels is Forget-Me-Not winery. Congratulations, Logan Parrish and all our new friends at Forget-Me-Not!"

The crowd erupted, and Diana lost track of Logan as he was encircled by well-wishers.

"We're leaving," Salvatore announced and stood, reaching for his wife's hand.

It was then that a man in a sheriff's uniform materialized in front of Marco. "Mr. Marco D'Salvo, you're under arrest." He read a laundry list of items. Then he said, "And once we've finished with you, the Las Vegas Police department is interested in discussing some of your business dealings from incidents a little over three years ago..."

Three years ago, right before Marco returned to Mountain Valley Vineyards, actions that set in motion the death of Logan's wife. Diana didn't know what to think. She just stepped away as Marco was read his rights in front of the entire crowd.

She couldn't see Logan for the swarm of people around him, but she decided it was time to leave, Brad right at her heels.

"Did you call the police?" he asked.

"No, I think Logan did," she replied.

"Did he tell you that?"

"Brad, it doesn't matter. Our client is a criminal. Give it up. We're done here."

"When you get back, we should have a meeting with Stephan. He will want to discuss several of the things I've seen."

"Have the meeting yourself. I'm not coming back."

"What?"

"I'm going to move in with Logan Parrish because I love him."

"Fine. Throw away your career."

"Shut up, Brad."

Brad started to speak but thought better of it. He wasn't going back to Mountain Valley Vineyards. She could tell his Panamera was packed. Obviously, he'd had it with the country life.

When neither one of them said another word, he stalked toward the lobby of the hotel. No doubt, he would get in his car and roar away in a cloud of exhausting ego.

Having lost Logan in the crowd, she made her way to the lobby and her waiting car. The rest of her life waited.

When she got back to the Merlot Cottage, she checked her watch. It was a little after eleven o'clock. She started her final packing.

Logan had won fair and square. He'd won!

Marco was probably enjoying a little vacation in the local jail. She wondered if there would be monetary damages for what he had done to Logan. She hoped so.

Still in her dress and heels, she walked around the cabin, picking up items that needed to be packed, and went through each drawer and cabinet for a last check.

She looked at her reflection in the floor-length mirror. The dress had been a good choice.

The knock on the cabin door had her almost falling off her heels. Her first thought was Marco. He'd hopefully still be at the police station. And if he wasn't, he wasn't stopping by to apologize.

Let it be Logan.

"Who is it?" she asked before opening the door.

"Logan," the voice called out as she threw open the door, smiled, and felt her heart give a little flutter.

He was still in the navy suit. His tie was off and poking out of his pocket.

"You still aren't leaving the porch light on. That's dangerous."

"It's my last night, so it doesn't matter."

"You left in a hurry. I was concerned."

"Well, it wasn't my party, not this time," she said. "And I needed to finish packing."

"I'm sorry you lost, but if you had to lose, I'm glad it was to me. I think we both won something tonight."

"We did. Congratulations, by the way. I wanted you. And I wanted you to win the competition."

They stared at each other for a good, long two seconds. She flew into his outstretched arms, and she murmured between kisses, "I always wanted it to be you."

He said, "I wouldn't have won without you. And I can't imagine anything without you, not ever again."

She shook her head and said, "You would have won without my help. Your wine is just better, I put up the best Mountain Valley had to offer, and they still lost."

"Even with a man on the inside," he said.

"I wish I'd known about it earlier," she said. "I'd have let you know and gotten out of the Wave contract. I expected it of Marco, but I'm surprised Salvatore went along with it."

Logan looked serious and shook his head, "I need to let you in on a little secret."

"Another?" Diana asked.

"This is a big one," Logan said and sighed. "I found my mother's old diary about a year ago. It talked about my father."

"Oh my god," Diana said, suddenly putting it all together.

She paused on the bag she was zipping. "I can't believe I didn't see it before. You have his eyes. Does anyone know?"

"Just you, me, and Salvatore, who apparently loved my mother but was engaged to a sweet little lady named Sophia he'd met back in Italy while visiting the family. He broke Mom's heart."

"I'm so sorry. I'm sorry for your mother, but I'm so thankful you don't have to claim Marco as a relative. But thank god you didn't inherit a snaggletooth," Diana said and crossed the room to hug him. "That's a lot to know, to take in. How do you feel?"

"It's too surreal. Someday, I think I need to talk to Salvatore about it, but I'm not ready. I like Sophia. I don't want to hurt her. And really, what does that solve in the end?"

"You're a kind man. I like that about you."

"Remember that first day back when you were in the vineyard? You wore that yellow dress."

"I remember," she said as he looked down at her.

"That was the first day I remember seeing color in over two years." His voice was somehow deeper in the muted light as he whispered, "I'm in love with you, Diana."

"How is it any different now from twelve years ago?" she asked.

"I'm no longer stupid with a sense of self-sacrifice that only hurt us both. And for the record, I never stopped loving you."

"I never stopped loving you. We have the rest of our lives for you to prove it," she said.

"Let's start tonight. Come home with me."

They packed her car, making sure the cabin was just as bare as when she'd arrived ten weeks earlier. He'd driven to Mountain Valley Vineyard, so she followed him as they left. Driving next door to Forget-Me-Not felt more right to Diana than she could say. But when Logan passed his house and parked in front of his aunt and uncle's Victorian, she didn't understand.

"This is a surprise," she said.

"I hope you'll like it as much as I do," he said. "I've loved this house my whole life."

"I thought it was beautiful when I saw it twelve years ago. I'd never seen anything like it."

"Let me help you with your bags," he said as he opened her trunk. Glancing at the four large suitcases, he said, "I'll need to make two trips."

"I don't need all of them," she replied.

He kissed her then, and she let him pull her close, settle her in his arms as his warm hands made soft, slow patterns over her skin, touching her, claiming her.

"Eventually, you are going to have a very large walk-in closet at your disposal. They'll fit."

Ginger was waiting just inside the front door with a stuffed animal in her mouth. When she saw Diana, she was beside herself with happiness.

As Diana greeted the dog, Logan brought in the second load of her luggage.

As he led her up the steps to what she thought was the master bedroom, he said, "Keep in mind, I didn't have a lot of time to prepare. I asked Tess to go out and do whatever she thought would look good. She has good taste, and I asked her to do something special, so I'm hoping for the best."

"You planned this, me coming here? Even before I said what I said?" she asked, feeling dumbfounded.

"The plan didn't come to me until this morning. I thought it was the right time to move back to the Victorian. You know, I've had a few things on my mind," he admitted as he stopped before a closed door.

When at last he pushed open the door, a large four-poster bed in peach and cream waited.

Peach and white rose petals led a pathway to the bed, which was turned down and covered with more petals.

"Wow," she said as he wrapped his arms around her. Taking

in the lit candles in large hurricane lamps and a bottle of Sparkling Chardonnay chilling in an ice bucket, she said, "It's beautiful."

"You're beautiful," he said and pulled her close.

Logan slowly undressed her until she lay bare, waiting for him in the soft sheets. As he undressed, she watched, knowing with each layer of clothing that was shed that something had subtly shifted between them. This wasn't young lovers' exploration or mutual satisfaction. This was the beginning of something much different.

As they made love, there was a freedom to their actions that had eluded them for months.

When Diana awakened the next morning, she was alone in the big bed, wondering where Logan had gone.

On cue, the door opened, and Logan entered with a breakfast tray, Ginger at his heels.

"Good morning," he said as he set the tray on a low table next to the bed.

"Good morning," Diana said as Logan dropped his robe, slipped under the sheets, pulled her close, and began kissing her.

Ginger went to her own bed, circled three times, and lay in a tight ball.

"I like waking up with you," she said as he kissed his way down her body.

"I missed this when I had to leave so early," he said as he left a trail of kisses along her ribs and up to her breast, where he lingered.

Shutting her eyes, she enjoyed the feel of his mouth on her nipple in sweet torture.

"No more hiding, no more sneaking around," she said.

"Seriously, is there another contract, or are you done with Wave?" he asked as his fingertips danced along her skin.

"Wave is part of my past. You are part of my future."

"I think we should go to Seattle, pack up your things and move you in here. Then, I'll put you to work," he said with a wink.

She smiled. "I don't have much to pack, but I think it will look lovely here."

Her cell phone chimed on the nightstand, but she didn't reach for it.

"You'd better get that."

"I don't want to," she replied as she reluctantly reached for the phone.

"Tell them you're busy," he said as he chuckled as he went back to her breast.

"Hello," she answered, a little breathlessly.

"Good morning," Stephan announced joyfully. They'd already discussed the final competition the night before. He wanted to "have a conversation about the partnership" when she got back to town. She needed to tell him there wasn't going to be a partnership with him. She couldn't figure out why he was calling her now unless it was to fire her. That would be alright by her.

"It's good so far. Why are you calling so early?" she asked, looking down at Logan, who was now watching her, his chin resting on the hand that covered her breast.

"I wanted to tell you about your next contract. Do you have a moment?"

"I need to talk to you about that—"

Logan's fingers danced along her skin.

"It's another winery—"

"Oh great. Do they know I just lost a large contest for a client?" she asked.

"There is a gentleman that is very impressed with your resume. And I have to tell you. I know you're going to like him. Coincidently, you already do. The contract is open-ended, and he suggested that you might not be returning to Wave. And that is too bad, because I'm making you a partner."

"Wait, a minute. What are you talking about?" she asked as Logan stretched out beside her and wrapped an arm around her middle as he watched her.

"Logan Parrish. He wants you to help him with his new Stark Hotel contract. We signed him yesterday afternoon. Considering that I think you're in love with him, I didn't think you'd mind. Sorry I didn't tell you earlier, but I wasn't sure he'd win. And I kinda wanted it to be a surprise."

"What? I—" she said to both men at the same time.

"Surprise," Logan said and took the phone from her hand. "Hey Stephan, she'll call you later, but I think you can consider that she's agreed."

Diana found herself nodding, and then she was kissing Logan.

"What just happened?" she asked as he gently rolled on top of her, her legs gently encircling him.

"You're officially sleeping with your boss," he said with a smile.

"No, I'm a consultant until I resign. You aren't my boss. I work with you. We're partners."

"Fine. Better. How do you feel about a fall wedding in the vineyard?" he asked as he slid into her warmth.

"Is that a proposal?" she asked.

"Yes. Will you marry me?" he asked.

"Yes," she said.

# EPILOGUE

T he wedding guests were the first to take up residence in the newly remodeled guest house that had once been Logan's home that he'd built for his first wife. It still served as his office, but the remodeling hadn't stopped there. The house now had six guest bedrooms and a staff to manage guests. A small vineyard restaurant was planned for the following year.

The renovations on Logan's uncle's house would take the historical structure down to the studs. To Logan, as much as to Diana, it was a labor of love. When completed, it would be the dream home they had once discussed years ago when they were young lovers in college.

The Stark Hotels' contract had proved more lucrative than they originally thought. The sales were coming in higher than they'd expected, thanks to Diana's marketing plan, which had made Forget-Me-Not one of the most sought-after wines in the Pacific Northwest. Daisy Stark was discussing an expansion of the wine to all their hotels—not just in North America, Europe, and the Middle East, but in Asia, South America, and Australia as well.

As Diana stood under a gazebo in the gardens that Logan had constructed, especially for the occasion of their wedding, she couldn't help but steal glances at all the people along the way that had a hand in making her who she was.

Bonnie Elder, who'd helped her pick out her wedding dress

and happily stepped in as the honorary mother of the bride, was in the front row with her husband. Next to them were Stephan and his partner from Seattle. They had planned today's event from the flowers to food and the invitations. Stephan was still a little angry with Logan for taking away one of his best consultants, but the contract for the wedding had softened the blow. Alex and Daisy Stark sat behind the first row, having become new friends.

Julianna's family had come for the wedding and supported Logan with surprising kindness.

Ginger wore a garland of peach and white roses around her neck, which held their wedding bands and perfectly accented her copper coloring.

The bride wore an elegant white satin dress adorned with yellow and white roses, which reminded the groom of the first day he'd reunited with her, that first sunny day down by the Persephone's Creek.

Salvatore and Sophia sat in the back. It had taken a while, but Diana had managed a peace between the two vineyards. It had been conditional on Marco's incarceration and monetary restitution to Logan. Once the information on Peter's burglary at Marco's instruction came to light, it didn't take long for Marco to admit his role and try to cop a plea. Salvatore hadn't known the depth of what he was up to until the final night of the competition.

Logan and Salvatore had taken to long walks together in their vineyards. The discussion of Logan's parentage didn't come up because if the information came to light, it would have ramifications and would no doubt hurt Sophia. But Logan, Diana, and Salvatore knew the truth. Logan was Salvatore's son.

After Logan slipped the eternity band of diamonds on Diana's finger, she did the same on his with a plain platinum band. They kissed and held each other as the evening light warmed them and shined softly on them.

In the end, fate had brought them together, and as they looked at each other and promised never to take their love for granted, Diana smiled at Logan with a mischievous grin.

He pulled her close and whispered in her ear, "I can't believe you allowed the pirates from next door to serve wine at our reception..."

"They aren't so bad," Diana said. "They can talk and pour at the same time."

"Well, Mrs. Parrish, you tend to know best."

"Is that why you married me? Because I'm the better marketer?"

"Sure," he said.

He stopped her ensuing laughter with a kiss.

✦━━━━━━⟡━━━━━━✦

*Six Months Later*

"I always knew Logan was going to win," Daisy Stark said as she and Diana had tea with Laura Stark at the very subdued lobby of the Stark Hotel in downtown Portland while their husbands played golf with Stark's visiting cousin, Spencer. "He had the best wine. It really was no contest."

"Yes, he did have the best wine," Diana admitted, pleased that the relationship with Stark Hotels was going so well.

"And I always sensed a little tension between you two, a spark," Daisy added with a wink. "And look, now you're married. I love it when I'm right."

"Yeah, I noticed that too," Laura said. "Were you sleeping with him during the contest? Because I think you were."

"Ladies! You are both sophisticated, lovely businesswoman and above such gossip," Diana said and took a sip of her tea.

"No, we are not," Daisy said.

"Nope," Laura said, shaking her head. "You were, weren't you?"

An elegant woman with a strong Italian accent sauntered up to the group and was introduced as Maria Medici Whitlow, wife of Spencer Whitlow who was Alex Stark's cousin and part owner of the Stark Hotels. Maria owned a chunk of the hotels in her own right.

"We are just talking about hot men and sex," Daisy said, bringing Maria up to speed.

"This is something I know a little about, even though my Spencer isn't Italian," Maria admitted as she turned up her nose at the offer of tea. Her accent was thick, but she spoke clearly, easy to understand. "He is Texan, which is very close."

"If you say so," Laura laughed.

"What does that say about your beverage specialist if I was having an affair with the competitor?" Diana asked. "That would be completely unprofessional." Not only was she Logan's partner, but the Starks had also asked her to step in and help them with a strategy for all the restaurants in all of their hotels. It was a huge undertaking and very exciting.

"She knows a piece of hot ass when she sees it," Daisy said. "I respect that in my beverage specialist."

"Makes her our kind of partner in crime," Laura said and smiled. Logan and Diana had commissioned Laura to redesign all of the Forget-Me-Not labels featuring her watercolor paintings of Forget-Me-Not, which were turning out beautifully.

"I should explain. Logan and I were in love back in college," Diana explained. "Then we found each other again during your contest. If you hadn't had it, I don't know if we'd have ended up together. It was a lucky coincidence."

"Something else would have come along to throw you back together, but I'm glad we had a hand in it," Daisy said.

"Remember, if it is meant to be..." Laura said.

"Is that a quote from personal experience?" Diana asked.

Daisy and Laura laughed. Laura said, "We need more than tea for those stories."

Maria put up her hands in frustration and asked, "Why are we talking about wine and drinking tea? Tea is for the English. Wine is for the Italians. And something tells me you are all honorary Italians today, especially if we are going to talk of passion and love."

"It is five o'clock somewhere. Let's switch over to a Forget-Me-Not wine?" Daisy suggested.

"Yay!" Laura said.

"My husband is Italian," Diana admitted.

Maria sat in an empty chair and crossed her legs, displaying four-inch heels. "Good for you for marrying a passionate Italian."

"He is passionate," Diana admitted.

"Oh god, we'll be good and drunk by the time all of our husbands arrive for dinner," Laura said. "They will know we were talking about them."

"I'd love to join you, but I need to stick to tea," Diana said.

"Because you're pregnant," Laura said.

"You owe me two dollars," Daisy said, playfully punching Laura's arm.

"Yeah, I knew you wouldn't forget about the bet," Laura said, smiling at Daisy.

"You bet on me?" Diana asked.

The ladies nodded and smiled, "We've all been there."

"Fine. Yes, I'm about three months along," Diana admitted. "We aren't telling people yet, but due to my age, I'm thirty-four, we decided to get started on our family. Ideally, we want four children if possible."

"You should have as many as you can," Maria said. "I just met you, and I see the twinkle in your eye. You are in love, and you carry your Italian lover's child." Maria then continued, "It is the ultimate happily ever after. After all."

And they all said, "Yes, it is."

The men arrived loudly in the quiet lobby, smiling and

sunburned, dragging lumbering bags of golf clubs with them. Logan made a beeline for Diana and kissed her in front of the others.

"Hello, Mrs. Parrish."

"Mr. Parrish," Diana said with a smile, and introductions were made.

Adam poked at Logan and said, "Tell her."

"I can't believe you haven't," Alex Stark added.

"I just arrived. I was getting to it," Logan said with a smile.

"Tell me what?" Diana asked.

"My golf partners had an idea," Logan said, "But it must be soon and before the baby arrives. And it is okay to say no."

"So, everyone knows I'm preggers?" Diana asked.

All the men and women nodded.

"Fine, what idea did you come up with?" Diana asked Logan.

"We—Alex, Adam, and I—came up with the idea because we are all happily married and know what it takes to stay that way," Spencer Whitlow said in a slow Texas drawl as he snaked an arm around his wife Maria's waist. He was rewarded with a quick kiss to his cheek. "Besides, we heard that due to the harvest, you didn't have a honeymoon.

"I'm still sorry about that," Logan said.

"As I told you, it is okay," Diana said.

"No, it's not," Laura and Daisy both said as Maria just shook her head.

"Redemption might be possible. You see, I seem to know some people in the hotel business, and they have made us an offer," Logan said, just as several waitstaff appeared with several bottles of Forget-Me-Not wine and enough glasses for everyone.

"Okay, what was the offer? As your consultant, you must run things by me first, even though I think I'm going to like this," Diana said teasingly.

"You are. It is a little tour of a few of their most beautiful hotels as a late wedding, early baby present. London, Rome,

Positano, Paris, Budapest, Berlin, Athens, Dubai, and lastly, New York. We fly first class, and we stay in beautiful suites in every hotel."

"Seriously?" Diana said, looking to Daisy, who nodded and smiled.

"And you don't have to name the baby after any one of us," Daisy replied as she gave Diana a hug. "Just make sure all the hotels are all serving Forget-Me-Not and spotlighting it properly. And, if you do name the baby after me, it is D-A-I-S-Y, no E. People like to add the E."

"If you agree, we leave next week," Logan said.

Diana grabbed hold of Logan's Forget-Me-Not polo shirt and pulled him to her. She kissed him and said, "I love you. Now, let's go home and practice for the honeymoon."

"I'll take that as a yes. I love you, Mrs. Parrish," Logan said, and he bent close and kissed his wife.

*The End*

# The Stark Hotel Competition Recipes
## &
## Diana's Other Favorites

**Mom's Oyster Stew**
½ gallon 2% milk
½ gallon half and half
½ cup butter
Combine and heat until almost to a boil. Add butter, salt & pepper to taste.

If you are making individual bowls, drop six to ten small raw oysters (per portion) into the soup and serve immediately. Add a thick pat of butter to the bowl and serve with Tabasco sauce and oyster cracker.

**The Beef Thingy**
Four to six nice steaks (I use Filet Mignons); cut into bite-sized cubes, trim off all fat
1 can Campbell's mushroom soup
¾ to 1 package of Lipton Onion Soup Mix
1 cup red wine you'd like to drink
Place cut up steak in a pot with a lid. Add mushroom soup, onion soup mix. Fill soup can ½ full with red wine, add to pot. Fill soup can ½ full with water, add to pot. Stir well.

Bake for one hour at 350 degrees. (Longer is better, feel free to extend to 90 minutes.)

When the meat is tender, and you are ready to serve, add ½ cup of sour cream.

Serve over egg noodles or rice.

Better on the second day.

# ABOUT THE AUTHOR

Mary Oldham is an award winning author, and three-time Golden Heart Finalist with the Romance Writers of America in the areas of Contemporary Romance and Romantic Suspense. When she is not sitting on her deck and looking at the Pacific in Yachats, Oregon—Gem of the Oregon Coast—Mary lives in Portland, Oregon.

# Also by Mary Oldham

Don't miss any of Mary Oldham's other books, available in Print or Digital at Amazon or Barnes and Noble:

**Stand Alone Titles**

*The Silver Linings Wedding Dress Auction,* October 2021

*Crush,* May 2022

**The Hotel Baron's Series**

*A Paris Affair,* November 2021

*A Summer Affair,* December 2021

*A Roman Affair,* April 2022

*A Hungarian Affair,* Available December 2022 (Tentative Title)

**Audiobooks**

*The Silver Linings Wedding Dress Auction,* Available April 2022

Narrated by Gildart Jackson

Mary loves to hear from her readers! You can email her to sign up for her newsletter at www.maryoldham.com.

# ACKNOWLEDGMENTS

The statement: *"I don't see myself spending my life with you..."* actually happened to me when I was in my early thirties, never was far from my mind, and motivated this novel. I'm very thankful it did. The man who said it to me is a friend, and if we'd ever married, I'm sure I'd be divorced from him now. Of course, after his proclamation, I didn't speak to him for around ten years.

As a real estate broker, a title account executive, and then part of the real estate team as an advertising account executive at *The Oregonian* and then *Gannett/USAToday*, I'm very familiar with real estate and terms related to real estate, such as riparian rights. I did, however, allow my creative spin on this story.

My knowledge of wineries runs more toward what I like to drink. Oregon is known for superb Pinot Noirs, which is why they are so prominent in my story. I'm a Prosecco girl myself. I realize names like Pinot Noir should not be capitalized, but they are to showcase the product in this book.

To all of my family and friends, thank you for sharing this lovely ride with me. I love you all.

Thank you,
*Mary*

Printed in Great Britain
by Amazon

19747673R00188